Not Quite Nice

Not Quite Nice

Celia Imrie

B L O O M S B U R Y
LONDON · NEW DELHI · NEW YORK · SYDNEY

First published in Great Britain 2015

Copyright © 2015 by Celia Imrie

The moral right of the author has been asserted

Bloomsbury Publishing Plc
50 Bedford Square
London
WC1B 3DP

www.bloomsbury.com

Bloomsbury is a trademark of Bloomsbury Publishing Plc

Bloomsbury Publishing, London, New Delhi, New York and Sydney

A CIP catalogue record for this book is available from the British Library

Hardback ISBN 978 1 4088 4687 2
Trade paperback ISBN 978 1 4088 6029 8

10 9 8 7 6 5 4 3 2 1

Typeset by Hewer Text UK Ltd, Edinburgh

Printed and bound in Great Britain by CPI Group (UK) Ltd, Croydon CR0 4YY

X000000 050 2910

To my pals who brought me here to Nice, and to the city whose beauty saved and inspired me.

Part One – Escape

I

THE SMALL TOWN OF Bellevue-Sur-Mer sparkled like a diamond on the French Mediterranean coast. Sprawling down from the foothills of the Alpes Maritimes to the beach, the town consisted of stately cream-coloured villas and old ochre houses with yellow, pink and lime-green shutters, hunched up, gazing out to sea. Dark alleys and bright pathways zigzagged vertiginously between pastel painted walls, and the one main road took a series of terrifying hair-pin bends in its descent from the corniches to the bustling cul-de-sac which bordered the harbour, with its railway station, souvenir shops, brasseries, hotels and a small but popular casino.

Everywhere you looked, the colours were almost startling in their intensity: vivid purples, pinks and reds of bougainvillea and oleander bushes crowded under the green boughs of umbrella pines, orange trees and palms, and all set against the turquoise and ultra-marine background which was the sea and sky.

Understandably, Bellevue-Sur-Mer had, like most places on the Côte d'Azur, seen more than its fair share of artistic and literary visitors: you couldn't walk five

3

hundred yards without passing a building which had been associated with Rudyard Kipling, Robert Louis Stevenson, H.G. Wells, Somerset Maugham, Jules Verne, Maupassant, Stendhal, Nietzsche, Chekhov or F. Scott Fitzgerald. In art galleries all over the world you could see vivid paintings of its streets and sea views, executed by the likes of Renoir, Cézanne, Picasso, Matisse, Cocteau, Chagall and Dufy. Nowadays rock icons and Hollywood movie stars lurked behind the virgin walls of impressive villas perched in the rocks above the Old Town, while many of the more garish seafront mansions along the bay belonged to magnates of world industry and Russian oligarchs.

As in most of the beauty spots on the earth, there were, dotted among the native inhabitants, a gaggle of Brits, people who, for one reason or another, kept a second home here or, in many cases, particularly of the older generation, had chosen to move, lock, stock and barrel to this magnificent village to retire in the sun. All of them, more or less, knew one another, if only by sight. They had their own local English newspaper, and even a radio station which broadcast English-speaking programmes from nearby Monaco.

This morning Theresa Simmons would be joining them. She walked briskly along the seafront, gripping the keys to her new apartment. She stopped a while by the harbour wall to take in the beautiful view – the glass-like sea, shining silver in the late January midday light, the little fishing boats tethered to the quay, bobbing and clanking, the sky dappled at the edges with pink haze, but at its zenith as blue as a kingfisher.

She knew she'd done the right thing. How lucky

that she had taken the plunge and chosen to come here. The flight and train ride might have taken less than three hours but Theresa's journey here had taken six long months.

The whole business of her transplant from Highgate to Bellevue-Sur-Mer started one night in July – a night of babysitting her three granddaughters. She always babysat, twice a week. But this one nasty night came after a horrible day, during which, quite against her will, she was forced into retirement.

Until that day, Theresa had hoped to go on working as long as she could and planned to carry on in the house in which she had been living for the last thirty-five years. Although she was coming up to her sixtieth birthday, Theresa was not expecting her boss Mr Jacobs to give her the heave-ho but, as she put on her coat ready to leave for her daughter's Wimbledon home, he had taken her aside and apologised, saying that in a few months he would be 'letting her go'. Theresa protested that she enjoyed working and didn't want to give up, but Mr Jacobs confessed that it was a cost-cutting effort. Like everyone else, Jacobs and Partners was going under financially and unless he did this to a couple of people now, in a few months they'd *all* be out of work, including him. He was very sorry, whether she liked it or not, Theresa had to go.

With a heavy heart she made her way to Wimbledon, for the usual dose of childcare. She rode at the back of the crowded bus, the warmth from the engine turning the back of her seat into a heat pad, leaving her sweltering in the already sweaty crush of the London rush hour.

She resisted the feeling that she was on a tumbrel, heading for the guillotine. Theresa knew that wasn't really right. She was only going for an evening's baby-sitting. That was all.

Two hours later she looked at her watch, horrified to see she still had three long hours ahead of her before she could go home. She was under siege on her daughter's taupe leather sofa, while the little bastards, her grandchildren, Chloe, Lola and Cressida, crawled around, ducking behind the sofa, whispering obscenities and insults: 'Granny smells! Granny pongs! Granny stinks! Granny wears make-up like a clown! Granny's fat! Granny's a mad cow! Granny's a witch! Granny's a bitch!'

She knew you were supposed to love your children. You were also supposed to love your grandchildren. In fact you were supposed to offer them all 'unconditional' love, a fashionable term which was merely a trite way of saying it didn't matter how badly your family behaved towards you, you had to love them anyway.

But Theresa had come to the end of her tether. Yes, it was easy to love the *thought* of them all, to love some idealised notion of what they ought to be: beaming daughter and giggling grandchildren running to darling granny, doling out love and hugs all round, while granny proffered foul-tasting bits of butter-scotch, which were supposed to make them all have fond memories of granny, even long into the future, when granny was under the sod and they themselves were grandparents.

But reality was nothing like the TV ads.

She thought about Mr Jacobs, and how he had

smiled at her so pityingly as he reminded her that she was nearing retirement age anyhow. It would be less hard on her, he had said, than it would be on the youngsters.

She pointed out to him that, at her age, the prospects of her getting another job were nil.

'So spoil yourself, Theresa, my dear,' he said, 'spend more time with your family, enjoy a dignified retirement.'

'Granny smells! Granny's got a fat arse! Granny's a mad cow! Granny's a witch! Granny's a stinkypoo!'

A dignified retirement indeed.

This night was not a one-off. It was like this every time. In fact, though Theresa first started babysitting a few years ago, the three children had recognised the opportunity for larks right from the start. Theresa had tried to win them round. She'd attempted bribery, with sweets and comics, brought round DVDs for them to watch, and board games for them to play (in some wildly imaginary world *that* would have been – an evening of Monopoly!), but within seconds the three girls had got bored with her baubles and resumed their ritual chanting, with Theresa as their totem pole.

Nowadays, for the duration of her twice-weekly stint, Theresa tried to ignore it. Nothing she did made any difference. She had learned to close her ears, but not well enough. It was impossible to use the TV to drown out the little bastards, they could always get even louder. It was also impossible to ignore them. She'd long ago given up on trying to read books. Even newspapers were useless, as all three of them had caught the idea of banging the back, cracking the paper, making her jump while they recoiled in spasms of laughter.

Today Theresa sat in the armchair with a cookery book. It was a new idea. Recipes could certainly be taken in small doses, there was no story to follow, very few complex sentences, and a few phrases on the page conjured a delightful world where she could imagine being at home in the calm of her own kitchen, stirring and chopping, pricking pastry and painting it with milk or egg yolk, buttering baking trays and popping things into the oven. In her mind she could even get as far as taking the completed dishes of her imagination out of the oven, placing them on the table and sitting down to eat.

'Granny's an old bitch! Granny stinks! Granny wears make-up like a clown! Granny's fat! Granny's a mad cow! Granny's a witch!'

Blah blah blah! She thought. Soon this purgatory would come to an end, she'd be released from her duties and she would go home, uncork a bottle and cook up a storm. A lovely cheese omelette – Gruyère of course – with champignons à la Provençale and a salad of sweet peppers. (No prizes for guessing she was deep into Elizabeth David's *Mediterranean Cookery* and thereby not only thinking of lovely food but lovely places too, with a sparkling azure sea and indigo skies.)

Theresa had worked in that office, a small solicitors' in Islington, for years. She'd been there ever since her husband Peter had buggered off with Annunziata the nanny, a nubile Italian girl with cow-like eyes and huge knockers.

And now what were her prospects? Years of

babysitting, no income – even her state pension wouldn't come through for another five years – and nothing else to do. The thought of this blank wall ahead of her, lasting for the rest of her life, couldn't be more appalling. Theresa was a get-up-and-go kind of person.

She dreaded days when she might wake up and have no reason to get out of bed. The income thing was a problem too. Just because no money was coming in didn't mean none would be going out. She had the last throes of the mortgage to get rid of, and there were all the usual bills. She had spent most of her savings buying things for the family – a car, school uniforms, expensive presents like computers, trainers and music gadgets, iPods and iPads – which her daughter Imogen told her they *needed*.

If money was going to be a problem the answer was simple: she'd sell the house. Sell the house, pay off the mortgage, buy something smaller and cheaper and leave herself a decent lump sum. She didn't need a huge place. A one-bed flat would be fine. Maybe she would give private tuition, a little reading and writing, helping kids swat up for exams, teach cookery even. She had always enjoyed cooking.

'Granny's reading a boring book, a boring book, a boring book . . .' This to the tune of 'Nuts in May'. 'Granny's reading a boring book and . . .'

Before they could finish, Theresa slammed the book shut and stood up. Momentarily she saw the girls flinch, expecting her to lash out at them. Instead she walked to the 'kitchen area' – as they called it these days. No one had a kitchen any more, just a huge carpet-free space which merged into one echoing kitchen-dining-living room which took up the whole ground floor of the Victorian house.

'Granny's going to teach you to cook some sweets,' said Theresa, tying on a flowery pastel-coloured apron which dangled from a hook but which had clearly never before been used. 'And when Granny's finished, if you don't want to join her, she's going to sit down on her own and eat them and make her arse even fatter. OK, girls?'

She shook her bangles further up her arm, and raised her chubby hands like a surgeon about to operate.

Like mice, the three sisters stood where they were, quivering slightly, eyeing Theresa keenly as she pulled open drawers and plonked pans on to the vast gas range.

'Come on, you lot, if you want to share the feast, you have to help make it.'

The girls edged a half-step forward, unsure.

'Granny's got a great big . . .' piped up Cressida, the baby at six years old.

She was neatly silenced by a jab in the ribs from her oldest sister, Chloe, nine. Theresa dropped a slab of butter into a pan, ladled in some sugar, syrup and cocoa, and slowly stirred while the warm aroma wrapped around the three siblings. Silent now, they crept imperceptibly nearer to her till they hovered a few inches from her elbow.

Theresa peered up at the row of cereals lined up on top of the fridge. 'Rice pops, cornflakes, biscuits or muesli?' she asked. She didn't mention the bran and other worthy-looking packets beside them.

'It smells of chocolate,' said Cressida quietly.

'It'll taste of chocolate too,' said Theresa, wiping some of the brown liquid from the edge of the wooden spoon and tasting it. 'Mmm. If we used biscuits we'd call it Tiffin. But Mummy doesn't allow biscuits, does she?' Theresa licked her little 'cook's' finger. 'Delicious. Here!'

She held the spoon out. Tentatively each child wiped away a small blob of the chocolate fudge and tasted it.

'Let's go mad, shall we?' said Theresa, tipping cereal into the mix. 'We'll have a bit of all three.'

'Please, Granny, can we have some more?' asked Lola, the middle one, holding out a finger.

'Wait a min, my little darlings, who wants to butter the dish?' Theresa pulled out a tin tray.

In unison they put up their arms, as though they were in a classroom, trying to get teacher's attention.

'Wipe this all round the tray,' Theresa handed Lola a piece of greaseproof paper dabbed with butter. 'Then in a few minutes you'll have something even nicer.'

The three girls started fighting over the paper, tearing it so that they could join in with the job.

'OK, OK,' said Theresa, as she ladled out the warm mixture into the roughly buttered tray. She handed Chloe the spatula. 'Smooth it over, then we'll all take a slice.'

Theresa marked out the dish into neat squares and cut deep, handing each child a flaky chocolate-flavoured slab.

The children ate.

Silence reigned.

Theresa turned back and wiped the tops of the counters, stacking the dirty pans into the dishwasher.

'How's school going then?' Theresa asked. 'Have you decided what you're all going to be when you grow up?'

The children opened up, gabbling with delight about teachers and ballet and art class. As they sat round the kitchen table, digging into the home-made confectionery, Theresa realised that she had finally found a way to connect with them. After all these years she had found a way to get through.

After about fifteen minutes of congenial chat, the children's focus changed with a united tilt of their heads. They jumped up from their seats and stood erect, listening. Theresa thought they looked like meerkats.

From the street, Theresa heard the slam of a car door, and feet clipping up the path.

In unison the girls' heads turned. They took a few steps towards the front door.

'Granny smells,' said Cressida, sotto voce.

A key went into the lock.

Knowing what would come next, Theresa braced herself, and moved briskly back to the sofa, slipped her book into her open handbag, before standing, arms folded, ready for the onslaught.

The key turned and as one, the three girls flung themselves to the floor, beating it with their fists, screaming, real tears oozing from popping eyeballs.

'Mama,' sobbed Cressida.

'We missed you so much,' wailed Lola.

'Why do you leave us with *her*?' Chloe cried, then quickly sucked the last drop of fudge from her finger.

Imogen dropped her bags in the hall and came into the living room. She shook her head and tutted.

'I do wish, Mother, that you would learn how to control them while I'm out. It's not much to ask.' Imogen bent low to hug her sobbing children and spoke in a strange cooing voice, as though addressing three little poodles. 'Did you miss me, my darlings? I know, I know. You poor babies. It's all right. I'm back now. Mummy's back with you.'

Theresa wondered why Imogen felt she had to collude with them in this way, why she treated them like helpless babies when they were in fact quite feisty children.

Suddenly, in a change to the usual pattern, Imogen took her arms away from her children. She stood up, held out her face and sniffed the air. 'What's that smell?'

'I showed them how to cook chocolate crunchies.' Theresa held out a piece for her daughter.

Ignoring the sweet, Imogen swept past the wailing children and hissed into Theresa's ear. 'I will *not* have my children eating this rubbish.' She grabbed Theresa by the elbow and dragged her into the kitchen space. 'They have allergies. You can't shovel this muck down their throats. Sugar, butter, biscuits? If this is what you live on, it certainly explains why you're so overweight yourself, Mummy.'

Theresa tried to defend herself but her daughter didn't draw breath. 'Never, ever, will you throw a stunt like this again. Do you understand?'

As she watched her daughter, advancing on her like a furious schoolteacher, Theresa wondered for a moment who was the parent and who the child.

'I'm sorry,' she said, feeling stupid for apologising to

her own daughter. 'I had to do something to entertain them. They're not the easiest children, Imogen.'

'What did you say? I don't know how you have the nerve ...' Imogen wiped the perfectly clean kitchen top with a damp cloth. 'So, you'll be wanting to get off now, Mummy. It's a long way from Wimbledon to Highgate. Same time Wednesday?'

'No.' Theresa winced. Why did she feel so bad about claiming her own life? 'I can't do Wednesday, I'm afraid.'

'Do you notice, Mother,' Imogen flung the cloth into the sink, 'how selfish you're becoming?'

Theresa felt herself stammering her reply. 'I'm meeting up with some friends.'

'Friends?' Imogen scoffed. 'Can't you meet them another night? You know Wednesday is my Pilates class.'

Theresa braced herself and said 'I can't really change it. It's a one-off. Schoolfriends, you know.'

Imogen wore a cold smile. 'Schoolfriends? You're fifty-nine years old. Why? How?'

Theresa felt her heart thudding, just like when she herself had been brought before the headmistress for disobedience. She said quietly: 'They found me on Facebook.'

'Facebook?' Imogen threw her head back and laughed. 'Facebook! Listen to yourself, Mummy. You're going on sixty, not sixteen.' She went back to rinsing the already sparkling sink. 'You don't think I have time to play about on computers and the Internet, do you?'

'I'm on the Internet all day at work, other things come through now and then,' said Theresa, wondering how it had come to this, what had happened that she felt it necessary to explain herself to her daughter.

'Oh really!' Imogen turned off the tap and pushed up her sleeves. Theresa could see that she was really spoiling for a fight. 'Perhaps I should phone Mr Josephs and tell him what you get up to on his time?'

'Jacobs,' Theresa corrected, under her breath. 'Please, Imogen, I'm not in the mood.' Theresa pulled away and went to the sofa to pick up her coat and bag. She noticed that the three girls were now sprawled out on the floor, happily playing with paper and crayons. How come it was never like this during her sessions with them?

'Anyway, Imogen,' she said, putting on her coat, 'for your information, Mr Jacobs has let me go.'

'He sacked you?' Imogen tutted. 'I'm not at all surprised.' She paused her kitchen cleaning, then perked up. 'You mean you don't have a job any more? You won't be going to work? Oh God, Mummy, how marvellous. If you're not working, you'll be able to come here more often and do days now as well.'

Theresa knew that she was cornered.

But why did she have to think of coming here as something bad? This was family, after all. The people who really had first claim on her time. She felt awful for resenting them. Was it she herself who was the problem? She steeled herself and resolved to work harder at being the perfect grandmother.

'Of course I'll do it,' she said. 'But you know, Imogen, I can't bear the thought of that endless tube journey up and down from Highgate all the time. Perhaps I'll sell up the house. It's way too big for me on my own anyhow. I could buy a flat somewhere round here.'

Imogen's smile froze on her prim, perfect face. 'Why? Why here?' She took a deep breath and looked Theresa in the eye. 'Look, Mummy, I hope you don't think that if you move to Wimbledon we're all going to look after you in your old age.'

The shock Theresa felt stunned her to silence. She had only suggested the move to save time, to make things easier, so that perhaps sometimes she could have the children to her home.

A small commotion took place as Michael, Imogen's husband, came in, and, with a cursory nod at Theresa, went straight upstairs.

'Better to keep a bit of distance, eh, Mummy?' Imogen laughed, steering her mother towards the front door. 'After all we don't want you spying on us.'

Spying?

Theresa had to turn away so that her daughter would not see the flush of embarrassment on her face, nor see the tears gathering in her eyes.

The front door clunked shut.

CHOCOLATE FUDGE TIFFIN

Ingredients
1 tablespoon golden syrup
1 tablespoon soft light brown sugar
1 tablespoon butter
1 tablespoon cocoa powder
A few drops vanilla essence
Pinch of salt
Crushed biscuits/cornflakes/muesli/rice crispies etc.
Raisins

Method
Put equal amounts (e.g., one tablespoon) of golden syrup, sugar, butter and cocoa powder into a heavy saucepan.

Add a few drops of vanilla essence and pinch of salt.

Stir over heat till it melts and bubbles.

Remove from heat and fold in a cereal of your choice: cornflakes, rice crispies, muesli or crushed biscuits and raisins.

Put into a buttered tin or dish and place in fridge to chill.

When cool cut into squares.

Eat.

2

THE WEDNESDAY AFTER THAT fateful night of babysitting, Theresa had met up, as arranged, in a hotel bar in Covent Garden with five of her old school-friends. She hadn't seen any of them in about forty years. They all exchanged memories and news of their old classmates and the nuns, laughed and drank a lot of wine.

'Another bottle?' asked Theresa, as she wiped away tears of laughter after another of Ann's tales of marital life. Ann had always been the class clown, the girl who, when reprimanded by a nun, always talked back.

She had just described the expression on her ex-husband's face the day she caught him in flagrante with one of his patients. 'If I'd wanted to I could have reported him to the General Dental Council and had him struck off, but my plans for revenge included a decent settlement and if he lost his job that would have been zip. So I simply dangled the threat.' She waved for a waiter. 'After the divorce came through I knew continuing my life in that town was unthinkable. My husband had slept with half the population, and the other half was baying for his blood. I didn't want to live the rest of my life getting sympathetic looks from the greengrocer, the butcher and even the paperboy. So I took the lump sum that the court offered and buggered off to the sun.'

Theresa sat back and watched the girls – though they were all sixty she found it impossible to think of them as anything but girls. Three of them, Catherine, Louise and Margaret, seemed so cowed and the lines on their faces spoke of struggle and disappointment, while the other two, Ann and Sarah, still had a youthful light about them.

'Are we all divorced then?' asked Theresa. 'Traded in for a younger model?'

Theresa, along with three others, raised her hand.

'And you two are still married?' Theresa said to Sarah and Catherine.

'I'm widowed,' Sarah said brightly.

'I'm still married,' said Catherine, who seemed so brittle and burdened, her inner light dimmed – old.

Perhaps it was losing her job, but Theresa feared she was on the edge of spiralling down into that same huge air of disappointment.

She wanted to be like Ann and Sarah, who appeared hardly to have changed since the days of hockey sticks and homework. Despite life's vagaries, both women seemed so radiant and full of energy. What was their secret?

'Mmm,' said Sarah, sipping the red wine. 'A lovely Tuscan red. But not nearly as good as the stuff I get from the next-door farm.'

'You get wine from a farm in Wiltshire?'

'Oh God, Theresa, keep up! I left Wiltshire ages ago,

about a year after Ron died. Too depressing staying. Too many memories, you know, so I sold up and moved to a run-down old shack without water or electricity a few miles south of Montalcino. Our local wine is Brunello, the taste of heaven.'

'You live without water and electricity, Sarah?' shrieked Ann. 'Gah! I have to have my comforts.'

'No, silly. The house has been my project. Fifteen years' work and it's almost like a real home. Every mod con you could wish for in Islington, but I'm smack in the middle of an olive grove with lovely views of the Tuscan hills. I even have my own private swimming pool.'

Theresa felt a stirring of envy. 'So are you in Italy too, Ann?' she asked, dreaming of olive groves, lemon trees and bowls of huge red tomatoes.

'Andalucía,' Ann replied. 'Cadiz, in fact. It's like a very hot, sunny, Spanish version of Liverpool.'

'Don't you get homesick?' said Catherine. 'I still live in the house where we brought up the kids. I enjoy the familiarity.'

'Me too,' said Margaret.

Sarah shuddered. 'Nothing on earth would get me back to the UK. I don't know how you all put up with it.'

'Me neither,' said Ann.

'I live just round the corner from my son,' said Louise. 'Though, to be truthful, I don't really see that much of him. Dan and his wife seem to spend half the year jetting off to exotic places. But they really need me there, you see, to take care of the grandchildren for them whenever they're away.'

'It's the grandchildren for me too,' said Catherine. 'My daughter wouldn't be able to manage without me. Or him indoors. I don't think Jonathan would want to leave Blighty. He'd miss the cricket. And anyhow all that foreign food disagrees with him.'

'He has a point. I couldn't live without my English tea,' added Margaret.

'Ah, Margaret,' said Ann with a wink. 'I don't miss England a bit. But I have to confess I occasionally pop over to Gibraltar to stock up on tea and Marmite.'

'I don't understand how you two can bear to live in some strange foreign land,' said Catherine, 'with nothing familiar around you and no family nearby.'

Sarah interrupted. 'Well, I don't understand how you three can bear *not* to break the ties and start anew.'

Louise sighed. 'How can you leave your children and grandchildren?'

'We have phones and Skype in Italy, you know,' said Sarah. 'Just cos there's wall-to-wall sunshine doesn't mean we're in a time warp.'

'And my lot come and visit.' Ann shrugged. 'Which feels like a lot more fun all round.'

'Change is the important thing,' added Sarah. 'Perspective. Not letting the familiar ties trap you like a fly in a cobweb.'

When the evening came to an end Theresa rushed along Long Acre towards the tube station, wishing she'd had the foresight to bring an umbrella. The vertical sheets of rain burned her face and froze her hands. So much for the English summer. She was glad to get home.

But the next morning Theresa called in estate agents

and put her house on the market. She liked the thought of change, blowing the dust away but, for the sake of the family, decided to stay put in London.

When she wasn't working, she spent her breaks looking at websites displaying flats in Highgate. After work she went round to see some of the places for sale.

She was not impressed. In comparison to her well-worn but lovely, quirky old house, everywhere seemed characterless and anodyne. Everyone with a place to sell seemed to have cleared out their space, chucked out the carpets, sanded the floors and painted the walls off-white. The pristine sleek kitchens had not been designed by cooks, that was certain, and the bathrooms looked like operating theatres. Nothing had any personality.

Theresa wanted somewhere in a lively area with a bit of heart, but all the flats she saw were more like dentists' waiting rooms than somewhere you'd like to curl up with a book on a rainy evening.

When Theresa got home from the viewings she was greeted by another accusatory phone call from Imogen.

'As you couldn't be bothered to come and babysit last night, might you be able to make it tomorrow instead?'

'I've put the house on the market.'

There was a small silence down the line.

'How could you, Mummy? All of our precious memories . . .'

It was at least eight years since Imogen had visited her here. That was how much she cared about her precious memories.

Theresa decided not to respond.

Another ominous pause.

'I do hope you haven't forgotten what I said about moving to Wimbledon, Mummy. It would be much . . . easier for you . . . if you didn't. We'd all prefer it, I mean, it would be better all round if you kept a decent bit of distance.'

Theresa braced herself, astonished to discover that it hurt just as much to be told this a second time.

'You're right, Imogen, of course.'

Theresa had no idea when in the thirty-five years since she had given birth to Imogen her daughter had become so high-handed. Was it Michael, she wondered, who had turned her into such a prig? She also couldn't think why Imogen was always so tense. She had no job, other than being a housewife and mother. She lived in a comfortable house with nothing more pressing to attend to than the calendar at the local gym. Perhaps it was because Theresa was always there, on hand. Perhaps she was to blame for being too ever-present.

Next morning Theresa asked Mr Jacobs for advice on buying abroad and he printed out a bundle of papers for her, which she pored over on the bus home.

She spent the weekend browsing the Internet looking at towns in France. She hoped that somewhere across the Channel should be a 'decent' enough distance. She browsed through articles about the Dordogne, the Ardennes, Provence and the Île-de-France. She came to the conclusion that the Côte d'Azur was the dream place for her: warm sun in winter to ease her aching bones, good food, the sea and lots of historical, artistic and literary connections. What could be better?

As much as anything because of the English meaning of the name, she plumped on Nice.

'I am going to Nice,' she said to herself. 'I am leaving Horrible and going to Nice.'

Theresa went to Nice for a fortnight. Just to look at the place, she decided. A little autumn holiday by the Mediterranean. Then, if the place made her heart sing, she'd come back in spring and look around for property.

Theresa was surprised at how easy it was to get from the airport into the city centre. A boy sitting next to her on the plane told her not to waste her money on a taxi, just take the bus, and she tried it, expecting the worst.

But the bus ride was cheap and rather wonderful. The route ran alongside the beach for the length of her journey, then she had a very short walk along the Promenade des Anglais to her hotel.

Her room had an old-fashioned window with a Juliet balcony that looked out over the huge blue arc of the bay. She had to drag herself away from the view to go out and explore the city.

The market was packing up as she swung into the Old Town. She bought herself a few pots of olives and tapenade to give to Imogen when she got back.

She was surprised that after crossing the avenue behind the Old Town that she was right in the middle of a proper city, with department stores and a modern tramline sweeping round and up into the hills. Although it was autumn the day was bright and warm, and the mountains, which rose protectively behind the town, were coated with a mantle of snow.

Theresa almost laughed aloud. Sun, sea, snow, mountains, city shops, historical ancient streets, a port, art galleries, even an opera house! Where else could you find *everything* in such close proximity?

She had a truly delicious dinner in a little restaurant at the port before turning in and spent the next few days doing the usual tourist things: taking a walk down the Promenade, visiting some of the many museums and art galleries, buying more souvenirs, mainly of the edible variety.

On the final day, on the advice of the girl on the hotel desk, Theresa took a bus along the coast to Monte Carlo.

It was unlike any bus journey she'd ever taken. The road was high, cut into the hillside, with dizzying views out to sea. If you looked down you could see magnificent villas with turquoise swimming pools and lush green gardens; look up and there were more pilastered houses, perched on rugged brown crags.

A little fishing village caught her eye, with its multicoloured awnings and pretty rows of cottages lining the harbour. But all too soon the bus swung round a bend and there was another gorgeous vista to admire.

But Monte Carlo was not quite so much her taste. The anodyne clean streets, with rows of absurdly upmarket shops and all the parking spaces filled by Porsches, Ferraris, Bentleys and Lamborghinis, left her feeling quite uncomfortable.

But as she had got there Theresa briskly did the sights. She viewed the Palace, which she thought a bit of a joke, very Disneyesque. The Opera House, designed by Garnier, who'd also done the Paris Opera, looked wonderful in the milky midday sunlight. Thinking of one of her favourite films, *The Red Shoes*, she knew she had to pop inside and take a look. But the theatre was closed for rehearsal and the only other option was a ticket to the casino.

Inside the ornate *salle de jeux* she couldn't resist having a go, and took a seat at one of the roulette tables. Theresa bought the minimum permitted number of chips, which still came to over a hundred and fifty pounds, with the firm plan of having only couple of spins then cashing in the remaining chips. She wasn't worried about losing twenty pounds or so for the thrill of imagining herself in some scene from a James Bond movie for a moment or two.

But half an hour later Theresa was still there. She had one chip left. Feeling hot and cold, and deciding she would not be telling anyone about this little escapade, she lay it down on a 6-line, all the numbers from 16 to 21.

'*Vingt*,' said the croupier as the ball fell into place, and he swept five pink chips towards her.

As the other players leaned over the table, placing piles of chips on multiple numbers, laying down thousands of pounds on a single throw, Theresa decided to cash in those last five chips and leave with at least a little dignity.

'*Rien ne va plus*,' called the croupier as she picked up her bag and climbed down from her stool. 'No more bets.'

The ball whizzed round the wheel and clattered into place.

Theresa strolled away from the table heading for the

cashier's window, taking a good last look at the sumptuous decor of the legendary salon.

Behind her the croupier called out '*Dix-huit.*'

Theresa laughed to herself. If she'd left the chip in the same place she'd have won another five.

'Madame!' called the croupier, urgently. 'Madame!'

Theresa turned.

He was pointing down towards a pile of pink chips he was sweeping off the board. 'Your number!'

She looked over her shoulder. He must be talking to someone else.

She looked at the table and saw what must have happened. Her last chip had remained in place on the corner of the board but had somehow been knocked a few millimetres from the sideline on to 18. She'd won thirty-five more chips. She'd more than doubled her money.

On the bus home she found herself humming 'The Man Who Broke the Bank at Monte Carlo'.

It wasn't a fortune, but it had more than paid for her break.

It seemed quite wrong now to go back to that hotel and pack. She had a pocketful of money – why not stop here, and find a place down on the seafront for a delicious late lunch?

On an impulse Theresa pressed the stop button just as the bus turned the corner above the colourful fishing village she had admired on her way to Monaco.

She got off and walked down a steep zigzag path, through ancient covered alleyways, passing quaint little shops selling pottery and a delightful-smelling bakery, eventually reaching the harbour. She took a table at a harbourside bar-brasserie and ordered a large glass of wine. What a day! The excitement of her win, the hypnotic spell of the beauty of this place and the radiant October sun gave her a feeling of exhilarating happiness.

The waiter arrived with her wine and Theresa asked if she could see the menu. He shook his head dolefully. The French had stiff rules on mealtimes, and she was too late to get any lunch and too early for dinner. It was apéro time.

She ordered another glass of wine and he brought a dish of little black olives and a few one-inch squares of pizza.

Theresa leaned back, enjoying the nibbles, and savoured the wine while taking in the stunning view of the harbour.

Right ahead of her, near the Gare Maritime, some workmen were hammering at a wooden sign.

She polished off the snack but still felt hungry. So, reluctantly, she left her harbourside seat and went off in search of that small bakery and a sandwich.

By the time she reached the entrance to the alley-ways, the men had finished erecting their sign and were gone. The sign read 'À VENDRE' – for sale. Theresa peeked over the little wall, trying to get a glimpse inside the front window of the property it advertised.

At that exact moment a woman came out through the front door. '*Puis-je vous aider?*'

Theresa jumped back in shock. She wasn't expecting anyone to be inside.

'Oh! I'm sorry,' she said, then remembered that she

was in France and needed to try it in French. *Je suis . . .'* she said, unable to get any further.

'English?' snapped the woman, gripping her clipboard and pulling the front door to. 'No problem. You want see inside? You want buy apartment?'

Theresa shook her head, then before the agent could lock up, stopped herself saying no. 'Why not?' she said, instead. *'Pourquoi pas?'*

As Theresa stepped across the threshold she heard her stomach rumble.

The estate agent handed Theresa a piece of paper with of a list of room measurements and at the bottom the asking price in euros. She then perched on the low wall by the front door, scribbling notes on her pad.

Theresa took the paper and walked through the cosy rooms. The flat was gorgeous – small, but with a lovely view over the harbour.

Theresa stood by the window for a few moments and imagined herself living here.

A wonderful feeling of calm swept over her.

The agent came back in, pointing at her watch.

'I have to go now,' she said. 'You like?'

Theresa felt a wave of excitement and said: 'I'll take it.'

The agent raised her eyebrows and bustled back inside, flipping over the pages of her clipboard. 'Can you come in the morning for the contract?' she asked.

'My flight home is at nine a.m.'

'So, OK, let's do it now. The office is by the station.'

Two hours later Theresa climbed aboard the train back to Nice.

In her handbag was a contract and a floor-plan of

the flat she had just bought. She felt as naughty as a fifteen-year-old playing truant. She also felt exceedingly happy. She'd spent too much of her life pleasing other people: pleasing her parents by going to secretarial college rather than art school, pleasing her husband by turning a blind eye to all the expensive presents he bought for this secretary and that work colleague while he regularly forgot her birthday and never once remembered their wedding anniversary, pleasing her boss by always being willing to put in extra hours for no extra pay, pleasing her daughter by being constantly on call. She was almost sixty now. It was time she pleased herself for once. She had just bought a little part of paradise for herself, and why shouldn't she?

French property law differs a lot from English and, once Theresa had shaken and signed on the deal, the flat went straight into the conveyancing process, no gazumping or procrastination and, subject to survey, she was given a predetermined end date upon which she would receive the key and be able to move in.

As winter drew in offers started coming in on her old home.

As she sat in Highgate, filling in forms and studying guidebooks, Theresa kept the information of her new purchase to herself until the whole process was all but complete.

Then, the night before the move, she went down to Wimbledon to pay the family a visit.

'Mummy! Have you got dementia?' asked Imogen. 'Who's going to babysit for me now on my Pilates nights?'

'How about paying a nanny or an au pair, like I did with you?'

'Oh really!' Imogen puffed. 'What a ridiculous idea.'

'What exactly is so ridiculous about getting professional help?'

Imogen rolled her eyes about and shrugged while casting about for a reasonable response, then said: 'It's just better if it's *family*.'

'Why?' asked Theresa calmly. 'It only makes the children think I'm one of your servants.'

'Oh, Mummy, don't be absurd.'

Theresa took a stab: 'Are you worried Michael will run off with an au pair like your father did?'

'Michael and I are fine. You can mind your own business on that score.' Imogen started frantically brushing non-existent crumbs from the shiny sofa. 'Well, Mummy, I predict you'll be back here in a few months, tail between your legs, begging me for help, so go.' She folded her arms and sat back, her lips pursed. 'I don't care. You'll never last out there in some horrid, strange place with no friends.'

'I'll be fine. Thanks for worrying.' Theresa made for the door. She didn't want to leave on a row. 'Tomorrow will be a long day.'

'Anyway, Mother, for a start, you barely speak French.'

'I have a smattering, *chérie*. Living over there can only improve it.' Theresa offered an olive branch. 'I will miss you all. Promise me you'll come over and have a holiday some time. It's so beautiful – and the sea is right on my doorstep. It's so lovely. Come to visit me in France, and you'll all be treated royally.'

'What?' Imogen laughed sardonically. 'You mean you're going to chop off our heads?'

Theresa laughed too. 'Well, I won't go that far, but I promise to lay on a feast worthy of Louis the Fourteenth.'

'You've got to watch your weight, Mummy,' snapped Imogen. 'And all you think about is food.' She stood with her hands on her hips and wearing a serious expression. Then she said: 'You'd better live frugally out there, Ma. We don't want you using up the children's inheritance.'

Theresa did not grace this parting shot with a reply.

As she clicked the garden gate after her and walked to the tube station, she wiped away a few more tears.

Theresa was shocked to realise that whatever she chose to do aroused this greedy disdain in her daughter. Making her way back to her now oddly empty and echoing house, she decided she must be resolute. Absence, she hoped, would make the hearts grow fonder.

She slept fitfully, and woke before dawn.

She left the key to the house with Mr Jacobs and, early that morning, flew out to Nice.

As Theresa stepped off the plane, her London house sold, the key to her new French apartment in her hand, the first thing that hit her was the heat. Then she looked up and had to shield her eyes from the glare reflected from the sun hitting the sparkling deep blue sea. Even though it was late January, Nice Côte d'Azur Airport was bustling with people.

She had arranged the sale of all her furniture and given most of her clothes to a charity shop, so she pulled only one suitcase from the luggage carousel. Of all her London treasures there was only one thing she had brought with her, a small painting that her mother had picked up for a few shillings back in the 1950s and which turned out to be an original Raoul Dufy. She would hang that in pride of place in the flat, and for everything else, well, she was looking forward to raiding the markets and bric-a-brac brocantes for furniture, painting it, hanging tapestries on the other walls, living the art-student life she'd dreamed of having before she'd sacrificed it to please her parents and, instead, taken the secretarial course at St Godric's College for young ladies.

Theresa rode the bus out of Nice, past the port (where she saw many enticing antique shops and signs indicating a flea market), up and over the hill, then along the coast, to the small fishing village which was to be her new home.

The views were stunning.

No wonder they called it the Bay of Angels.

It was coming up to noon when Theresa let herself in to her bright front door.

SALAD NIÇOISE

Ingredients
Jar of fine albacore tuna in olive oil
Small plum tomatoes
1 stick celery
Lettuce – cos or little gem
Spring onions
Fine green beans (blanched)
Black olives (naturally, Niçoise if possible)
Anchovies
Hard-boiled eggs

Dressing
Olive oil
Balsamic vinegar
Salt (fleur de sel, if possible)
Black pepper
Dijon mustard
Honey

Method
Dip the fine green beans in boiling water to blanch then immediately run through with cold water.

Lay the tuna in the centre of the plate, and layer on chopped celery, lettuce leaves and quartered hearts, halved tomatoes, green beans and chopped spring onions. Lay small black olives on top, and place quarters of hard-boiled eggs alternating with anchovies in a circle on top of the prepared salad.

Mix the dressing and pour on just before eating.

I T WAS NINE YEARS since Sally Connor had moved to Bellevue-Sur-Mer.

When she bought her house, nestled in the heart of Old Town, she was told that it had once belonged to a dancer from the Ballet Russes of Monte Carlo, and that, according to legend, he had entertained Diaghilev, Stravinsky, Isadora Duncan and Mata Hari in his dining room. Though no one knew whether this was at the same time or on separate occasions.

Not on the same level, obviously, but Sally herself had once been famous. Back in the 1970s she had been a TV presenter on a very bumptious Saturday morning kids' TV show, and for a few loud years had had her face plastered over every magazine cover on the supermarket shelves.

On this bright January afternoon, a few months short of her sixty-second birthday, Sally came out of her little house in the milky winter sunshine, a canvas bag slung over her arm and strode along bound for the market down on the quay.

Today Sally had guests for dinner.

Outside the boulangerie, Monsieur Mari was chalking

up the sign for his 'Sandwich du jour'. Sally gave him a smile and a wave. She'd stop to buy the baguettes for dinner on the way back, thereby catching the latest warm batch.

Sally liked to think that her home was the hub of the English set. Only Zoe Redbridge had lived here longer, but as she was that much older than Sally, she felt Zoe didn't count.

She shivered as she plunged into the cool darkness of the alley which zigzagged down to the harbour.

Sally had been to the best-known ballet school, Elmhurst where, a few years before her, Hayley Mills had been a pupil. After this she had gone on to study at RADA and for a few years a successful career in the theatre followed, where she played leading roles in repertory companies from Dundee to Exeter.

When offered the TV presenting job she accepted for one reason only: the irresistible lure of money. She planned to save up, put aside a nest egg 'to fall back on', then, when the show finished, go back into proper acting, only with a slightly raised profile.

However, things didn't work out like that. The show made her very famous, and the image of her in spotted, baggy dungarees, throwing buckets of brightly coloured goo over visiting stars, overshadowed any serious chance she had of establishing herself in roles like Hedda Gabler or Lady Macbeth. When her name was suggested directors in repertory theatres sneered. Only companies that spent all their time working with children or touring schools, were interested in using her.

Sally's years of fame had not lasted long, but her renown did attract a handsome husband in the form of

Robert, an insurance broker. Due to her celebrity, their wedding was reported, with photos of the grinning couple, in all the women's magazines.

During the first few years of her marriage, when filling in forms, Sally still styled herself an actress, even though she had no professional engagements. But, after her first baby, a bouncing boy, Tom, came along, she started telling people that she had left the stage *for the moment* to concentrate on bringing up her family.

A few years later she gave birth to a daughter, Marianne.

After this, when people asked, Sally styled herself a 'stay-at-home mum'.

Soon after both children were settled in school, Sally made another feeble attempt at getting acting work. When she failed to land anything except a few unsuccessful auditions for tiny parts in regional TV soaps, if people asked her whether she still worked she would shrug and tell them 'No, she didn't have the time any more.' As a full-time wife and mother, she said, she had a far more fulfilling life than any glittering acting career could have given her. Every time her children had a birthday party, to Sally it was equivalent to another first night, every exam they passed was as though she had won an award.

At around the time the menopause hit her, both kids left home. Tom, having dawdled around 'finding himself', rather than going to university, took himself off on what he called a gap year. But once he arrived in Goa he found some kind of nirvana and never came back home, just kept wandering aimlessly round the world, painting, playing instruments and living, as

Robert put it, 'like a lazy, useless, money-sucking hippy'. Tom never asked his parents for cash. But he had no ambition in the financial world either, almost in opposition to his father's obsession with money.

Robert had made a major event of disowning his son. He cut him off and refused to have any communication, while devoting all his energy towards helping Marianne succeed in her brilliant academic career. Tom's 'gap year' lasted more than a decade.

Publicly, Sally gave a show of support for her husband, but secretly she kept in touch with her son, sending regular emails from computers in Internet cafes to Australia, Indonesia, Vietnam and Sri Lanka.

Marianne finished university with flying colours and immediately took a management job with an international oil company in Aberdeen. She was following in Daddy's footsteps, aiming high in the business world.

Empty-nest syndrome shook Sally hard. She hated being alone. And now, with the kids gone, she only had Robert, who became more preoccupied with work and seemed to lose all interest in her.

Sally suspected he was having affairs, but could never prove it. Then one day he was found dead in his secretary's bed.

All it took was one lone tabloid journalist, who worked out that the errant corpse's widow was Sally, the beloved star of the old Saturday morning television show, and suddenly all the newspapers and magazines remembered her again. The story made vivid headline news.

It didn't take long either for it to become clear that

her husband had not been the financial whizz-kid he always boasted of being. He died in debt, having blown not only all of his own money but also every penny of Sally's TV nest-egg.

At his funeral a number of women turned up, none of whom Sally recognised. They all wept profusely.

At the age of fifty-three, alone, broke, embarrassed and humiliated, Sally sold up and, using every penny left from the proceeds of selling the house, moved to Bellevue-Sur-Mer. No one in France had ever had the vaguest idea who Sally had once been, and now that her dark brown hair was streaked with grey, even the visiting English package-tourists who piled out of cruise ships no longer recognised her.

As she swung out into the warm sunlight of the harbour Sally's eagle eye was alerted to some men removing the 'For Sale' sign in front of the ground-floor flat of the old apartment block near the Gare Maritime. It had had a slash across it saying 'VENDU' – sold – since the day it went up.

When local properties bore a sign reading 'À VENDRE' – for sale – English eyes watched keenly to see whether their number would swell with a new couple from Surrey or Kent going into retirement, or maybe something exciting like a writer, following in the footsteps of Graham Greene or Somerset Maugham, moving out here to concentrate on writing a new book . . .

This sale had been presented and snapped up without a by-your-leave. What was going on?

Sally had more reason than the others for watching out for these property sales.

Last year her parents had died in quick succession

and the money from their house was now sitting in a bank. Like everyone else, Sally was very aware of the precarious banking situation and was keen to get the money tied up in property, rather than risk it vanishing overnight in a surprise bank collapse.

On top of this her daughter Marianne had told Sally she was looking to buy a holiday home. She hadn't actually talked about buying here in Bellevue-Sur-Mer, and was actively looking in the Dordogne and Tuscany, but Sally felt that if she could show her something lovely here Marianne wouldn't be able to resist and that would mean that, hopefully, Sally would see her daughter now and then. A few days ago, Marianne had phoned her mother to tell her she might drop in on her very soon for a weekend between business meetings in Zurich and Rome.

If only Sally could buy a house or flat here, to let out during the high season and bring in a little income, maybe Marianne would like to come and stay in it, out of season.

But Sally wasn't having any luck. All the decent places in this village were pounced on within days of going on the market.

As she shopped for fish, cheese and vegetables, she gritted her teeth.

'Penny for your thoughts, dearie.' It was David Rogers. 'You look as though you're preparing to play Cruella de Vil. Surely we're not that hard to cater for!'

David and his wife Carol, American neighbours who lived further up the hill, were two of her dinner guests.

'I hate cooking. I'm going to buy almost everything pre-cooked. Sorry, David.'

'Oh, dear. Let me carry the shopping bag, sweetie.' David thrust out a hand. 'You look all done in.'

Sally envied Carol having such a charming partner, so attentive and thoughtful. Perhaps it was an American thing. David was always so well dressed too. This morning he was wearing a navy blazer, pale slacks and a panama, and looked as though he was about to head off to a party at a tennis club in some novel by P.G. Wodehouse.

'Look at the red of those tomatoes! It makes you wish you were a painter, doesn't it?' David grinned. 'Or a juggler!'

'That flat by the Gare Maritime, the one that was for sale ... someone's moved in.' Sally realised she had blurted this out, for no apparent reason.

'So I believe.' David shrugged up his shoulders. 'According to my friend in the immobilier's office, it's an English woman of a certain age.'

'I'd my eye on it.' Sally gave the stallholder the money for a jar of honey. 'It's silly of me but I'm starting to feel as though the world is conspiring against me.'

'The old widow Molinari's place will go on the market soon. Those children of hers don't want the responsibility. You wait and watch. They'll cash in their inheritance by the end of the summer.' David picked up a lemon and paid for it with a handful of coins. 'For Carol's gin and tonic!'

He took Sally's arm and they walked along together. 'I gather practically the whole town will be in attendance at Villa Sally today.'

'No, no.' Sally smiled, but realised he was almost

right. It certainly felt like the whole English-speaking set in town anyhow. 'It's only me, you two, William and Benjamin and Ted.'

'Doesn't Ted have Sian, the Welsh she-dragon, in tow at present?' David pursed his lips and gave Sally an arch glance. 'I heard she was seen at the airport this morning.'

'Oh, no,' said Sally, panicked. Secretly she was terrified of Sian. And, with Sian round the table, everyone would have to be on their best manners, even the irrepressible William and Benjamin. 'I thought she wasn't due here till tomorrow.'

'I myself may have caught a glimpse of her just now, leaving the House of Poetry. It was a woman anyway.'

'You're sure that was *Sian*? You know Ted and holidaymakers.'

'Oh dear, yes – while the cat's away . . . But I'm rather afraid that the cat is back.'

'Miaow!' Sally laughed, but her heart sank. 'Oh, well, I'd better cater for her. Just in case.'

As Sally made her way back to the *traiteur* to buy another slice of pre-cooked salmon, a shadow fell across the sun.

4

FIRST THING THERESA DID was fling open the shutters. Warm light flooded into her kitchen and living room–diner at the front of the building, over-looking a little patio garden. Beyond the wooden fence lay a quiet winding road into the old village, and across it the harbour sparkled. She could hear fishermen in their boats shouting at one another as they tied up after a morning out at sea. A little launch was setting off from the Gare Maritime, heading presumably for the huge motor yacht anchored in the harbour.

Theresa lugged her suitcase through to the large bedroom and she pulled out a few things – her silk throw, which she laid out on the bed, her washbag, nightie, a book and the lovely pen Mr Jacobs had given her as a parting gift. The pen was only a ball-point, but was a lovely pearlised turquoise, with her initials engraved in tiny letters on the brass band round the lid.

She peeled its bubble wrap and newspaper from the Dufy painting and hung it from a hook in the living room. A Prussian-blue sea, azure sky, a pink house and three white sailing boats. A perfect addition to the flat.

She looked at it for some time and felt sorry that her mother wasn't alive to see it, hung in its new home so near to where Dufy had probably painted it. It could almost be the view from her front window.

Then she flopped down on the bed, pulling the flimsy throw over her, and smiled, happy to be safely installed in this, her dream apartment.

She had barely been there a few minutes when she heard a thud and a yelp, followed by a sharp rap on the back door.

As she remembered, from her viewing a few months ago, that this door opened only to a dark little courtyard surrounded by steep stone walls, she was cautious, and, before opening up, peeked through the net-curtained window.

She could see a man crouching low, huddled in the corner.

He was naked.

Theresa armed herself with the only thing that came to hand – a broom – and called through the closed door the only thing she could think of to say in French.

'*Qui êtes vous?*'

'*Au secours*, Madame,' the man replied in a hoarse whisper. '*S'il vous plaît.*'

Jamming her suitcase under the handle so that it couldn't open very far, Theresa teased the door open a crack.

'*Pardon, mais je suis Anglais,*' she said. '*Je ne parle bien le français.*'

'Thank God for that, nor do I,' whispered the man. 'I'm Australian. We don't *do* language. Wife's after me. No clothes. Almost caught in a compromising situation.

Jumped out of a window. Got to get home before she does.'

Theresa opened the door and peered upwards. The man had had quite a lucky fall.

'Well,' she said. 'I don't actually have much clothing and none of it men's.'

'Here!' said the man, grabbing the silk throw from her bed and wrapping it hastily round his waist, sarong-style. 'You're the new girl in town?' he said. 'No doubt we'll meet again. Name's Ted. Ted Kelly. I'll drop the net thing back through the letterbox. Better dash.'

Grabbing the fabric tight to his skin, he scarpered through the living room to the front door, peered in both directions and ran for it.

Theresa watched him darting along the street, nodding politely to people as he rushed through the throng.

She smiled.

If this was how things were going to be in Bellevue-Sur-Mer, she was in for an exciting time.

5

AFTER A STROLL ROUND the town, Theresa took her dinner in a small brasserie on the harbourside.

Having been warm all day, once the sun went down she was astonished at how cold it became.

'The wind is blowing from Italy,' a waiter told her. 'This means bad weather is coming.'

Theresa couldn't quite understand the logic of this, but other people around her nodded, knowingly.

'Wind from Italy rain, from Spain sun.'

She returned to find her home was very cold indeed. She went to the little box room and fiddled with the central-heating switches. Nothing seemed to do anything. She feared she was being stupid, but after an hour, gave up, and went to bed, emptying all the clothing from her suitcase on to the bed to help her get warm.

She woke with a start just after midnight. A woman's laugh had woken her. She lay still in the bed. Was someone inside the flat? She could hear whispering, a man and a woman. Silently she rose from the bed and slowly pushed the bedroom door open.

The light spilling in from the moonlight illuminated the living room. No one was there. Then she heard an Englishman's voice, saying 'Shall we open another bottle?' It appeared to be coming from her yard.

She tiptoed to the back door and peered into the dark well. There was no man or woman, clothed or unclothed, in the yard.

Gingerly she opened the back door and peered out into the darkness.

A bright ray of light spilled across the sheer wall, it was coming from an open window in the hotel above. The voice again. 'Here you are, darling.'

It was coming from the hotel.

Theresa relaxed. How bizarre that the sound from that high room should be so clear. But at least she didn't have intruders.

After a night of fitful sleep Theresa rose, rinsed her face in the cold water and went out to buy some groceries.

The difference between the weather today and yesterday was enormous. Black clouds hung low and a stiff wind blew a steady drizzle, which seemed to penetrate her very bones. She was not prepared for this at all. Embarrassing as it was, Theresa had the choice of being soaked to the skin or buying and putting on one of those plastic macs favoured by tourists. It was really little more than a gigantic piece of bright yellow cling-film in the form of a giant hooded poncho flung over her clothes. Moving up into the sheltered alleyways of the Old Town she found the small boulangerie with attached café–tabac, which she had passed on her first day here, the day she found the flat. The smell of baking

47

bread was so enticing she decided, rather than buy a loaf and take it home, to sit inside and take a petit déjeuner. After all she'd have to eat it in the damp flat, sitting on her bed – currently the only place in her new home where she *could* sit down, except the floor and the loo.

She pulled off the tourist mac, huddled up on a small table near the oven and ordered a tartine – a baguette sliced open and spread with butter – and a *café crème*.

On a rack of newspapers she saw, nestling between the morning copies of *Nice Matin* and *Le Figaro*, an English tabloid newspaper, and considered buying it, till she saw it was yesterday's, the very paper she had read on the plane from London.

There was only one other person here. Sitting at an adjacent table, was a lady dressed in what looked like evening dress. She couldn't be sure as the woman was also wearing a sensible faun Burberry mac. She had a pretty face, and well-coiffed hair.

The woman nodded a breezy smile in Theresa's direction.

The proprietor arrived carrying Theresa's breakfast on a little tray, and laid it out in front of her while giving a sly look at the woman at the neighbouring table.

Theresa tucked in to her bread. Then suddenly out of the corner of her eye she saw the woman flop forwards, her head hitting the table with a crack.

'Madame? Madame?'

When the woman didn't respond, Theresa got up and called the proprietor back from the counter.

'Monsieur! Monsieur!' she said. '*La dame! Attendez! Elle est malade.*'

'*Elle est complètement défoncé,*' replied the proprietor, giving the woman a shake. '*Allons,* Madame!'

He was right. The woman was drunk. From where she stood Theresa could smell the fumes of alcohol. She checked her watch. It was nine in the morning.

The woman lifted her head from the table. 'Ah, Stéphane! *Un cognac, s'il vous plaît.*'

Stéphane shook his head and shrugged in Theresa's direction.

'*Ami?*' he asked her in an accusing tone. '*Votre ami? L'anglais bourée?*'

'No, no,' Theresa was no friend of this woman and didn't have the language to deal with the situation. '*Je suis étranger,*' she said, grasping at a dim memory from the musical *Cabaret.*

Stéphane pulled a face of exasperation and went back to serve a customer.

As Theresa ate her tartine, the woman sat there inert, face back on the table. Theresa sipped her coffee. The woman started snoring loudly, with long pig-like snorts. Theresa looked around the tiny cafe, feeling as though she was on some TV prank show.

Suddenly the woman sat up, looked across at Theresa and said, in imperious English, 'And as for you, I'd be grateful if you would stop staring. I am not an exhibit in a museum.'

Clutching her sparkling evening bag with hands that Theresa thought looked very much older than her taut face, the drunken woman staggered to the front of the shop, giving the proprietor an airy wave as she passed.

'Tourists!' She cried, flicking her head in Theresa's direction. '*Oh là là! À tout*, Stéphane. *Ciao bella*,' she cried and teetered out into the rain.

After her breakfast, Theresa caught the bus into Nice and wandered round the big shops in Avenue Jean Médecin. While she bought some cardigans, a hot-water bottle (surprised that the French went in for such things – the pharmacy was positively stacked with them), a small electric halogen heater and various other things to keep her warm, she thought about that drunken woman and wondered if that's how she'd end up, alone in a cafe, out of her mind on booze at nine in the morning.

Why had she done this? Why had she run away from everything familiar and landed up here, where she was in danger of being run over by cars coming in the wrong direction, with only a smattering of the local language, with no friends to phone or meet up with, and her solitary consolation being a freezing cold place with no furniture.

The woman from the estate agent's office had said she would come over that evening and show her how to turn the boiler on, but if she had a viewing, which was a possibility, she would come instead tomorrow in the morning before the office opened. Theresa thought it better to be prepared for another cold night.

She felt ungrateful for being so negative.

Perhaps when the boiler was on she'd feel better, have a long hot bath, do a bit of cooking.

As she crossed the main road, looking both sides for trams, just to be sure, the rain changed from steady drizzle to a major downpour.

She dashed into Galeries Lafayette.

As she passed through the departments, her hair plastered to her scalp, dripping a trail of water wherever she walked, she felt about as low as she could go.

How Imogen and the grandchildren would laugh to see her now.

'Granny's a witch! Granny's a bitch! Granny's a soaking wet, miserable, lonely old freak!'

She pulled a turquoise mac from the rack and, tearing off the plastic thing, tried it on. She looked at herself in the floor-length mirror, her mascara streaked from the rain and her hair flattened, overweight, over made-up, over the hill.

She was a walking disaster.

She felt a stab of misery.

No wonder Imogen didn't want her living near her family. She gazed at herself in the harsh grey department-store lighting. What a sorry sight. The grandchildren were right. She did look like a clown.

A tall, elegant blonde woman crept up behind her, trying to share the mirror.

'Excuse me.'

Theresa stepped aside, ashamed and embarrassed to stand next to this slender, beautiful thoroughbred, but relieved to hear her speaking English.

'My grandchildren are always saying I wear clothes which are too bright.' Theresa started taking off the mac. 'It's too young for me.'

'Poo! Grandchildren! What do they know?' the

slim woman said, over her shoulder. Her voice had a strong American accent and was deep and warm. 'You've a pretty face. And an interesting character. Colour suits you.'

Theresa watched the glamorous American inspect herself in a figure-hugging sleek red dress while she put the mac back on its hanger.

'Pardon me for saying so, dear,' the woman caught Theresa's eye in the mirror's reflection. 'But you look utterly done in.' She turned and faced Theresa, her hands on her hips, and said: 'Whenever I feel done in I treat myself to something I can't afford. Look, honey, take my advice. Don't even pause to wonder what other people think about you. Who *cares* what they think? Buy that raincoat. Once you've dried off, you'll feel better.'

'I have to be careful with my money.' Theresa wished she hadn't said this. She knew it made her sound mealy-mouthed and stingy.

'Poo!' said the American. 'We're a long time dead. Happiness is more important than money. And so is looking good. So, while we're on the subject, get yourself that lovely pink scarf to go with the raincoat, it's darling. I can see that today you need cheering up.'

Theresa knew that the woman was right. She took the scarf from the rack and laid it across the mac on her arm.

'Who doesn't have to be careful with money these days?' said the American, back to smoothing the dress down and squinting at herself in the mirror. 'But you know what? We only live once. You don't need to creep around in beige just to please your family, dear.' She spun round and winked at Theresa. 'And I'll tell you a secret. If my husband finds out about how much this dress cost, I am dead meat. There we are. I won't tell on you, if you don't tell on me.'

Theresa felt much better as she stepped out into the street wearing her new turquoise mackintosh and pink silk scarf. She pulled up the collar as she strolled down through the Old Town to the port, where she wandered round the many stalls of the flea market looking for a table and chair so that at least she could eat in, and use her laptop.

The first stall was full of dusty chandeliers and garish, lumpy 1950s paintings of Italian women. The next seemed to specialise in jewellery and postcards, the one after that bits of old bicycles. The only tables on sale in the market were really ragged and far too small. Theresa walked back up the hill towards the antique shops.

The shop that caught her eye resembled a huge cave in which gorgeous gold-leafed chairs were piled up on top of fabulously ornate Boulle tables. Gilt mirrors, complete with candle sconces, hung from the walls, dustily reflecting other, even more ornate mirrors on the other walls. It was a cavern of delights.

Theresa passed through into a back room, a second wonderland of furniture – and there was *the* table. She wished now she hadn't bought the mac, because this table was a beauty, a wrought-iron masterpiece that looked as though it came from some Parisian-set Gene Kelly ballet. All swirling treble clefs and golden balls, it came with four lyre-backed chairs. Being metal, Theresa thought it had probably been made for the garden, but she was in love with it, and it would not only look gorgeous in her dining area, but every time she looked at it, it would make her heart sing.

She moved back to the main room to ask the manager for the price.

A supercilious young man in a velvet jacket and bow tie came through with her and said coldly '*Mille*' – A thousand.

A thousand!

'*Six cent*,' she said. Six hundred.

'*Neuf cent*,' came the swift reply.

Nine! Oh God. Now that she had started bartering she realised she really wanted this table – but nine hundred? She could never pay that for a table and chairs.

'*Sept cinquante*.' Theresa bit her lip. Seven hundred and fifty.

With a sudden rush of relief and hope, she realised she had been thinking in pounds and wondered how it would convert – less surely?

'*Avez vous un . . .*' Again that language barrier. 'Calculator?'

'Another British skinflint,' said the man in perfect English, sotto voce but quite loud enough for her to hear. 'Clearly you want to bankrupt me. Typical tourist scrounging for a bargain.'

'If I were you, Monsieur, I'd think seven-fifty was better than nothing on a miserable January day. Look around, I am your only customer.' Theresa shrugged, and hoped he would relent. 'Who's going to come in here on a soggy wet winter's afternoon and buy a garden table?' she said, adding, 'And for your information I'm not a tourist.'

'No,' he said. 'No deal. Not interested. Go away!'

She held her position.

'Go on! Shooo!'

'*Qu'est-ce que tu fais*, Benjamin?' A curtain behind him was pulled back and another man, hastily fastening the buttons of his jacket, slipped into position behind the till. He gave Theresa an ingratiating smile. 'Madame?'

'I was offering seven-fifty for the metal garden table.'

'*Non.*' The leather jacket puffed his lips in distain. His English was good, but he was undoubtedly French. 'Not seven-fifty . . . But eight hundred and it's for you.'

'But you can't sell it to her, Pierre. She's a barbarian.'

'It's sold,' said Pierre, the manager.

'*Cochon!*' The Englishman shoved past him, slipped round the edge of the counter and strutted towards the door. 'You *know* I have a friend who wanted that table.'

'Do you deliver?' Theresa asked Pierre, ignoring the Englishman. 'To Bellevue-Sur-Mer?'

Benjamin, the Englishman, stopped in his tracks and briskly looked Theresa up and down. Then, holding his hand up to cover his face, he darted out into the street.

The man in the leather jacket smirked and gave another Gallic shrug.

'*Livraison ce soir,*' he said. 'I deliver you tonight. To Bellevue-Sur-Mer.'

As Theresa, still damp and feeling utterly bedraggled in her new mac, put her key into her front door, a voice called from behind.

'Hello! I'm Sally. Well done buying this place. I rather fancied it myself.'

Theresa turned and said 'I'm so sorry.' Theresa felt as though she must have met the lady before. Her face was very familiar. 'Who knows, I may not last,' she said. 'Things haven't been working out spectacularly so far.'

'Never mind,' said Sally. 'It's a gorgeous flat. I'm sure you'll settle down soon.'

The estate agent arrived shortly after Theresa got in and spent half an hour fiddling with the knobs on the boiler, searching for the booklet, reading it, fiddling again.

Theresa had already done all this. From their telephone conversation, she'd imagined that the woman *knew* how it worked.

Just when she was getting exasperated and wishing the woman would go, there was a loud rap on the front door.

'That'll be the table,' said Theresa.

'I can't stay any longer.' The estate agent was already pulling on her coat. 'Perhaps the deliverymen will have a look at the heating. But I say you'll need a plumber.'

She pulled out a notebook and glancing at her mobile phone, scribbled down a number. 'This is the man we use for our rental homes. He's very dependable.'

While Pierre installed the table and chairs, Theresa dialled the plumber. She hoped, should she run out of language, he might help her. The plumber informed her he might arrive later that evening, but it would probably be next morning.

Theresa couldn't stand another night shivering and she wanted a bath.

After putting the phone down she asked Pierre if he knew how to work a boiler. He had a tinker, then phoned a plumber friend of his own, who came round and had a look just as the estate agent's plumber arrived. Between the three of them the men decided the thing was kaput. Theresa would need a new one, they all told her. The system was ancient and not worth repairing. It would cost her maybe five thousand euros, perhaps more, excluding where they'd need to take up the floor and to redecorate afterwards.

Then they left her, alone with her new table and chairs and her turquoise mac.

She filled a hot-water bottle, rested it on her lap and sat down to do some sums.

As she took the lid off her turquoise pen she realised it wouldn't take Stephen Hawking's mathematical genius to see that if anything else unexpected came along she was going to sink like a stone and that therefore she would need to set up some kind of home business, and earn herself some cash. *Vite!*

6

B EFORE THE HAMMERING ON her front door started, Sally had heard the sound of running feet clattering down the alley leading to her home.

Wrapping her dressing gown tight, she opened up.

Before her stood William, looking frazzled, despite his immaculate velvet jacket and freshly ironed mauve shirt.

'William! What on earth has happened? Is Benjamin ill or something?' She stood back to let him in.

'That house,' he panted, fluttering a palm to cool himself down. 'You know, the boarded-up one . . .'

Sally shuffled to the kitchen to put on the kettle.

'The empty one, you mean. Owned by the old Italian family? The Molinaris' place? Tea or coffee?'

'There's no time for a drink, Sally. You must get dressed, now. The Molinaris have obviously decided to sell the place.'

'Good. But it's eight o'clock in the morning. What's the rush?'

'I saw the immobilier going inside, just two minutes ago.'

'Naturally he has to measure up . . .'

'No. *With people*!'

'People?'

'He had a couple with him. They had brochures for other properties. They're definitely buyers.'

Within minutes, Sally was fully dressed and running behind William up the steep hairpin bends of the paths leading to the higher part of town.

When they arrived, panting, at the house, William gave her a thumbs up. The front door was ajar, so Sally called out and walked inside.

The immobilier poked his head down the staircase.

'Madame Connor! *Bonjour. Et* Monsieur William.'

Sally explained that she, too, would like a viewing, and the immobilier signalled her up the stairs to join the prospective buyers. 'Two English,' he said.

There was another knock and, letting Sally and William past, the immobilier bowled down the stairs to answer it.

In the main bedroom she found an elderly lady, dressed in grey.

'Oh, hello. I'm Faith. Faith Duckworth.' She held out her hand and Sally shook, while trying to look round and get a measure of the place.

If Marianne didn't fall for this place Sally would be amazed. Although the ceiling was rather low on this upper floor, Sally liked the bedroom a lot, with its glimpses of the harbour. It was bathed in morning sunlight. Quite the best aspect for a bedroom.

'Are you moving out here to Bellevue-Sur-Mer as well?' asked Faith. 'It certainly is a beautiful spot.'

'I already live here,' said Sally, realising she sounded a bit of a know-all.

'Just having a snoop then?' A man came into the room behind her, giving her a wry smile.

'As a matter of fact,' Sally answered, 'I'm looking to buy somewhere near me, for my daughter.'

'Excuse Alfie,' said Faith. 'He means well. He's my son.'

Alfie was shortish and sturdy, with a thick head of curly dark hair setting off a cherubic face and a roguish smile. He gave a breezy 'Hi!' and strolled across to look out of the window, blocking out the light.

'Alfie's helping me look around,' said Faith. 'He's taken a week off work to come out here. He's a good boy.'

'My daughter's looking for an investment, you know, doubling as a holiday home. She's a business executive.'

The more Sally went on, she realised, the more smug and awful she sounded. But she was desperate. And knowing the local ropes she knew she had a good chance of beating them to this house. If she got a move on.

'Excuse me.' She went back to the landing. 'I'm in a bit of a rush actually, so I'll nip round to look at the other rooms.'

She left mother and son gazing out of the window at the delightful view of the bay. As she quickly took notes on the spare bedroom, she heard Alfie, in the next room, whispering to his mother. He said the name of the TV programme Sally had been on.

Oh God, she thought. He'd be about the right age to have watched it as a kid. And once you'd appeared on TV everyone thought you were loaded, which she certainly was not.

She went down the stairs and found the immobilier

sitting at the table in the kitchen with a largish grey-haired man wearing smartly pressed chinos and a navy blazer.

'Your wife is obviously loving it here,' said Sally, presuming he had something to do with the lady and her son upstairs.

'Single gentleman, actually. Don't have a wife. But if you're offering . . . !' With a beaming smile, the man stood and presented his hand. 'Brian Powell. They just sent me down from the office. I'm looking to buy somewhere round here too. This is a lovely little house, no?'

She looked down at the suitcase by his feet. 'Are you moving in today?' Sally joked, hoping there was not some special twist to his sudden appearance.

'Wouldn't that be nice?' He shrugged. 'This one's a little bit above my size and budget, I'm afraid. I was looking for something more in the way of a bachelor pad.'

'Monsieur Powell was 'oping to stay at Villa Bougainville while 'e looked, but zey double-booked.'

'Up the creek without a paddle.' Brian pulled one of those wincing 'look-at-me-I'm-such-a-twit' faces, and Sally laughed. 'Only just got off the plane and I'm already homeless.'

'Try the little hotel up by the railway station. They may have rooms. Or there's another hotel just above the Gare Maritime. Though it's a bit rougher, I'm told.'

'Already tried. All the hotels here are full this week. It's half term or something. The estate agents have been ever so kind, but turned up nix. It's quite a bore. I've got to lug the old case behind me wherever I go till

I find somewhere. After I've had a look around I'm going to nip over to Nice and find somewhere to lay my weary head until I get settled.'

'I'm sorry not to be more help,' said Sally, leaning in to touch the estate agent's arm. '*Je dois parler avec ma banque. Je vous parlera.*'

This house was more expensive than Sally was expecting. It would cost all of the money she had inherited, and she would need to supplement it with money from elsewhere. Perhaps Marianne would part buy it with her?

With a brief smile at Brian, Sally rushed out into the alleyway, dialling her daughter on her mobile as she walked down towards her home.

'Oh, Mum, what's the rush?' wailed Marianne down the line. 'I'll get my accountant to look into it.'

'You'd better get a move on, darling. The whole property thing is different here in France.'

'Stop panicking, Mother,' replied Marianne. 'No one ever said no to a bit of gazumping. Palms can be greased anywhere in the world.'

Sally knew better, and, as she put her key into the lock of her front door, tried to interrupt.

'No buts, Mother. Remember, I am the business-woman here. You made a right old hash of it all. You earned all that money and have nothing whatsoever to show for it. You never had any idea of how to capitalise on your investments.'

'But your father . . .'

'My father always did his best for us. He had to work hard, not earn his money prancing around in silly costumes. Anyway I can't get away to visit for a month or two, so don't start airing your spare room for me quite yet.'

'Where are you now, darling?'

'Look, Ma, I can't talk now. I'm in Europe for a flying meeting. Speak soon.'

Marianne ended the call.

Crushed to the heart, Sally slammed the door behind her and threw the mobile phone down on to the sofa. Europe? How vague could you get? Was she in France perhaps? Surely she would have said. Probably the reason was that she was in one of those places in Uzbekistan or somewhere with an unpronounceable name.'

She went into the kitchen to make herself a coffee and tartine, but the milk was off, she hadn't bought bread and what she did have left from yesterday would be better used as a table leg than food.

She slumped down on to a kitchen chair.

Why did she bother?

Why?

Ah well. Another property within her financial range would turn up soon, preferably before any bank crash. There was no reason to be upset. Her neighbours in Bellevue-Sur-Mer were very sweet and generous, after all, and she had lots of friends.

The trouble was they all had someone special of their own. Benjamin had William, Carol had David and Ted had Sian. True, Zoe was alone, but she was barking mad, and also much older.

Sally longed for some company.

She jumped to her feet and grabbed her bag.

Damn money and saving, she'd take breakfast in the

brasserie down by the port. Why not? It would only set her back a few euros and at least she'd have someone to talk to, even if it was only the waiters.

As though to prove her right, the moment she took her seat at a table on the cafe's terrace, the sun came out, bathing her with warmth. She ordered and sat waiting, gazing out at the boats bobbing around on the choppy waters, wondering where she had gone wrong.

'I suppose you wouldn't care for a little company?'

Sally looked up to see the man in the blazer, Brian, hovering.

'You look sad, which is all wrong for a pretty woman in such a beautiful setting.' He gave a solicitous look. 'Perhaps I could help?'

Sally pulled out a chair.

'There's nothing to be done,' said Sally. 'I am always astonished at how, no matter how hard you try, you can never please your children.'

'No need to tell me about it.' Brian smiled. 'I know exactly how you feel.'

'You have children?'

'A daughter.' Brian looked down. 'Let's say I understand the role of *King Lear*.'

'Yes. Me too. Oh, I don't mean, I, er . . .' Sally laughed. 'Did you find anywhere to stay yet?' She handed the menu to Brian. 'The croissants here are always warm and fresh, and the coffee superb.'

'I saw your plate and was toying with ordering exactly that. Now that you have verified my thoughts, I shall order the same,' said Brian. 'Once I've eaten, the plan is to head for Nice, as I said. I think I'm going to try and find a room to rent. That should work out better for me than the extortionate rates the hotels charge round here.' He laughed. 'I presume you know what it's like, living on a fixed income!'

Sally tipped a spoonful of sugar into her coffee and watched it sink slowly through the froth.

She had that spare room which she always kept prepared, ready for Marianne should she want a short break. Perhaps she could do this man a service and, while she was at it, make a little pin money for herself. It would be nice to have a man around the house and some company.

'I wonder whether you might like to take my spare room,' she asked tentatively. 'I'm hoping my daughter might come over soon. She's a businesswoman. Very smart. But at the moment it's free.'

Brian waved his hand for the waiter. 'You're very kind, but I couldn't dream of it,' he replied. 'But thank you for the offer.'

7

THERESA TRAIPSED UP THE hill to the boulangerie for a fresh loaf and to stretch her legs. Despite
having no hot water or heating she was looking forward
to her first breakfast in her new home. She'd got the
coffee and a lovely-looking pot of apricot jam and a
sweet little percolator to brew up the coffee.

Coming out of the little Huit-à-8 shop with some
milk and butter, a packet of paper plates and cups,
which for the moment would have to do, she thought
she saw the lady from yesterday who had persuaded
her to buy the mac in the Galeries Lafayette going
into the wine shop. She was looking superb in a neat
black-and-white outfit, matching gloves and scarf,
simply too well turned out for this time of the morning. Theresa scurried along hoping the woman wouldn't
turn and catch sight of her in her sloppy old clothes.

Then while the coffee brewed, she turned on the
radio and sang along as she polished up the new table
ready for eating. She pondered phoning Imogen to ask
whether she or Michael might be able to give her a
loan towards getting the boiler done and decided
against it.

The spluttering of the percolator coincided with the delicious aroma of the warm bread coming from the oven. Perfect timing! She lay it all out on the new table, got her penknife from her bag and spread out a paper napkin for a tablecloth. Then she poured herself a steaming cup of best arabica.

Bang! Bang! Thump! Thump!

Theresa jumped out of her chair.

Somebody was battering on her front door in great agitation and, whoever it was, they were surely desperate. Theresa prayed that it was not the police with bad news.

She opened up.

'You whore!' A tall woman with long blonde hair screamed into Theresa's face, then, pushing her out of the way, strode through into the living room.

'I'm sorry,' said Theresa, still by the door. 'I think there must be some mistake.'

'A mistake? You're dead right there is.' The furious woman swung round, hands on hips, and looked Theresa up and down. 'My God! Look at you! How low could he sink? He must be getting desperate in his old age. I never thought he'd go for such a frump!'

'I think you must have got the wrong flat,' stammered Theresa, leaving the door open so that, should it be necessary, there was a quick escape from this raving madwoman.

'His standards have certainly fallen if he's down to fucking over-painted fat old cows like you.' The woman took a step forward and slapped Theresa across the face. 'So back off, bitch. And in future, you superannuated Jezebel, *leave my husband alone!*'

The woman turned towards the door, plunged her hands into her pockets, then swung around. 'I believe this grubby *thing* is yours.' She dropped Theresa's silk scarf on to the floor as though it was infected with leprosy.

With no further ado, the woman left, swept out by the same whirlwind upon which she had arrived.

Theresa stood, leaning against her new table, mouth open, stunned.

She put her hand up to stroke her still stinging cheek.

She could see clearly enough what had happened. The naked man who had landed in her courtyard must be the madwoman's husband. Lord, she'd only wanted to help. Now look at the trouble. What had she done? By lending that naked man her throw, she was now the accused.

Oh, what a ghastly start to her new life!

She slumped down into a chair, lay her head on the table and wept.

Why had she come out here to this strange town where she knew no one and had nothing, not even proper cutlery? She wiped a tear from her eye and stooped to retrieve her scarf, which was now dusty and rather badly ripped.

When Theresa looked up, standing before her in the doorway, like a guardian angel, perfectly made-up, resplendent in her stylish suit with matching scarf, gloves and clutch bag, stood the glamorous American from the department store.

'Oh dear, we meet again!' said the woman in her casual American drawl. 'I feared it was you. So now you've met the dragon-woman, Sian. I'm Carol Rogers, by the way.'

Carol stepped inside and gently shut the door behind her. 'I heard the brouhaha from the street. Do you have another of those paper cups? I'd love a coffee.'

Carol sat at the new table and tore off a piece of baguette.

'Come along, honey, sit down. Let's eat this lovely breakfast.'

She buttered a strip of bread and laid it in front of Theresa's coffee.

'My, what a lovely table and chair set. I adore that 1950s look. So chic.'

Theresa still stood in the centre of the room, clutching her hanky in one hand, her torn scarf in the other.

'You mustn't listen to these people, dearie. They're minnows compared to you or me, and that's why they dislike us so.'

Theresa sat, bemused by this beautiful woman sitting at her new table, spreading butter and then crunching into a piece of baguette.

'I haven't slept with *anyone's* husband, you know,' said Theresa. 'There's been a mistake.'

'Make the most of it. You're the talk of the town, darling.' Carol guffawed. 'There may be a logical explanation, but, you see, Ted *was* seen running naked from your house.'

'But nothing happened . . . he'd jumped from the window above and landed in my little yard.' Theresa stood pointing towards the back window. 'I just lent him a scarf to cover his nakedness and let him out.'

'How typical of him.' Carol shook her head. 'Ted may think of himself as a poet, but at heart he's really just a silly little boy. He enjoys getting Sian worked up. She's so busy with her business projects she doesn't spare much time for him. It's his way of getting attention. In my humble opinion she's asking for it, but poor you. It's a terrible pity you took her wrath. And on your second day here.'

'I've just about had it, Carol,' said Theresa. 'All I do is keep running away. But the problem is that wherever I go, however far I run, I always bring myself and, you see, I'm beginning to realise that it's *me* I'm running from.'

'Bah!' said Carol popping open the jar of jam. 'Stop being self-pitying and absurd. Let me tell you, in my time I've had my share of mockery. I *really do* know what it's like. And I'll tell you now, the best method of defence is indifference. Let them rant and rave. They're the ones who'll make themselves ill, poisoned with their own venom.' She rose. 'If you don't join me and eat something I will finish that whole baguette all alone, and what would that do to my figure? I'd blow up like a balloon, then I really wouldn't forgive you.'

Carol strolled into the kitchen and refilled the percolator.

'I adore this apartment,' she said. 'It's perfect. How many rooms?'

'Bedroom, box room, this one, kitchen and bathroom,' said Theresa, blowing her nose on a paper napkin. 'I'm very lucky.'

'I know we'll both be fired up with caffeine overdoses, but why not? We're going to sit down and you're going to tell me all your problems and plans, and I am going to see how we can get them sorted. And before you open your mouth, you are forbidden to say no.'

Avoiding telling her about the trouble with her daughter, instead Theresa told Carol about her worries about the boiler and money, and her doubts over the move to Bellevue-Sur-Mer.

'Don't doubt that moving here was a good idea, darling,' said Carol, sipping her coffee. 'Best thing you ever did. Money however is another matter. It doesn't grow on trees here any more than it does in London. What are you good at?'

'I used to work for a solicitor.'

Carol put down her cup and looked at Theresa, her eyes sparkling.

'Wow!' she said. 'A solicitor? That's a kind of English pimp, right?'

Theresa was momentarily puzzled, then worked it out.

'Oh, no! Nothing so exciting, I'm afraid. A solicitor is a kind of local lawyer.'

'Oh. An attorney. I was thinking that it was a kind of thrilling world to be admitting to leaving.' Carol took another sip of coffee. 'Going back to the subject of Ted – you say he'd jumped from a window?'

'So it appeared.'

'I don't understand. Why jump? Why not walk out of the front door?'

'I know it sounds mad. I suppose you don't believe me now.'

'No, no. But think about it. He had no reason to risk life and limb, especially while he was in the altogether, did he?'

'His wife was after him, he said.' Theresa tore off a piece of baguette. 'There was no other way out.'

Carol chewed, screwing up her forehead, like a detective on a case. 'Can I look at the drop?'

They walked to the back door and stood for a while in the small yard peering up the sheer rock wall to the hotel windows above.

Carol shook her head and blew a whistling sound of awe.

'That is some jump! Is he a goat, like the god Pan? I've heard he has similar attributes.'

'Really?'

'Covered in hair like a gorilla, with a huge ... you know ... well of course you probably do know, very much the rutting male.'

'I wasn't really looking. I was in too much of a panic.'

'That's the Hotel Astra, which makes the puzzle with Sian coming here to attack you, all the more intriguing.'

'How's that?'

'Think about it. If Sian was really coming into the hotel, after Ted, because she thought he was in there, what would make her now believe that he'd actually been *here* with you? It doesn't add up.'

'No. I suppose not. Look, Carol, I really didn't have anything to do with him you know ...'

Carol flapped her hand, silencing Theresa. 'No, no. I'm sure you didn't. But there is a mystery here. Why was Sian going into that hotel within minutes of arriving in the town? There has to be a reason.'

'Maybe she didn't. Perhaps Ted imagined hearing Sian's voice.'

'Don't be silly. You've heard her. They don't only call

72

her the dragon because of the temper. She has the vocal tone of a corncrake. And why else would he jump? No. If Ted was so convinced that she was coming after him that he jumped naked from one of those windows, he must have had reason to believe she was there.'

Carol took the sputtering percolator from the hob, strolled back to the table with it and flopped down into a chair.

'Oh, by the way, Theresa dear, I really didn't mean so much to ask you "how did you earn a living back in England?"- but rather "how would you like to earn a living here?"'

'Not soliciting!' said Theresa. 'I'm too old and fat.'

'You'd be amazed, my dear,' Carol laughed. 'Men have a very wide spectrum of taste. What are your hobbies, the things you enjoy doing?'

'I like reading.'

'No money to be made out of that, I'm afraid.'

'Cooking?'

Carol pursed her lips and screwed up her eyes. 'Now *that*, my darling, might just be an idea we could run with. How about you . . .'

Carol was interrupted by a hammering on the front door.

Theresa cowered. 'Oh, not again . . .'

'Come on.' Carol rose. 'Stand up to her. This time I'll be right beside you ready to land her a hefty punch if she goes too far. And believe me I've got quite a powerful uppercut.'

Wincing, Theresa went to the door, took a deep breath and opened up.

A man stood on the threshold. 'Oh, sorry. I'm looking for Carol. Someone told me she came in here?'

'In here, William, darling. Come meet my lovely new friend, Theresa.'

Theresa held the door wide and William edged into her living room.

'Your taxi awaits, Divina!' He stopped, open-mouthed and flung his arms out in a gesture of amazement. 'Oh, Theresa, my dear, *where* did you get that wonderful table? Carol, isn't it just divine!'

'*Divine*, as is its owner. Theresa – William. We're all going to adore one another, aren't we, darling?'

Carol reached for her clutch bag, gloves and scarf. She moved towards the door and linked arms with William. 'You're going to sign up, aren't you, William?'

'Oh, God, Carol, you devil!' William gave her an old-fashioned look. 'What are you getting me into now?'

'It's wonderful – so exciting – Theresa is going to give us all classes in cooking.'

In unison Theresa and William exclaimed.

'Thirty euros per person per session. Ten weeks, isn't it, Theresa? Such a bargain. Good Lord, William, look at the time. I'll never get all my things done before the midday gun. Pip, pip!'

And Carol was gone, leaving Theresa standing in the middle of her front room, holding a chunk of buttered baguette, her mouth agape.

8

SALLY SAT ON THE sea wall, swinging her legs, watching a young couple quarrelling as they tried to get the engine going on their little motorboat. What fun it must be to have a boat, she thought. When things got on top of you, you could go down to the harbour, get in, start up the engine and drive off into the sea, away from everything. You might see dolphins, or maybe go fishing for your supper. Think about that!

What would everyone think when they turned up to one of her dinners and not only had she cooked the fish, she'd actually caught it!

'Put the bloody rope back in the box,' snarled the man in the boat.

'It's soaking wet,' sobbed the woman. 'It's too cold and dirty. My hands are filthy. Argh, look at my nails!'

'For Christ's sake,' hissed the man, giving Sally a brusque and insincere smile as he pulled on the throttle and the boat spurted off into the bay, causing the woman to lose her balance and fall into the rear seating well.

It was a beautiful day, and Sally decided today must be the day when she started anew, with fresh hopes and dreams. She was in a rut, and she knew she had to pull herself out. She had every reason to feel happy but kept giving herself artificial hopes which only led to crashing disappointments.

She remembered once, years ago when she was in her teens, being lured into some place full of weirdos on Tottenham Court Road, and put through various stress tests. Then they took her into a curtained room and a rather smelly bearded man in sandals told her the reason that she was stressed was that she wanted to achieve too much – she wanted to be successful at work, and to get married and have a house of her own. If only she'd stop wanting those things she could attain happiness.

What bunkum!

Now that she thought about it she really had achieved all those things she had then wanted. Not that they had really brought her the wild happiness she thought they would, but she'd had fun along the way, and, as to the test, well, she'd only gone into the place to escape a heavy shower.

Eating breakfast yesterday morning with the bluff Englishman Brian had been very cheery. She was sorry he hadn't taken her up on the offer of staying in her spare room. It would be lovely to have someone else in the house for a bit, some company, someone who'd banter comments on the TV programmes, and with whom she could share dinner and breakfast. Cooking for one was never much fun. You always cooked far too much and either had to throw it away or couldn't bear the waste, so ended up eating the lot till you felt sick and put on another inch or two round your waist.

She looked up from the ripples on the water just as

David and Carol's sports car gave a toot as it went bowling up the hill, roof down, with Carol in the driver's seat, David at her side and William in the back seat, heading off in the direction of Nice. Those three were clearly off to town for the day, having fun.

A car! That was an idea. If Sally got a car she could give lifts to people and feel she had a purpose in life, even if it was being the unpaid taxi service. But Carol already had a car. If she got one too and everyone preferred taking a lift from Carol rather than her, wouldn't she then feel even worse?

What she really needed was a project. Something to go to bed thinking about and which made waking up such fun because you couldn't wait to get up and at it again. But what?

The problem with being an ex-actress was that you couldn't just go back to it after years out. And even if you did, then what? You couldn't decide to play Goneril or Blanche DuBois in your living room. You had to wait for other people to ask you, and Sally knew well enough that she'd been out of the loop far too long to be asked to play *anything*, even a cough and a spit on a ropey afternoon soap. Not only that, if she wanted to get back into the acting world, she'd have to move back to London and the rat race, and that was something she *really* could not face.

She adored it here in Bellevue-Sur-Mer. She loved the weather, the light, the scenery, the people, the food, the ambience. And look at all those historical painters who had come here for the same reasons. Years ago Sally had painted. Now that was something you could do of your own volition without other people being involved. Maybe she should try again. Perhaps she'd go and buy a canvas and some acrylics and see how she got on. If she was still any good she could spend a morning standing out here on the quay trying to sell her work to unsuspecting tourists off the cruise ships. She felt a pang of worry at the thought of being judged or, perhaps, recognised by those awful tourists. Not painting, then.

Maybe she should try something new, take classes in something.

That was it.

She'd learn something exciting that she'd never tried before, like Mandarin, or lacemaking.

She walked briskly along the front to the little tourist office which had a lot of handwritten cards up, advertising everything from boats for sale to childminders available. The section of 'classes and private tuition' was surprisingly long, though most of them were courses in French and English, and would therefore be of no use to Sally. She browsed for a few minutes, noting down a few details of classes which looked interesting, then marched back up to her house to make a few phone calls.

On the sharp bend just before the medieval arcade she bumped into Zoe.

'Good Lord, Sally, where are you off to in such a rush?'

'I've decided to take up evening classes, and you're going to join me. Think of the fun we could have.'

'Sally?' Zoe peered over the top of her spectacles. 'Are you feeling quite well?'

'So, Zoe, what do you think?'

'In what subject are you planning to take this course?'

'Oh, I don't know.' Sally felt quite fired up. She threw her arms outward in a huge circular gesture. 'Anything!'

'Sally, dear,' Zoe took a step back. 'Now you're worrying me. Have you completely lost your marbles?'

'I have too much time on my hands . . .'

'Never a truer word was spoken.' Zoe's quavering voice boomed out in the echoing tunnel-like arcade. 'Your problem, Sally, if you don't mind my saying, is that you never stop talking about your children. You spend your hours tirelessly maundering on about your tiresome adult offspring. Don't you realise that there is nothing so boring as other people's children, except, perhaps, other people's dreams? Whoever heard of such an inappropriate subject for a woman, especially of our age?'

Sally was somewhat taken aback. Zoe was from a different generation. She must be at least seventy-five. When you thought about it, she was technically just about old enough to be Sally's mother, so how could she lump them both together under the phrase 'our age'?

'My children need me, Zoe. I'm just trying to be a good mother—'

'Good mother? If you really mean that, then ignore the selfish little bastards. Forget about them for a bit and concentrate on yourself. Look at you. You're quite the frump now. No longer the glam TV star of yesteryear.'

Sally was so astonished she was lost for words.

Zoe steamed on.

'*Good* mothers, Sally, let their children go. Look at lions.'

'But I'm not a—'

'Your children will like you ever so much more if you pay them no attention. Really. Start enjoying your life and then they might be persuaded that it would be fun to visit you here. If I was your child I couldn't be bothered to come. The very thought would give me claustrophobia. Too much pressure. Ugh.'

'But Zoe, I really—'

'As young people say, Sally: get a life.'

'Zoe, why are you being like this? I just told you that I was going to start concentrating on something else, didn't I? Evening classes.'

Zoe threw up her arms in despair. 'Evening classes! Evening classes? Since when did taking evening classes constitute having a life? You need to live a little, girl. Get out of your comfort zone. There are some wonderful discos in town. Dance the night away. Meet some interesting people.'

'Bellevue-Sur-Mer is crammed with interesting people.'

'Bah!' exclaimed Zoe. 'You need to let your knickers down a little, dear.'

'What I do with my knickers is none of your business . . .' Sally stopped when she saw that Faith and her son Alfie, the two who had been at the house viewing yesterday morning, were standing only a few feet away, staring. They had come out of the tiny tabac, holding a small map of the town while deciding which way to go.

'We're looking for the Hôtel Astral,' said Faith, blushing.

'Astra,' corrected Zoe. 'The Hôtel Astra. You need to go up the way and along a little alley. Bougainvillea all the way. It's heavenly.'

'Oh good.' Faith smiled. 'As it's so cheap I was fearful that it might be rather rough.'

'It *is* rather rough,' said Zoe. 'It's the *path* leading to it which is heavenly. The Hôtel Astra is a dump.'

'It's not that bad,' said Sally.

'Oh, dear. This is my son.' Faith winced. 'Alfie, well, he thinks it's a good idea for me to stay here, on site as it were, till I settle in. Our bid was accepted, by the way.'

Sally swallowed. Another chance gone.

'And, anyway, we've just booked a room there for two months.'

'No probs, Mum. If the place is a dive full of marauding sailors and tattooed prostitutes we'll soon find you somewhere else, minus the low-life, and more suitable to a lady of your age and tastes.'

'Who said anything about low-life?' said Zoe. 'Low-life would be terribly exciting and would certainly be preferable to the actual clientele of the Hotel Astra, which consists in the main part of Australian rucksackers and British obese, illiterate lobsters sporting dayglo shorts.'

'Gap-year kids and package tourists, mainly,' said Sally, wondering why she felt obliged to apologise for the hotel. 'It is all pretty basic.' She hesitated before going on, afraid that Zoe might start up again.

'Everywhere else seems to be full,' said Alfie.

Sally had an idea. 'I have a spare room in my place,' she said. 'You could pay me less than you'd pay the Astra. It would give me a little pin money.'

'No doubt to spend on lessons in astronomy and motorcycle maintenance.' Zoe gave a little wave to no one in particular and walked on. 'Good luck to the lot of you.'

'Don't worry about Zoe,' Sally whispered. 'She's a little eccentric.'

'Heard that,' shouted Zoe without turning round, as she beetled up the hill, round a corner and out of sight.

Sally went with Faith and Alfie to see the only available room at the Astra. It was a dark poky space with a tiny window looking out on a wall. It had a shabby rug on the scratched wooden floor and was not easily reached, necessitating a hefty climb up a complex set of irregular stairs. Sally asked the manager if that was the best he could do, and he explained that there was a much nicer double room but it had been booked a month ago by a local person on behalf of a young lady who had been already installed, though she might be leaving in a day or so. But the room was reserved for her with a retainer on a short notice basis.

'In other words,' snapped Sally, 'it's already taken. Why not just say so?'

Sally took them up the road to her house.

There it was agreed all round that, rather than pay to take the dingy box room at the Hôtel Astra, Faith would spend the waiting weeks in Sally's better spare room, the one she kept pristine at all times in hopes of a visit from Marianne.

'Let me give you a deposit,' said Alfie, pulling out his wallet as he flopped down on the bed.

'It's all right, I'll do it.' Faith took a while to get her purse out of her bag, but *she* handed Sally the money.

'Here. This is what I would have paid the hotel for the whole stay. You must have it.'

'But I couldn't . . .'

'Please,' said Faith. 'It will make me feel better knowing it's all settled.'

'If you insist. Look, you make yourself at home, while I go downstairs and rustle up a cup of tea. Would that be nice?'

'Lovely,' said Faith.

'Strong please,' said Alfie, 'with one sugar and a tiny bit of milk.'

'He's very particular,' said Faith. 'Alfie likes things just so.'

As she pulled open the tea caddy Sally felt elated. Still clutching the wad of euros she picked up the phone and dialled one of the numbers she had written down from the cards on the noticeboard, the class that earlier this morning she thought would be way beyond her means.

'Hello,' she said. 'I'd like to sign up for the power-boating course.'

9

THERESA WAS TOTALLY PANICKED at having been thrown into this cookery class idea of Carol's, though it would certainly be one way of raising the money for a new boiler.

Wrapping her new turquoise mac tightly around her she opened the front door, and peered out, scanning the road for hysterical blondes on the rampage. When she saw that the coast was clear she furtively darted up the street in the direction of the main town and the railway station.

She only had a few minutes' wait on the graffiti-smeared platform before a train pulled in for the ten-minute journey into Nice. Her plan was to find a bookshop and buy a few recipe books to pore over, and also to get a basketful of goodies from the vegetable market.

In the central part of town she bought a shopping trolley. After a quick browse through a second-hand bookshop she found some interesting-looking old recipe books, and by the time she reached the market she was just in time to catch the last of the stall-holders packing up before the market space was taken over by the bars and cafes for the afternoon. Somehow Theresa just managed to buy some great cheeses, a bag of olives and a random selection of vegetables.

Exhausted but inspired, Theresa flopped down at a sunny terrace table and ordered a coffee. The waitress was rather snippy with her as the tables were already being laid up for luncheon. Theresa had forgotten how strictly the French took their ritual of mealtimes. Luckily the girl relented – for the moment.

As she relaxed in the warm rays of the sun Theresa's phone rang. It was Imogen. She picked up.

'So how's it going in Fantasy Land?'

'You mean Bellevue-Sur-Mer.'

'Wherever . . .' Imogen gave the usual world-weary sigh. 'I thought you were moving to Nice?'

'Well, it's not quite Nice, Imogen, but very near. I'm in Nice now.'

Theresa told her daughter that it was lovely and suggested that she should come out at half term to see for herself, and bring the children.

'How will I have the time for that, Mother? It's all right for you. You live in a daydream. I'm in the real world and I have obligations.'

Theresa couldn't help but wonder what these obligations consisted of, as Imogen didn't go out to work and even had a cleaner. All she really had to do with her day was look after her husband and children and go to her Pilates classes.

'Imogen, I am sitting on a sun-kissed terrace with a bag full of beautiful fruit and vegetables which cost me substantially less that it would have cost me in

Wimbledon. I am a few steps away from a sparkling azure sea and surrounded by beauty wherever I look. I imagine you have the lights on inside today because of the dark and the freezing drizzle, while I am sunbathing.'

'You're so impractical.' Imogen sighed. 'Weather isn't everything. You'll soon get bored of sunny days.'

'You're right, I probably will. But I just thought that a break from England's miserable bleak February might be nice for you. There's a carnival in a few weeks' time.'

'A carnival!' Imogen let forth another long world-weary sigh. 'That's fine, Mother. I'll leave you to your rosy spectacles for another week or so. No doubt the scales will fall from your eyes. Michael says he gives it a month before you'll be running back to us for help.'

When Theresa put the phone back into her handbag she felt furious, but even more determined to make things work. Michael! What a cheek. She thanked God she hadn't been tempted to ask them if they would lend her the money for the boiler.

She gathered her things together and walked up through the winding alleys of the Old Town, heading for the bus stand and a bus home.

On the bus, when Theresa could tear her eyes away from the stunning views over the Bay of Angels, she took out her turquoise pen and scribbled some words on to a scrap of paper, composing an advert for her cookery classes. Maybe classes sounded too formal. A cookery club sounded more fun. She scrawled the word 'club'.

She totted up some figures and made the decision to borrow the money from her capital, even if it did mean losing a whole year's interest as a penalty. But at least if she did that she could get the work on the boiler done right away. If she was going to be doing lots of cooking she'd need running hot water.

If she could only make this thing work, she would recoup the money over time and, once it was paid for, have a small income.

And also, while she was putting up the signs on noticeboards and in shop windows, she could search the boards to see if anyone needed some typing done, or maybe bookkeeping. If she could get a little income from anywhere she would be fine. As the bus neared the stop she put the pen into her handbag.

She climbed out of the bus and realised she'd made a mistake not coming back home by train as the bus stop was right at the top of the town, while the railway station was only a main road away. Now she had to bump the heavy trolley down an endless set of stone steps before reaching the alleyways of the old village and home.

She slung her bag from her shoulder, balanced the trolley in front of her and took it slowly, wheeling it down one step at a time, while gripping tight to the rusty iron handrail.

Then she heard a clatter of feet coming down swiftly behind her. She clung on to the handle of the trolley and stepped aside, to get out of the way.

The feet got nearer but as they reached her, instead of passing her, someone shoved Theresa from behind, knocking her down. She tripped over the trolley's wheels and stumbled down a few steps before landing palms down, sprawled out on a stone step. As she came to a stop, the man moved in close and wrenched her handbag out of her grasp. She could smell the cigarette smoke on his leather jacket. He shoved her handbag under his arm and then kicked her trolley, so that it tumbled down ahead of her, spilling fruit and vegetables, which bounced away, then rolled into the dark little alleyways at the bottom.

The thief followed the trolley, rushing down the rest of the steps, and disappearing out of sight into the dark warren of the old village before the trolley and its contents finally came to rest.

Theresa reached up for the rail and tried to pull herself up, but her hands were badly grazed and she was shaking. A blue throbbing lump was already swelling up on her knuckle.

She tried to yell out, but her voice came out in a weedy kitten-like mewl.

She heard the thief stop running. His steps turned into a casual stroll as he walked away, all innocence.

Theresa pulled herself into a sitting position and took a few deep breaths. Then she stood and took a tentative step, but her legs were shaking so violently she was scared that she would fall, so she sat again. She could feel the cold and damp of the stone penetrating her coat.

'I say! Are you all right down there?' A man's voice from above.

Theresa twisted her head round to see a tall man in an old-fashioned navy blazer and chinos making his way down the steps.

'I was mugged,' said Theresa. 'He took my handbag.'

'You're English too. Oh dear, look at all your shopping,' said the man. 'How awful. I'm Brian, by the way. Oh Lord, poor you. You stay there. Let me help.'

He walked briskly down the steps and started retrieving as much of the shopping as he could. 'I'll just put it all together,' he said. 'Then I'll come back and get you. Don't worry. Sit still and take some deep breaths.'

Brian helped Theresa all the way down to her flat, holding his arm out for her to clutch, wheeling her trolley with his other hand.

'You should make yourself a stiff drink,' he said. 'You've had a shock. Do you have any whisky or brandy?'

At the front door, Theresa realised her keys were in her stolen handbag.

'I can't get in. He's got my keys.'

'Oh, good Lord,' said Brian. 'That's unlucky. I wonder what's French for a locksmith?'

'I was due to have it done, anyway,' explained Theresa. 'I've only just bought the place.'

'The estate agents will know a locksmith,' said Brian. 'They must have to organise it all the time.'

'I don't have a phone!' Theresa realised she had no wallet, no credit cards and no way of paying. 'He's taken the lot.'

'Let me sort it out,' Brian pulled his own phone out of his blazer pocket. 'I was only going round a house with the gentleman myself this morning.' He cupped his hand round the phone and pointed down. 'Oh, by the way, your leg is bleeding.'

Theresa looked down to see that her tights were ripped and torn, with dirty black patches, and blood was oozing through a hole at the knee.

She sat on the small wall surrounding her front yard and burst into sobs.

Talking on the phone Brian walked out to the street, phone on one ear, his hand covering the other. He talked for a while then came back smiling.

'It's lunchtime. But I did manage to speak to a very nice girl, who is going to get a locksmith down here as quickly as possible. She says that you must talk to the bank, and they can arrange for you to get cash. I'm hoping you didn't have your passport in the bag?'

Theresa was numb with it all. She didn't move. 'I don't know,' she said.

'Do you have a friend, whose place you could go to?'

Theresa shook her head. 'I'm new here.'

'Oh dear,' said Brian. 'Like me. Look, borrow my phone. I'll pop back for it in an hour or so. I have a few things I need to do. Will you be all right if I leave you?'

'Thank you so much.' Theresa's voice came out this time in a feeble reedy croak. 'You're very kind.'

She spent ten minutes on the phone to the bank, who told her she must first report the robbery to the police, and then come into the bank, which was in Nice, near the Promenade du Paillon.

She then tackled the call to the police.

They too needed her to come in person to report the theft.

Theresa realised that the only thing she could do,

for now, was sit and wait for the locksmith. Then after she'd got inside and washed up she would tackle the rest.

She pulled an apple from her trolley and took a bite.

S ALLY HAD AN IDEA. She phoned Ted to put it to
him, but Sian answered.

'You're not after his body, too, are you?' she joked.
'What did you want him for?'

'Well . . .' Sally was at a loss. She actually wanted to
persuade Ted to join her taking one of the classes, but
knew she could only do that kind of thing to Ted
himself. 'As you were in town, I was phoning to ask
you both to lunch today.'

Sian accepted. 'Ted can't come though. He's in the
doghouse, with me,' she said. 'So, while I had a meeting, I've sent him off on a nasty chore. He's taking the
car up to some nearby hilltop village for the annual
service. I doubt he'll get back before coffee.'

A couple of minutes after Sally put down the phone,
the doorbell rang. She couldn't imagine Sian could
have got up the hill so fast.

She opened up, expecting to see the postman standing there with a parcel, but it was her daughter
Marianne, leaning against the side of a limousine with
its engine running.

'Hi Mama! I told you I would whizz by. Can only

manage a hello–goodbye cos I have to be at the airport in twenty minutes.'

'But darling, surely you can come in for a coffee or something?'

'Absolutely not. But I knew you'd be furious if I was passing so near and didn't say hello.'

'But where ... what ... ?'

'Business along the coast. Just a whistle stop. I'm off to Rome now. Can't be late for the flight.'

Sian appeared, waving at Sally from along the street.

Marianne formed her hand into the shape of a mobile phone. 'I'll phone you.'

She climbed back into the car. The car sped off.

'My daughter,' said Sally, crushed but putting on a brave face. 'She's in business too, as I told you.'

'Nice,' said Sian, watching the car disappear along the twisty uphill road.

'It's a work thing,' replied Sally. 'She's a high flier.'

'So I see,' said Sian.

Half an hour later the two women managed to change the subject and Sian sprawled on a chair at Sally's dining table, safe in Ted's absence, talking about him. She also had much to say about the new inhabitant of the flat on the seafront, which Sally had coveted. The new woman had, it seemed, seduced Ted.

Sally had seen the woman involved, shopping in the village earlier. She found it hard to believe Sian's story as the new woman was rather on the large side and not at all Ted's usual type. She felt sure that Sian had got things wrong.

'Have you asked him outright?'

'I don't need to. Enough people witnessed him running away from the scene of the crime. Anyhow, I gave her what for, so I don't think she'll be likely to try the same again.'

Sally was starting to get tired of the way Sian never stopped going on about Ted and his errant ways. She began to wonder if Sian didn't work at keeping his rampant sexuality inflamed by her jealousy as some weird fetish of her own. Why else, if she was so upset by his gallivanting, was she always going off, leaving him behind? Sian never stopped treating him like a naughty boy who would lose his pocket money if he didn't obey her. She never included him in her plans, even today she had made sure he got uninvited here, and, not content with that, she then spent hours slagging him off to Sally and anyone else who would listen.

Poor old Ted. He was so bored and lonely he spent much of his time making a great play for every passing woman who came through town, which in the summer was a very high number. All he needed was to ask a girl in a cafe to pass the sugar, and within half an hour they'd be together in her hotel room.

After what seemed an eternity of listening to Sian going on and on and on while she toyed with the salad on her plate, not eating anything, Sally came out with it.

'I always wonder, Sian, if you are so frightened of losing Ted, why you don't take him with you when you go off on all your high-flying business trips?'

'Oh, Sally, you just don't understand Ted.' Sian gave Sally a pitying smile. 'Your husband was a businessman. He would have been able to keep up in a world like mine. But Ted isn't like that. Ted is a poet.' She gave Sally a beatific smile. 'It's a totally different mindset. Ted needs his freedom and independence, and to be somewhere beautiful, which is why I bought the place here. For him. So that he can concentrate on his poetry.'

Sally wondered when was the last time Ted had written a poem, let alone had anything published. His main claim to fame was having once, back in the 1980s, written some long hippy-style ode along the lines of 'Desiderata'. It had been reproduced *ad nauseam* on postcards, tea towels and posters which hung on students' walls all over the English-speaking world and made him quite a bit of money.

But that had been years ago, in the days when Sally herself was making money and still had a TV career.

'I just think . . .' Sally started but Sian interrupted her.

'I don't need marriage guidance from you, Sally. I have my own way, thank you very much, and it has worked well, thus far.' She held up her hand to prevent Sally interrupting. 'Ted really wouldn't know one end of a business deal from another. Can you imagine him grappling with a PowerPoint presentation or a spreadsheet? It's ridiculous.'

'He's bored, Sian, bored and lonely.'

'Well . . .' Sian seemed to hesitate before delivering the news. 'I've got a lovely new PA. She's English, got a very good degree from a real university, not one of those cornershops that dole out MAs in sewing, and from now on she's going to help me out on the business side of things.'

'And how will that help Ted, exactly?' Sally realised she sounded tart, and poured herself and Sian another glass of rosé.

'This girl is so impressive. She'll take a lot off my mind. I'm hoping to groom her up so that she can organise much of the business, and then one day soon I'll be able to retire. Well, not *really* retire, but I'll be able to take a lot more time off. What's the point of owning a lovely house here if I'm always on the road?' Sian took another swig of wine and, barely pausing for breath, continued. 'Now as you know, Sally, despite the recession, my shops in the UK are beating the downwards trend, and so I'm thinking about doing some business locally, maybe open up a small boutique here or hereabouts.'

'Here?' Sally couldn't believe it. Sian's London shops were temples of high fashion.

'It won't be like the London ones,' Sian added. 'It'll be more of a novelty shop, something on the lines of those old Carnaby Street places, you know, which not only sell cheapish clothes, but fun things too, like posters and mugs with amusing things written on them.'

Sally had no idea how to react to this stuff. And the very thought of a horrible shop like the one Sian was proposing here in Bellevue-Sur-Mer was awful. It was as though Sian wanted to turn the place into a fake tourist trap, just as so many surrounding towns and villages had become. What made Bellevue-Sur-Mer so nice was that it still kept hold of an everyday reality – the majority of shops and restaurants were for locals, not tourists.

'So, for a while this girl is going to be my right-hand

woman. She will join me on important trips, but, when I need things overseeing anywhere else, I shall put her in charge. I just thought you should know.' Sian chuckled, leant forward and whispered confidentially, 'When she's down here she has strict instructions to keep an eye out on Ted, and report back to me.'

'Like the Stasi?' said Sally. 'Ted won't like that.'

'He won't know.' Sian glugged her wine glass empty. 'I'm hiding her from him. I haven't told him about her, and I'm not going to. She won't be staying with us. I've got her a room in a local hotel, where she can come and go.'

'When does she arrive?'

'So you can warn him?' Sian wagged a finger. 'No, no, no, no. Anyway, for all you know she may be here already.'

Sally couldn't help herself wincing. How sorry she felt for poor old Ted, having some brainy business whizz-kid, paid by his wife, whose main purpose appeared to be spying on him.

She also felt rather miffed that Sian hadn't thought of approaching Marianne if she needed help with the business. Marianne had a degree too, and all kinds of certificates in business management – and, if she'd used Marianne, Sian wouldn't have had to run to the ridiculous expense of a hotel.

'My daughter is qualified you know, Sian, in business studies. If you ever . . . ?'

'Yes, yes,' snapped Sian. 'You deal with your business; I'll deal with mine.'

There was a rustle, rather than a knock, on the architrave round the kitchen door.

'It's only me. Sorry to interrupt.'

Sally had entirely forgotten that Faith was upstairs.

'Oh, Faith, do come in.' Sally stood up. 'Please feel free to use the kitchen whenever you like.'

'I only want to fetch myself a cup of tea,' said Faith. 'This whole morning has been pretty exhausting, I'm afraid.'

'Sian, this is my house-guest, Faith. She's just buying the Molinaris' old place. Sian is a local businesswoman. Very high-flying.'

Sian gave a glacial smile.

'You're lucky, though, Faith,' said Sally, filling the kettle. 'You have that lovely boy of yours helping you out. He must be quite a support. There's not many young men who take such an interest in their mothers, you know.'

Faith bit her lip and nodded. 'I'll just get that cup of tea and get out of your way.'

'Ted'll be in *her* knickers next,' said Sian, as soon as Faith was up the stairs.

'Oh, Sian, really . . .' Sally hoped that Faith hadn't heard Sian's remark.

'I don't know what's wrong with him, Sally. He needs treatment.'

Sally had had enough. She decided to come out with her opinion, no matter how much it might annoy Sian.

'You know the problem with Ted, Sian? You treat him appallingly. That's what's wrong. You behave as though you're his mother and he's a wayward adolescent boy, so he acts like one. Ted needs something to care about, some project to keep him feeling, I don't know . . . wanted.'

'He has his poetry.'

'Oh, for God's sake, Sian, you know what I mean.' Sally sipped her glass of rosé and watched Sian's face harden. 'Yes, we're all so envious of you because you still have a husband around. But why not value him? Put *him* in charge of your new shop. Let him have the business to care about and take him away with you instead of some fancy assistant.'

Sian looked at her watch and rose abruptly from the table, grabbing her handbag and coat from the back of the chair.

'You said it. You're jealous of me, that's what it is. Jealous.'

Before Sally could contradict her she continued.

'I'm late for a meeting.' She bent forward and made a feeble attempt at kissing the air on either side of Sally's face. 'And I have a flight to catch. Must rush. Thanks for the snack.'

And she was gone.

Snack indeed, thought Sally who felt she had spent the better part of the morning putting together a fancy three-course lunch for Sian. They'd not got to dessert, so now she had two portions left. Sally put them on a pair of side plates and laid a tray. She knew she mustn't get into the habit of behaving as though she was running a hotel, but she felt sorry for Faith. Also, Sally had already laid down the rent money Faith had given her on her new course, so she didn't want Faith moving out and asking for it back.

She took the tray upstairs and knocked on Faith's door.

When Faith opened up Sally could see that she had been crying.

'My friend had to leave before pudding,' she said. 'So I thought it would be nice for us to eat them.'

Faith smiled. 'You're very kind.'

'It's only two tarts, from up the road,' Sally said, then laughed. 'I could have phrased that better,' she added.

Faith tidied away a sheaf of paperwork about her new home.

'It's a lovely house you're buying.'

'A little large for me.' Faith shrugged. 'But I suppose if I'd spent the same amount of money in London I'd be lucky to have got a bedsit.'

'True,' said Sally. 'Will your son be living out here with you?'

'Oh no,' said Faith. 'He works in London, in the City, you know, finance and all that stuff.'

'Another one.' Sally laughed. 'So *he's* to blame for the world's troubles!'

Faith looked so upset by this remark that Sally hastily covered for herself.

'Poor bankers, no one likes them any more, do they?'

'He's not exactly a banker,' said Faith. 'He is a financial advisor.'

'That's lucky for you. I wish I'd had one of those when I was earning.'

'I feel a bit like a fish out of water, here in France,' said Faith. 'It's very daunting leaving everything you know in England and coming out to a place you don't know at all.' She sighed. 'I don't even speak French.'

'Oh, don't worry, Faith. You'll fit in in no time.' Sally smiled and laid the plates of fruit tart on the bedside table. 'It really is beautiful here, and it's very kind on old bones, you know. And as for the language, well, you can get by with only a few words. Most French people speak English, to some degree.'

Sally felt quite drained from the day so far. The most cheering thing was the scenery outside the window. She smoothed down the bedspread and added: 'Remember, Faith, you have us. We're quite a gang, you know, the Brits of B-S-M!'

11

SUDDENLY, AS EVENING FELL, Theresa's flat was like Piccadilly Circus. While the locksmith fiddled with the front door, a plumber and his mate were busily dismantling her boiler.

Theresa herself, calm now, sat at the glass-topped table, writing out a stack of index cards and putting them into two separate piles, one with details of her Cookery Club meetings and the other with ads for the spare room, which she had decided to let out for the moment, until things settled down. She had looked around for the turquoise pen Mr Jacobs had given her and realised, with a groan, that it must have been in her snatched handbag.

Carol was whirling around making cups of tea, while her husband David was measuring up all the walls and radiators for the plumber.

Ted was in the kitchen helping the plumber.

Theresa had been startled when she saw Ted standing on her doorstep, but then Carol stepped up behind him with a bright grin. 'I'm gathering the troops,' she cried, while Theresa stood open-mouthed.

'What?' Ted had joked as he crossed the threshold. 'Don't recognise me with my clothes on?'

Naturally Theresa went into a flat panic.

'But your wife . . . She thinks . . .'

'She's wrong,' replied Ted. 'You know that. I know that. It was a very nice English girl I met in a bar. Didn't even have time to exchange names, as it happens. And, now my beloved wife isn't here to suspect anything between you and me. Flown off to New York this afternoon, only gave me two seconds warning, as usual, so . . .' he gave Theresa a saucy wink, '. . . in the meanwhile I am your slave. I know I owe you one for the roasting you had from her. Very sorry about that, mate. Oh, and I didn't tell her, you know, I think it was one of the pesky waiters at the bistro who saw me running along the way with me family jewels on display. He must have thought I'd gone troppo. Or was jealous of me physique.' Ted rolled his sleeves up. 'Anyway, let's get at it. 57, here, rounded me up as I do know a bit about building and so on.'

'57?'

'Don't worry about it. It's my pet nickname for Carol.'

Earlier, as Theresa sat waiting after Brian had left her on the doorstep, clutching his mobile phone, the locksmith had phoned to say sorry but he couldn't be there for a few hours. Desperate to get things moving, Theresa had gone straight up to the police station, then headed back into Nice, where she had a very productive talk with the French bank manager. He had not only arranged for a new card and some immediate cash, but also proposed that, rather than touch her capital, which was on a deal where she couldn't touch the money for a year without penalties, Theresa take a small loan towards the new central heating. His only condition was that she moved fast and paid it off quickly, maybe got some income coming in soon, from the classes and perhaps letting the spare room.

As she came out of the bank, Theresa ran into Carol and David, who were waiting at Place Garibaldi, for the same bus back to Bellevue-Sur-Mer.

'Lent the car to William,' David explained. 'So we're reliant on public transportation. Which is fun, once in a while.'

When Theresa told them her tale of woe, both husband and wife got on to their respective mobile phones and started getting things moving.

Within an hour the plumber was in Theresa's kitchen, along with everybody else.

Theresa marvelled that anyone could be so kind. But Carol was even more radiant as she corralled people into coming forward to help a neighbour in distress.

Just when Theresa was wondering how many people could comfortably fit into her flat, the locksmith popped his head round the door and ushered in William.

He made a ta-daa sound, and stood there grinning and waving the car keys.

'Carol, you called? Your car is at your service.'

'Darling, I know you won't mind running Theresa round the town while she puts up her little signs all over the place, will you?' Carol shooed Theresa out into the waiting car. 'Thank you, sweetheart. You're a darling.'

What would have taken hours by foot, with all the steep hills, took all of ten minutes in a car. They darted round from the tabac to the library and the tourist office and a few other places along the way.

Though, for Theresa, the conversation was at first rather stilted, mainly weather, the majestic views and similar small talk, once William discovered that Theresa had moved to Bellevue-Sur-Mer from Highgate they chattered away. As a student, William told her, he had had a small flat in Jackson's Lane. He was studying at the Slade at the time, before he moved into the interior design business. Once he made a bit of money he'd moved down to Wimbledon.

Theresa told him that she spent much time there too, babysitting her grandchildren.

'Very twee, Wimbledon,' said William. 'But I got lots of work. Everyone was remodelling their kitchens and living rooms,' he said. 'They all wanted their house to look exactly like the one next door. Mysterious.'

He changed gear as they sped down the hill towards the water's edge. 'I adore that table set of yours, by the way. Well done you, picking up something so fabulous.'

'It was my big extravagance,' said Theresa.

'Always be extravagant.' William pulled the car into an empty space in a central car park. 'The horrors you'll feel from being extravagant are never as soul-destroying as the ones you get when you're tight and deprive yourself of the things you crave.'

'Depends whether you mean tight drunk or tight mean!'

'I'm sure you're never drunk.'

'No, never.' Theresa laughed. 'Can't afford it.'

When they arrived back at the flat, the new boiler was already being fitted.

'He's going to attach the thing to the taps, then see about replacing the radiators next week,' Carol explained. 'But at least in the meanwhile you'll have patchy heat and plentiful hot water.' Carol indicated down to the small halogen heater which was glowing in the corner. 'I must say that's a very effective little thing.'

Theresa paid the locksmith and had just closed the front door after him, when the bell rang again.

'He's forgotten something.' Carol looked around for a misplaced tool box.

'Or he's angling for a drink,' said William.

Brian was standing on the step clutching a bottle of wine.

'Oh, you've come for your phone.' Theresa stepped into the bustling living room. 'Everything has changed since I last saw you. It's like a miracle.'

Brian adjusted his tie and blazer and came in.

'Oh, Lord! Actually, it's all a bit of a coincidence.' He held up a piece of paper. 'I was just at the tabac, looking at the "rooms to let" signs and I came across this one. I had no idea it was my damsel in distress till I arrived here at your front door!'

'Another Limey!' Carol rose and held out a hand. 'My my, our little Anglo-Saxon community is growing like mint. It's sprawling all over the place! I'm Carol, by the way, and, if you hadn't guessed from my accent, I'm an American. And the fellow over there being very butch with some copper piping is my husband, David.'

'Brian Powell.' Brian gave a little deferential nod as he shook Carol's hand. 'What an enchanting place this is.'

William also introduced himself, while Theresa

went off in search of Brian's phone, which was on a bench in the kitchen, surrounded by wrenches and tins of Plumbers' Mate.

She grabbed it and handed it over. 'I'm so grateful, Brian. I don't know where I'd have been without you.'

'Oh, don't worry.' He held up the bottle of wine. 'I brought this because I was heading here to give it to you to help cheer you up after ... what happened.' Brian shuffled from foot to foot. 'Could I see the room now, or should I come back later?' he asked.

'Oh – you seriously want to see the room!' Theresa walked him through and showed him the spare room. She couldn't believe how an afternoon could turn round so quickly and how her despair had turned to excited hope and happiness.

'I know it's a little dark,' she said, pulling open the curtains. 'And there will be a bed, of course. I'm off furniture hunting first thing in the morning.'

'It's not anything permanent,' said Brian. 'You do understand I only want somewhere till I get settled?'

'That's fine with me,' said Theresa. 'You're exactly what I'm looking for.'

'Then I'll take it,' said Brian with a smile to the roomful of people. 'Aren't I lucky!'

'Stay for a drink, Brian?' Theresa turned to the assembly. 'Anyone got a corkscrew?'

'Yay,' said Ted, producing a penknife from his pocket. 'It's wine o'clock.'

12

SALLY ARRIVED BRIGHT AND early for her first lesson in power-boating.

The school was round the corner from the port in Nice. The building itself, a dark shop with painted-out windows, was up a small shabby alleyway off the busy road leading to the ferries which sailed night and day to Corsica and Sardinia.

Her teacher, Jean-Philippe, a tattooed, brawny bloke with a beard, who looked like something out of a motorbikers' convention, greeted her at the door.

The first thing he did was sneer at her attire.

'We're not going for a picnic on the beach, lady,' he said. 'I need concentration and hard work. I've no time for time-wasting charlatans.'

Sally shrugged and tried to smile to cover her embarrassment. Her clothing did look more like a woman in an ad for some exotic luxury jewellery line than a woman going out in a boat.

Jean-Philippe showed her along a dark corridor to a dirty classroom piled high with parts of outboard motors, skeins of rope and old tarpaulins. She drew up a plastic seat and, feeling quite out of place, prayed that the other people on the course would show up soon.

Jean-Philippe took a piece of chalk and scribbled a lot of mysterious symbols on to a large blackboard. He turned briskly and glared at her.

'So how much do you know about reading a chart?' he asked.

'A little.' Sally wasn't sure whether she was blushing at her own lie, for the truth was she knew absolutely nothing about chart reading and just hoped that it wouldn't be too different from geography maps she remembered from school.

'Navigation?'

'Not that much, to be honest.'

'Do you recognise any of these symbols?' He stabbed at the board with a long plastic ruler.

Sally shook her head.

'Knots and knotting?'

Sally winced.

Jean-Philippe let out a profound and deep sigh, then turned and flopped down on the table.

'You housewives,' he said, pulling his knees up and exposing rather dirty toes in old brown sandals exactly at her eye level. 'You come along here to get your seaworthy certificates, thinking the sea is this pretty vista on a greetings card. But it isn't. The sea is a ferocious, capricious, murdering monster. You will never control the sea, you will never dominate the sea, you will never even predict the sea. The least you can do is find out how best to master yourself so that, when the sea pulls one of her surprises on you, you might have a fighting chance of survival. It won't be comfortable and cosy, but what you will learn here may teach you how to manage her in all her fury, how to respond to her deceptively soft touch and how to survive her piques, her tantrums and her rages.'

Sally gulped.

This was not the picture of a power-boating course she had imagined.

But Jean-Philippe was right. She had seen herself lazily turning a large polished wooden wheel as warm zephyrs blew through her hair and a glamorous but powerful white gin-palace, packed with happy drinking chums, cut through the calm aquamarine sea.

Jean-Philippe slammed his chalk down on the floor. 'As I am giving my time here to teach you, the least you could do is listen to me.'

'I am listening.' Sally sat up. 'But are we going to start before the others arrive?'

'What others?' Jean-Philippe stood up and glared at her. 'It is just you and me, Madame.'

Sally wondered whether, if she pulled out now, she would get her money back, but was too frightened to say anything.

'We start today,' said Jean-Philippe, 'with basic safety procedures, a look at charts and tying essential knots.'

Sally took a deep breath and resolved to work hard, and win Jean-Philippe round.

By late afternoon when her first day was over, her brain was dizzy with the differences and advantages between various types of motors: outboard, inboard and outdrive, and how to choose and use different fuels. She knew which was land and which was sea on a nautical chart, and recognised various symbols for rocks, wrecks, lighthouses, shipping lanes and forbidden areas. She knew the difference between the signs and regulations for an anchorage and a marina, or, as the French called them (which Sally preferred), a port de plaisance.

As Sally put on her coat to leave, her hands were freezing, dirty and grazed with rope burns. But she could now do a round-turn-and-two-half-hitches knot. She also knew how to create a bowline, a sheet bend and a clove hitch.

As he wished her a good evening Jean-Philippe did not smile, but only told her that next time she should wear some real waterproof, windproof, sensible clothing and more suitable shoes, for, after some more theory, regardless of weather, next time they would be actually going out on a boat.

Sally got into a taxi, noticing that the wind was up. Motoring over the hill, she glanced out at the bay. The sea looked magnificent and picture-perfect azure blue. But a small motor yacht coming into Villefranche was pitching all over the place and even the huge cruise ship anchored in the Rade rocked from side to side.

It was funny how she had never really noticed things like that before. If the sun was out she imagined that all at sea was fine and dandy. Driving home along the coastal road, Sally observed the sea, trying to get herself mentally prepared.

As she climbed out of the car and paid the driver, the sun was setting. She took out the large canvas bag which Jean-Philippe had presented to her as she left the sea school. It was heavy. She lugged it over her shoulder and let herself in.

She put on the kettle and sang to herself for a good half hour then, once she had a cup of tea and some biscuits, she flopped down on to the kitchen chair. She pulled the bag on to the table and poured out all the books and things she had been given to swot up on. Everything looked daunting, from a book of sea rules and regulations, much like the Highway Code booklet, a card with diagrams of semaphore and Morse code symbols and photos of clouds and boats with various different lights on, to local sea charts, a pair of pincer things, a strange plastic slide rule. There was even a length of rope.

Good Lord, there was so much more to this course than she expected.

She pored over a page of the book. It concerned light-houses and the meaning of the lights emitted from them and from buoys. She went to the window to watch the two lighthouses at the end of nearby caps. The rays came at different intervals. She counted the seconds.

In the silence she heard a creak upstairs.

Her heart stopped. Had someone broken in?

Only then did she remember about Faith renting her spare room, and felt really badly that she hadn't called out Hello or some greeting when she'd come in, which must have been almost an hour ago. How rude must that seem?

She put the kettle on again, then called up to Faith that she was brewing up a pot of tea.

After a few moments Faith appeared on the stairs. 'I really don't want to be any bother.'

Sally sighed to herself. She really didn't want some-one who was going to bring down her mood like this. But having taken the money – and already spent it on her course – she had to make it work. She put on a bright smile.

'It's no bother really – just a cup of tea and a chat.'

Faith came down and sat. With light, careful fingers she inspected the books and pamphlets.

'Do you have a son?'

'Yes I do, actually. Tom.'

'Does he live locally?'

'No. He's in India. I believe.'

'But . . . ?'

Sally suddenly realised that Faith must have thought that the books were his.

'No. These are mine,' she said. 'I'm trying for a certifi-cate in powerboat-driving.'

Faith looked aghast. 'Is that like Formula One, those huge red racing things?'

'No, no. It's anything really from what we might have called a rubber dinghy with an outboard motor up to those huge white boats which millionaires all moor at Monte Carlo and St Tropez. Here in France you need certificates before you can drive anything with a motor, even a little wooden fishing boat.'

'Oh dear,' said Faith. 'It's all so alien, isn't it?'

Sally was mystified. Everything about this woman seemed to indicate that she wanted to stay in England. Why was she moving to Bellevue-Sur-Mer? Sally didn't like to ask straight out, but it certainly was a mystery to be solved.

'Did you come to the Côte d'Azur, before?' she asked

tentatively, hoping it might spark a conversation explaining everything. 'And fell in love with the place?'

'Never.' Faith sipped her tea. 'It's the first time I've been anywhere, really.'

'So what made you chose to settle here, exactly?'

Faith put down her cup. Sally noticed the saucer tremble slightly.

'My son picked it for me. He chose the place and the house. He knows me very well.'

Sally doubted that.

'It's certainly a lovely house.' Sally ripped open a packet of biscuits and poured them on to a plate. 'Do you have plans?'

Faith suddenly rose and moved to the stairs. 'I'll fetch them,' she said.

'No! No!' Sally laughed. 'I meant did you have plans for things to *do* here.'

'I'll get them anyhow,' said Faith, disappearing up the stairs. 'I don't understand any of it, but maybe you can explain it all to me.'

'It's very big,' said Sally, looking at the house plans a few minutes later. 'Lots of rooms for one person.'

'Too big,' said Faith. 'But it is quite beautiful. I can see that. It's only that I . . .' Her voice trailed off.

'Wanted to stay in England?'

'It isn't that either, really. I always thought, as I got older, that I would be able to start doing those things I always wanted to do, and couldn't afford to do. I worked hard all my life in the civil service, and I always saved. When my husband died I thought . . .' She paused. Sally thought she noticed a tear welling up.

'Ah well . . .' Faith sighed. 'But I suppose most people don't get what they wish for in life.'

'It depends what you wish for.' Sally smiled. 'Once upon a time I thought I'd be famous, a Dame by now, turning up and signing autographs at the stage door before going in to play Cleopatra at the National Theatre, waving to the stage-doorman, putting on the slap and walking on stage each night to enormous rounds of applause. Well, none of that happened because I accepted the shilling from low-brow commercial kids' TV. But, you know, in the end I think, accidentally, I got the better bargain. It's lovely here, and the people are so nice. And I think I'd hate living in some awful house in Dulwich or somewhere, trudging into some draughty, rat-infested dressing room each night, panicking about learning my lines.' She bit into a biscuit. 'Listen to me going on. We were talking about you, Faith. So tell me about the dreams you have. The ones that you feel you won't be able to have here?'

'Oh, I don't know.' Faith took a sip of tea. 'Little things. Travelling by taxi. Going out to a posh dinner at the kind of places that cost two hundred pounds for one person. Taking a little cruise, here and there.'

'I may be able to take you out for a few boat rides to St Tropez or San Remo once I get the certificate.' Sally pointed down at her books. 'And what's to stop you going out for one of those three-star dinners? There are plenty of places like that round here. This is France – the home of gastronomy.'

Sally noticed Faith's fingers contract around her cup.

'You don't have to buy that house, you know, Faith. You could always wait and get something a little smaller, cheaper. Just go up to the estate agent and tell them you've changed your mind. I'll help you find somewhere cheaper. They allow you a few days, you know, to change your mind.'

'No, no, no, no!' Faith started violently shaking her head. 'I can't do that. I just can't.'

'Of course you can.' Sally was frightened at how upset Faith seemed. 'It's your life. You can do whatever you want. You can, you know. Really.'

Faith seemed to collapse internally, as though in total surrender.

'That's the point, you see, I really can't. If I don't go ahead and do it, I'm afraid of what Alfie might do.'

13

AFTER A VERY JOLLY night in her living room, eating pieces of pizza brought in from the brasserie next door, and drinking Brian's Côte de Provence wine, Theresa got up bright and early and went out shopping for furniture. She tried a French version of that cheap Swedish shop, but after a quick walk about decided she would be happier spending a little more and getting things that she would like to keep, things that were more likely to be robust and that she didn't have to assemble herself with a pot of glue and an Allen key. She went back to the furniture cave near the port and bought a lovely French double bed for her own room – she'd need a new mattress, but the one on it would do for the moment. She would move the bed she already had into the spare room for her new tenant. She also bought some chairs, both comfy and upright, and for her own room a small ebonised desk with panels, brass caryatids and little painted china plaques.

She arranged for the delivery and headed towards the bus home, before remembering she needed sheets, pillows and blankets, both for herself and Brian.

Again she grabbed what she could manage to carry and arranged for the remainder to be delivered then, as she made her way to the bus stop, another thought struck her: if she had a paying lodger he would need a bedside lamp, and they both needed plates, cups and cutlery in the kitchen.

When finally she did get home she began to panic about how much she had spent today. At this rate she'd have no money at all to live on, even after getting a bit of an income and paying it into the bank.

She looked at the Dufy on the wall. If she sold that she could be rid of all her problems. But it wouldn't seem right, and after all it was the only thing she still had left of her mother's. She also realised it was not the kind of thing you could sell just like that. By the time you'd had it valued, put it into the auction house, and they'd printed photos in their catalogue and waited for the right sale to come along, and after that all the usual red tape . . . well, it would be the best part of a year before she saw a cent. And she'd never have the chance to get something so lovely again. She would find a better way of managing.

As soon as everything started arriving, Theresa worked like a dervish. She managed somehow to persuade the deliverymen to move the old bed from her room into the spare room, which was quite a pala-ver. She rewarded the men with a bottle of wine.

Then she made up both beds with new sheets and blankets, and made the guest room look as comfort-able as she would like it to be, if she were paying to stay in some stranger's home.

With a spray can of polish, she got all the dusty newly bought furniture to look rather splendid, especially her desk.

As she scrubbed and rubbed, her hair kept getting in the way, so she tied it up in a scarf, like a wartime housewife.

By the time the light started to fade, the flat was looking and smelling divine.

The doorbell rang and it was Brian, complete with suitcases.

He raised his eyebrows at the sight of Theresa in her rubber gloves, apron and headscarf.

'Rather daring a costume for a cook,' he said, lugging the two cases over the threshold.

Theresa laughed and showed him through.

'So where will you be taking the class?' He asked, after making a few complimentary remarks about the newly furnished room.

'Next door in the living room. It has the kitchen bit at the back so that'll be all right.'

'If you like I can give you a bit of a hand, you know . . . assist you putting things in and out of the oven, clearing pans away.'

'Yes,' said Theresa. 'You can be a Johnnie for my Fanny.'

It was only when she saw Brian's shocked expression that she realised that her joke hadn't sounded quite as she had intended it to sound.

'I meant like Fanny Craddock, you know, and Johnnie, her long-suffering husband – I mean, not that you're going to be long-suffering . . . or my husband. Oh dear. Sorry.' She bit her lip and winced. 'But, yes please, Brian. All help accepted. But don't feel obliged, just because you're renting the bedroom.'

Brian rubbed his hands together and surveyed the room. 'I'll just get myself smartened up a bit before everyone starts arriving.'

'Arriving?'

'For tonight's Cookery Club.'

'Tonight's?'

'That's what it said on the card.'

'But I ...' Theresa gasped. 'Didn't it say tomorrow? The third?'

'Today *is* the third. The same date as the room became available.'

Theresa realised what must have happened. In all the kerfuffle around her, while she was writing out the cards for the room to let, she had written down today's date as the start date. She must have also put it on at least one of the cards, maybe more, for the Cookery Club.

She glanced at her watch.

'Good God!' she exclaimed. 'They'll be here in half an hour. I've got to get this room looking decent. I spent all afternoon working on the bedrooms.'

She pulled off the rubber gloves and headscarf and ran into the kitchen.

'Oh *God*!' she cried. 'I don't have any pans. Or ingredients.'

Brian stepped forward. 'Let me help. I could go out to the Huit-à-8. That'll still be open.'

'No, no,' cried Theresa. 'You won't know what I need. I'll have to go.'

She grabbed her wallet and pulled on her coat.

'I'm so sorry to ask you this, Brian, but could you arrange the chairs and make it look a bit nice? I'll be back as soon as I can. If anyone arrives ... well ... Sit them down.'

She ran up the hill to the little corner shop. It was tiny. She knew it would be hopeless in there, quite impossible to find ingredients that would make anything impressive. But there was no choice. It was here, or nothing.

She glanced along the shelves. They held rows and rows of tins. There was also a freezer full of frozen ready meals.

Theresa grabbed a basket and darted round the aisles. She started at the hardware section, which held mainly cleaning things, mops, bleach, dusters. The only pans she saw there were one very small, thin frying pan, a baking tray and a pile of shallow cake tins.

She put them all into her basket, along with some wooden spoons. What on earth could she make in those? Quiche? How boring.

She went next to the fresh produce. Mostly it consisted of wilted aubergines, most of them on the verge of being ready for the bin. There were some oranges, a few large apples and some very nice-looking tomatoes.

Her cooking dictum had always been that the most important thing to have in any kitchen was the best, most fresh, top-quality ingredients. Well, the tomatoes qualified, so she ladled all of them into bags. Tomatoes! What was she going to make? Salad du tomates? Tomato soup?

Tomatoes and cake tins!

She picked up an apple and inspected it.

Well, with cake tins and an apple she could make an apple tart. She snatched any fresh herbs that looked half decent before rushing up the other aisle and grabbing some rolls of pastry and, for good measure, a few more things from the small chiller compartment: butter, a few cheeses. Then she stormed the grocery shelves, picking out all the usual essentials that any cook kept in a kitchen: flour, olive oil, sugar, salt, baking soda, mustard, eggs. All the while her head was whirring through recipes she had read and dishes she had cooked or eaten.

She stopped in front of the cabinet of wines. She put six bottles into the basket and immediately it was both full and too heavy, so she staggered over to the counter left it there and grabbed another.

Once all the pupils – customers – attendees (what on earth would she call them?) arrived, everything would be all right, for a moment at least, if she passed round some wine and nibbles. Then, while everyone socialised, she could tell them that this first class was going to be more of an introduction, a taste of what she planned to do in the future classes.

She grabbed packets of crisps and nuts and got a large pot of olives.

She quickly paid and, laden with six heavy plastic bags, she staggered back to the flat.

When she got in, Brian was chatting to some very nice young girl with very long blonde hair and a very short skirt.

'I'm so sorry,' said the girl, standing up and smoothing her skirt down to prevent exposing herself. 'I'm

Jessica, by the way, and I'm awfully early, I do realise, but I'm new here, you see, and I had no idea that this address was so near to my hotel.' She smiled apologetically. 'On the map it looks miles away!'

'No problem at all, Jessica.' Theresa plonked the shopping bags on the floor and Brian took them and carried them through to the kitchen.

'I hope you don't mind waiting, Jessica. Do take a seat, while I make a few preparations. Would you like a glass of wine?'

'That would be lovely.' Jessica hesitated for a moment. 'Whom do I pay?'

Theresa shuddered. She found the whole subject of asking for money deeply embarrassing.

'If you like,' Brian shrugged. 'I can take care of that.'

'Would you, Brian? And open a pair of bottles and sprinkle some crisps around the place.'

Theresa turned the oven on, then frantically opened the cupboards and, seeing how dusty they were, knew she had no choice but to don the rubber gloves and give them all a quick wipe before putting everything away.

She still had no idea what she was going to make during the class, but to soothe herself, she decided immediately to make some cheese straws. It would certainly get the welcoming smell of cooking into the room.

Using one of the wine bottles as a rolling pin, she rolled out the puff pastry, then spread it with mustard and grated some Cantal (the nearest French cheese she could find to Cheddar) on to it, before folding over, adding more mustard and cheese, and rolling again. She glanced over and saw Brian chatting merrily to Jessica as she cut the pastry into straws and laid them on a baking tray, ready to pop into the oven. She put some cayenne pepper into a bowl, ready to dip them all when they came out, to make matchsticks.

She looked at her watch.

Zero hour.

Only one taker! Two, if you counted Brian. Perhaps this was it. Maybe no one in Bellevue-Sur-Mer wanted to cook in public. But Carol and David had definitely said they were coming, hadn't they? It was all Carol's idea, for heaven's sake.

Perhaps there was only the one sign out there with the wrong date, and Jessica would be her only taker tonight, and then Carol and David and a second batch of cookery students would turn up tomorrow.

She wondered which day Carol had put down. She hoped she would arrive soon. At least Carol always made things go with a swing.

While Theresa rinsed all the cake tins she wondered why Carol was so damned nice to her. Everyone here in Bellevue-Sur-Mer, really.

Everyone except Sian, of course. But Sian was clearly demented.

Whenever there was a pause in Jessica and Brian's conversation, Theresa felt that the quiet was extremely disturbing.

'You two all right?' she asked, a tad too brightly. 'I won't be a moment.'

The waiting seemed so stilted. She wished she had a music player of some kind, or a radio, anything to break the awkward silence.

While the oven warmed up she made her way over to the others.

'Have lots of people signed up?' asked Jessica. 'I'm really looking forward to picking up a few cookery tips. I can barely boil an egg.'

'Quite a few people have said they're coming,' said Theresa, crossing her fingers and hoping for the best, but fearing that it would be just the three of them.

'Oh, goody,' said Jessica. 'I'm really looking forward to meeting the locals. Have you been living here long?'

Both Brian and Theresa laughed.

'I'm afraid we're the newbies,' said Theresa. 'But hopefully some of the long-time residents will be coming along tonight.'

Seeing the other two sipping, Theresa poured herself a glass of wine.

'I suppose all we can do is sit and wait for them to arrive.'

Theresa winced, and hoped that Jessica hadn't seen it. With only two takers, the proceedings would be acutely embarrassing and at the same time she would have to continue on for years and years before she recouped.

She took a great gulp of wine and perched herself on the edge of a seat.

Sally had cooked a little dinner for herself and Faith. They were almost through the main course, accompanied by a bottle of local rosé. Pale pink with a light delicate flavour, the wine was deceptively intoxicating.

Sally had managed to draw Faith out of her shell,

though she was cleverly steering away from anything to do with any of their children.

She told Faith about the writers and painters who had all settled in Bellevue-Sur-Mer and the surrounding hilltop towns and villages in the nineteenth and twentieth centuries, and about the lovely houses that were open for viewing. Sally's favourite was Villa Kerylos, the mad dream of a Hellenophile who, in the 1900s, had recreated an Ancient Greek villa just down the road. It came complete with Ancient Greek furniture and few, if any, concessions to the modern age. Sally laughed as she told Faith how, when she had first gone round it, she had thought that if she were the man's wife, and was expected to live in those conditions, she'd have made a mighty fuss, and, as soon as he was away, arranged for a comfy plush settee and a decent bath to be brought in.

'Go on.' Sally poured the remains of the bottle into Faith's glass. 'You have the wish.'

Faith's face crumpled again.

'Oh, thank you very much for being so kind.' Faith downed the glass and closed her eyes. 'Poor Alfie. I don't know that I can have been a very good mother.'

'No one thinks they have been a good mother, believe me. And from what I can see, the only people who imagine themselves to be Mother of the Year have truly awful children.'

'I spoiled him, you see. I think that was the problem. I gave him too much. When his father died, that was the final straw. His father stood up to him, you see.'

Sally dreaded what was coming next – tales of paternal beatings, perhaps?

'At his father's funeral, Alfie came to me for money.' Faith wiped a tear from her cheek. 'I couldn't believe it. But he looked so forlorn, so troubled. I knew it must be something pretty serious, so there and then I wrote him a cheque.'

Sally had no idea how to respond, so she sat still.

'That was the first cheque of many. I wanted him to make a life for himself, get a wife, settle down, start a family ... but the girls came and went. And all the while he kept running back to me for money. Five thousand here, eight thousand there.' Faith looked up from her glass. 'I'm so sorry. You don't want to hear all this. He's a good boy, really. Just unlucky.'

The doorbell rang.

Sally excused herself and answered. It was Carol and Zoe.

'I'm gathering people to come and support Theresa. You know, the one who bought the flat you fancied? She's starting up a cookery club.'

Sally lowered her voice.

'Another time, Carol. Tonight, I just can't.' She indicated towards Faith with her head. 'Tricky. Hello, Zoe. My God, don't tell me you're going, too? I thought you disapproved of classes and clubs.'

'I do. But Carol's giving me a lift to the airport. I'm off to Montreux.'

'To the music festival?'

'Skiing,' said Zoe. 'As you know, Sally, I'm never happier than when I'm on the piste.'

'Yes, Zoe. We've noticed.'

'There's no need to be bitter,' said Zoe. 'It'll only end in wrinkles.'

Sally shrugged to Carol.

'Well, Zoe, have a nice time, and give my love to the waterspout.'

'That's in Geneva.'

'I'm sure you'll make up for it.'

'Girls, girls, girls!' Carol laughed. 'Break it up.'

Sally briefly considered turning to Faith, breaking the tense atmosphere and suggesting they go along with Carol to the Cookery Club, but realised this was not the time.

'Maybe next one, Carol. We could both come. Sorry.'

Sally shut the door and returned to the table.

'You see, Faith. It's a lovely place, here in Bellevue-Sur-Mer, and there's quite a local support group. I'm sure you'll love it here, once you settle in.'

Sally uncorked another bottle and took some ice cream out of the freezer to thaw a little.

But she was intrigued to know more about Faith's son.

'Alfie? Is he an only child?'

'Yes.' Faith sighed. 'We both doted on him, his father and I. Though his father was stricter than I ever was.'

'Didn't you say he works in the City? Surely that should bring in a decent wage. Bonuses. All the things that make people so envious.'

'He never seems to last long anywhere. And on top of that he keeps investing in projects that fail.'

Sally wondered why that would affect his personal finances. Didn't people who did that kind of thing lose the bank's money, never their own?

'Is he part of that financial sector that places bets on currencies and things?'

'Oh, don't ask me, Sally. I don't understand any of his business stuff, I'm afraid.'

'My daughter's in business too. We should try to get them out here at the same time and they can talk money together!'

A short silence ensued. Sally topped up their glasses.

'You know, from what I saw, Alfie seemed to be quite perky at the thought of you moving here. If you were just the money tree you think he thinks you are, he'd want you to stay in England. He's obviously trying to make it up to you for past indiscretions.'

Faith made no comment.

'With that lovely house he picked for you he's probably making a hint. Boys are like that. They can't ever say what they really mean. He must want to come over and stay with you, but doesn't have a way of suggesting it.'

'And your son?' asked Faith. 'What does he do?'

'He's – well – he's a traveller.'

Sally thought about her own children and how seldom she saw them. She looked at Faith and realised it could be wonderful to have someone who had similar worries, someone to share a confidence with.

'I have to confide in you, Faith, that if one of them wanted to come out and stay here with me that would be my dream come true. My own two kids never come to see me. My daughter arrived yesterday and stayed for all of a minute. That's all the time I seem to deserve.'

'I'm sorry to hear that,' said Faith. 'You are a lovely person.'

'I don't think my children think so,' Sally replied. 'But I suppose the thing we forget is that though we think of them as bound to us in some mystical way, they think of themselves as individuals, not connected much to us at all. Just as we did with our own parents.'

'You're right.' Faith nodded. 'I only really realised how much I loved my mother when she died, and I no longer had her to turn to. It must be the same for them.'

Faith took another gulp of wine.

'I think Alfie changed when I wrote him out of my will.'

Sally resisted the urge to gasp. This whole story was unravelling like some Victorian sensation novel.

'In the new will I left the lot to cancer research. That's what took his father. Prostate cancer. I believed it would be for the best. I thought that, if Alfie didn't think he'd have all our money to come into when I turned up my clogs, it would make him sit up and concentrate on work, and stop running to me for money, praying for me to die so that he could have the rest.'

'I'm sure that isn't it.' Sally could see how agitated Faith was, and feared for her. 'If you've written him out of your will, surely it must be in his interest to keep you alive!'

'Yes. And he certainly seems a lot more cheerful since I agreed to buy the house here. Like a new boy. He doesn't ask for money, and has become again like the little boy I loved so much. That's why I have to buy the house, even if it means I have to do without in order to do so.'

'But surely if you bought somewhere smaller . . .'

Faith shook her head. 'He chose it and I don't like to upset him. You see, the last time I did that he . . .'

The sentence dangled. Faith swigged down the remains of her glass.

'He . . . tried to kill himself.'

Sally found it hard to fill the ensuing silence. She wondered how *she* would react if Marianne or Tom had ever tried anything like that, the cry for help.

She said one word only.

'How?'

'Pills.'

'Oh Lord, Faith. How awful. What did you refuse that made him do that?'

'He wanted, no, I mean he "needed" one hundred and fifty thousand, right there and then. But that would have been half my savings – the money I need to live on. I couldn't do it.'

'I see.'

'He took a bottle of paracetamol. Twenty pills. Luckily he said they'd gone straight through him, and all that happened was a nasty case of diarrhoea.'

Sally froze.

Alfie was not to be trusted.

She knew that this story of his had to have been made up – a tactical lie.

Sally knew all about the real dangers of paracetamol. In her early theatre days she had known a fellow actor who had accidentally overdosed on it. He'd only taken nine pills over a short period after some heavy dental work. The toothache went, and the boy had seemed fine for a few weeks. Every day he came into rehearsal, as usual. Then, during the technical rehearsal, he had suddenly keeled over. He was taken to hospital, where he died the next day.

In the few days between his death and the funeral the whole company had asked the same question: how?

Sally, being who she was, had gone into the hospital and asked for answers. A kind nurse had explained how easy it was to kill yourself with only a few paraceta-mol tablets. Once they got into your system they worked silently and, worse than that, irrevocably.

And so Sally knew that if those tablets had reached Alfie's abdomen he would have been doomed, and a few weeks afterwards would have died of total organ failure. Only if he had had his stomach pumped within an hour of taking the overdose would he have survived. But the way he had told it, he would not have had a chance. Therefore Sally could only surmise that the episode had never happened.

Alfie was using emotional blackmail to steer his mother into doing something he wanted her to do. Something that Faith appeared to have no idea of.

Sally wanted to know why.

'Did you give him the money?'

'I did. The best part of the remaining half is going to pay for the house.'

'When are you next going to see your notaire to sign the documents?' Sally asked.

'At the end of the week,' replied Faith.

'Then I'll come with you,' said Sally. 'You'll need a witness, anyhow.'

Having heard Faith's story, Sally knew that some-thing terrible was going on. Faith was being taken for a dupe, and Sally was determined that she would get to the bottom of it.

* * *

Theresa had downed three glasses of wine before the doorbell rang again. She felt herself sway slightly as she got up to open the door.

It was Carol.

'Darling, we're so sorry we're late.'

Carol breezed in, followed by a gaggle of people.

'As you can see, I dragged along a little crowd for you. Where shall we put ourselves?'

Carol sniffed the air.

'Delicious smell, Theresa! I can't wait to get going. I am one lousy cook.'

Theresa ushered everyone to a chair.

'Red or white?' she asked, heading for the oven to rescue the cheese straws. 'Brian is playing sommelier, for the evening.'

She spilled the hot cheese pastry pieces on to a pair of large brand-new plates. She started dipping each one into the cayenne and realised it would take for ever to do the lot, so she grabbed the bowl and shoved it on to the tray beside the plates. If people wanted to dip into the cayenne they could do it for themselves.

Carol raised her voice to say 'There should have been one other, my dear old friend Zoe Redbridge, but she's just off for a week in Switzerland.'

'How lovely,' said Theresa passing around the cheese straws. 'Skiing?'

'That's what she'd like us all to *think* she's doing,' said Carol tartly. 'But she goes for secret beauty treatments. She gets injected with lamb's glands or something. It's supposed to stop you ageing.'

William looked up. 'You never told me about this!'

'Really? She's being doing it for years. It must

certainly make her bank account lighter. It costs an arm and a leg.'

'And does it make a great difference?'

Carol raised her eyebrows.

'No.'

'So why . . . ?'

'Oh, in her youth everyone used to do it.' Carol waved her arms in the air. 'It was the chic thing to do back in the forties and fifties. Charlie Chaplin, Marlene Dietrich, Jackie O . . .'

William made an excited 'ooh' sound, and nudged the young man sitting next to him, while Carol continued. Both men wore similar velvet jackets, colourful shirts and bow ties.

'. . . Cary Grant, Gloria Swanson, Charles de Gaulle, Somerset Maugham, Pope Pius XII.'

'There you've lost me,' said William.

Theresa laughed and offered cheese straws to the two men.

William spoke. 'Oh, Theresa, this is my husband, Benjamin.'

Theresa and Benjamin caught eyes. They recognised one another at once. But in the few seconds during which she was remembering how, on her first full day here in the furniture cave Benjamin had so rudely tried to stop Pierre from selling her the prized table, she just missed the nanosecond during which Benjamin signalled her to pretend they had never met.

She blurted out: 'Oh, Benjamin and I have met.'

Benjamin was shaking his head in a warning fashion, while maintaining a desperate eye contact with her.

Theresa finally understood and realised she should

not continue. William had been kind to her after all, and she liked him. And both men were her neighbours. There was no point making enemies of them.

'Really?' said William. 'How? Where?'

'We ... er ...' Theresa had no idea what story she could make up.

'We met in the Huit-à-8,' said Benjamin. 'It's the *only* place to meet. So divine a rendezvous, beloved by all the inhabitants of Bellevue-Sur-Mer.'

'I have to confess,' said Theresa to the assembled company. 'That, due to unforeseen circumstances, this evening's recipe is limited to produce I bought in that very shop about an hour ago. So please forgive me.'

She turned to her piles of cake tins and the ingredients on the kitchen tops.

'There are eight of us here and I have four cake tins. So if we get into pairs we can all make something together.'

William and Benjamin, Carol and David already stood in ready-made pairs. Carol noticed that Ted made a beeline for Jessica, while Brian moved towards her, Theresa's, side.

'Go Fanny!' he whispered into her ear.

'Well,' said Theresa, suppressing a giggle. 'I am going to show you all a little spin on the French staple, tarte tatin. Only, tonight, we're going to use tomatoes.'

She picked up her cake tin. 'And as in most recipes, the first thing we do is butter our pans.'

William spoke. 'Is it me, or does that sound vaguely obscene?'

Everyone laughed, Benjamin the loudest. He gave Theresa a conspiratorial wink.

It took less than forty minutes for everyone to produce and bake a very handsome dish of tomato tarte tatin.

As Theresa and Brian brought them out of the oven, everyone cooed and aahed over their own product.

Theresa lifted her own tart on to a plate and cut it into slices, she tried to deliver an old joke about pies – but changing the word pie to tart: 'What is the best thing to put into a tart?'

Everyone stood round, pop-eyed with anticipation.

As she prepared to give the answer Theresa realised the joke had gained something in translation.

'Oh Lord! The answer should be "your teeth",' she said, totally embarrassed. 'But I can see that only makes it worse.'

'As the actress said to the bishop,' said Benjamin.

Everyone crowded round the glass-topped table where they sat down and ate.

At the end of the evening, the members of Theresa's Cookery Club left her flat, laughing and happy, each couple clutching their own take-home tart on a paper plate, wrapped in tin foil.

Theresa wondered who would actually eat the tart made jointly by Jessica and Ted or would they be going somewhere now to share it?

Brian helped Theresa clean up the kitchen and put all the dishes, tins and glasses into the dishwasher. Then they bade each other goodnight and went to their separate rooms.

Theresa lay in her new bed staring out into the moonlight spilling down into the dark courtyard. She felt happy and positive. Things *would* work out here. All would be well.

She had done the right thing in moving from Highgate.

The first club meeting had gone so perfectly that she really looked forward to the next one, for which she planned to be better prepared.

She'd made a bit of money to put straight into the bank, and had more coming in from Brian's rent. So far, he was proving to be the exemplary lodger.

She pulled the blanket up over her shoulder and rolled over nearer the window so that she could see the tiny square of starlit sky above the Hôtel Astra. She could hear the voices of the people in the hotel room. It all sounded very romantic.

In the darkness, she smiled to herself.

What would Imogen make of all this? Her mother running a cookery club and sharing a small flat with a good-looking eligible bachelor?

Brian was quite a catch. He was such a gent, and him making that little joke into her ear before the cookery session started had really given her the confidence to go for it. There was nothing to relax the atmosphere like a slightly rude joke.

She wondered about him. What was he thinking, lying there in that rather uncomfortable tiny room? Was he in bed next door thinking of her?

For all she knew, Brian had designs on her.

And indeed he did.

In the small box room across the corridor, Brian was indeed thinking about Theresa. He thought about how generous she was, how kind-hearted and how much she had to offer.

Oh, yes, Brian certainly had designs on Theresa.

His room was very small, like a prison cell, but that was something Brian was quite used to. For, only two months earlier, under his real name, Ronald Arthur Tate, Brian had been a prisoner, doing time in Wormwood Scrubs.

TOMATO TARTE TATIN

Ingredients
Small plum tomatoes
Honey
Puff pastry
Basil
Salt and pepper
Egg yolk or milk

Method
Place the tomatoes, bunched together, in a cake tin.
    Drizzle over a little honey, salt and pepper.
    Cut the pastry slightly larger than the cake tin and lay over the top, tucking in to make a tight fit.
    Brush the top with milk or egg yolk.
    Bake at 180° for about 15–20 minutes.
    When cooked cover with serving plate and tip over so that the tart turns on to the plate upside down.
    Decorate with basil leaves.
    Serve.

Part Two – Bagna Cauda

BAGNA CAUDA
(From Nissart – the Niçoise dialect –
meaning, literally, hot bath)

Ingredients
200 g butter
100g olive oil
Jar of anchovies
4 cloves of garlic
Salt and black pepper

Raw vegetables: carrots, celery, spring onions, chopped peppers, quartered little gem lettuces, radishes, hard-boiled egg – anything you fancy.

Method
Prepare and arrange the vegetables in a basket.

Melt the butter with the oil, add the crushed garlic, and then the anchovies. Stir vigorously over heat until the anchovies dissolve into the mixture.

Season and serve in a dipping bowl (if possible, kept warm by a candle from beneath).

Gather round and dip the vegetables into the 'hot bath'.

14

ALL ALONG THE CÔTE d'Azur, from Marseille to Menton, the yellows of February – the lemons, daffodils and mimosa – made way for the purples, reds and shocking pinks of March and April. Oleander plants with their poisonous splashes of blood-red peered out from behind every stone wall and bougain-villea bushes spread lushly up the sides of houses and spilled over fences.

The carnival was over, Lent almost done and Easter was imminent.

The famous Riviera heat, now at its most pleasant, brought people out on to the streets to drink and dine. The sun shone almost every day. The sky was blue, all day a perfect cerulean, darkening at night to a faultless Prussian. The sea dazzled with its ever-changing shades ranging from pale turquoise to dark navy, always sparkling with diamonds of light.

Bobbing upon it, the cruise ships, so scarce during the winter when most of them were off on world tours or in the Caribbean, returned to their regular summer Mediterranean circuits. Almost every day saw a huge white liner unload its passengers in

Villefranche-Sur-Mer or Monte Carlo, from where they dispersed in coaches for the day to all the towns and villages along the coast.

Daily, tourists arrived from the airport, having taken up spring bargain flights to Nice. From there they moved along the coast to picturesque spots where they wandered around the shops, buying postcards and souvenirs, and filled the beaches and the pavement tables of all the cafes and bars.

For the English-speaking residents of Bellevue-Sur-Mer it was business as usual. For them nothing much had changed.

As ever, they were all in and out of one another's homes and lives, laughing, sharing, eating, drinking, gossiping and being very good neighbours.

In March, one by one, they had all gone down with a nasty cold, and then took it in turns to watch out for each other, turning up with supplies of fruit, ibuprofen and bottles of whisky for hot toddies.

Carol and David continued to drive around, nipping in and out of Nice, and taking their friends off for trips to local olive farms and vineyards to stock up with *produits de terroir*, while William and Benjamin could be seen most evenings in their matching jackets, drinking wine on the terraces of the local bars.

Sian spent quite a bit more time at home while she searched for a suitable local location for her new boutique. People couldn't help noticing that for some unknown reason she seemed oddly serene. She declined attending Theresa's Cookery Club, as, she told everyone in a very loud voice, she had a blue ribbon in cookery from a course she had taken while at Lucie Clayton's School when she was twenty. She allowed Ted to go. He was, he told people, writing again, though no one really believed that.

The new girl, Jessica, told everyone she was having an extended stay in the town while recuperating. She never told anyone what she was recuperating from and no one believed her anyhow. When pressed further, by Zoe, naturally, Jessica simply said that she had had a lung infection – the modern term for a bit of a cough. She was a writer, she told them, working on a small picture book about the Rolling Stones' album, *Exile on Main Street*, which had been recorded a few miles along the coast on the edges of Villefranche-sur-Mer one stoned summer.

No one really believed this either. They were all certain she was working for Sian as her mole. Sally was the first to come to that conclusion and she told Theresa and Carol as much. As a result, all three woman kept a sharp eye on her, especially when she was in Ted's company. Ted did appear to be quite taken by her, and they all noticed little intimate moments of familiarity between them. No one dared to warn Ted that Jessica was a spy just in case they were wrong, and also because they knew the heat of Sian's wrath. Anyhow, the only thing that really could be pinned on her was that, while at Theresa's Cookery Club meetings, Jessica always took copious notes in a little red notebook. Theresa even made a joke one evening, asking Jessica if she was going to publish a book of her recipes. Jessica laughed and explained that her memory was very bad, and she certainly wanted to make these things again, on her own, at home and how on earth could she do that without notes?

Faith had moved into the old Molinari house and, since the move, seemed entirely composed, and no longer the nervous, timid woman who had so feared becoming an inhabitant of Bellevue-Sur-Mer. She was frequently seen in the bistro, taking dinner, alone with a book, or waiting at the bus stop all prepared for a day out exploring somewhere along the coast. She had even spent a night at the opera with Zoe, seeing *La Ballo in Maschera*, and including a late-night drink in a cafe in the bustling Cours Saleya after the final curtain. When Zoe had suggested they go on to do a bit of dancing in a fabulous little gay disco club in the Ponchettes along the way, Faith had drawn the line and found a taxi to take her home.

Faith spent a fair amount of time with Sally, because Sally had helped her out with the move, and particularly in handling and dealing with all the legal complications that she had so feared. Sally knew all about buying property out here and the pair of them had contrived an excellent contract, which would be to their mutual benefit. Sally had in fact invested in the house, leaving Faith enough money to enjoy life, and alleviating Sally's own worries about leaving her money in the bank.

After a rough ride with her tutor at the sea school, Sally had finally got her certificate in power-boat driving, and was now looking out for a small boat to buy. Ted had been unable to join her in taking the course, but he had decided that he was going to buy the boat and register it in his name, with Sally as his certificated skipper. Sally spent most days helping him in his search, the pair wandering round local marinas, and occasionally taking a boat out to sea for a test run. So far nothing had met their fancy. Sally was attempting to teach Ted all the things she had learned at sea school, but Ted's attention span was not great, and Sally found his eyes were more often roving to inspect a gaggle of passing tourists, than paying attention to the details of making a round-turn knot with two half hitches. His knowledge of engines on the other hand was, to Sally's surprise and delight, supreme.

Sally frequently thought and worried about him. Sian's girl spy was surely the enigmatic Jessica, who didn't ever have much to say, but spent much time cosying up to Ted at Theresa's Cookery Club sessions, which Sally enjoyed attending, now that she had passed her power-boat test. There was no other new woman in town who could possibly fit the bill. She still wasn't sure whether or not to warn Ted. Would that be interfering in his marriage and bring Sally a visitation from Sian in dragon-mode? It was best left alone, she decided.

The only cloud on the horizon was a spate of burglaries in the town, though, it must be said, that none of them were very serious. There was never any violence, and mostly it happened when people were out for the day, or away on holiday.

Understandably, the victims did feel unnerved to get home and find their front doors open and all their cash and the TV or a digital radio gone, but everyone was insured, and the actual damage done never amounted to much beyond a new lock or window, so it was more of an inconvenience than a tragedy.

Zoe Redbridge had been the first to have been burgled. She arrived home from her 'skiing' trip to Montreux, the skin round her eyes and neck tauter than ever, her lips inflated to three times their normal size. The door had been propped shut, the lock picked. Someone had broken in and taken her costume jewellery, only the pieces she had left behind when she went to Switzerland, which wasn't that much, and a jar of petty cash in the kitchen. But, as she was obeying the clinic's orders and resting her face after the treatments, she didn't want to make a huge fuss, just thanked the Lord it had happened while she was out of town. If she had been in residence, she told people, she thought she would have died of fright. 'Can you imagine what a shock it would have been, just for the sake of a few measly euros and a couple of really unattractive brooches?' she said to anyone who would listen. 'Waking up and finding a man rummaging around inside your drawers?'

Most people were too busy staring at Zoe's new strangely stretched face, now in an expression of perpetual astonishment, or searching her visage to see whether they could recognise any remaining traces of the pre-Switzerland Zoe, to listen to any of the words that came out of her swollen trout-pout mouth.

The local view was that the burglaries were being done by kids or teenagers. The police took a low-profile outlook on the crimes too.

'Albanians on day-trips from Italy,' they said.

'Perhaps tourists? Or petty crooks, coming over for the day from Marseille.'

A man had been reported, on a couple of occasions, lurking in the streets of Bellevue-Sur-Mer, peering through windows and letterboxes. His unkempt, straggly long hair and unshaven face had attracted attention, not to mention the fact that his clothes were rather dirty.

'A *clochard*!' exclaimed the local businessmen indignantly. 'A tramp!'

The tramp had not been seen in Bellevue-Sur-Mer for a few weeks, but the gendarmerie had received calls about his presence in many towns and villages along the coast from Cannes to Cap d'Ail. But, so far, he had never been discovered in the act of anything more sinister than walking about looking intently at houses, so no action had been taken.

Theresa made the occasional phone call to Imogen, but had learned to brace herself and never to dial before taking a deep breath, sitting down and pouring herself a glass of wine. She went on inviting, while Imogen went on sneering. Despite the hurtful comments, Theresa loved her flat more and more. She had no regrets about leaving Highgate and moving to Bellevue-Sur-Mer.

Theresa was really enjoying the whole process of the Cookery Club now. She was sitting at her table early one morning, totting up the figures, when she realised that since the first session the numbers had doubled and if any more people turned up she would have to start doing two sessions a week as there would not be enough room in the flat to accommodate them all. She brought out her calculator and after a few minutes tapping in numbers she could see that from her calculations, she would have repaid the loan for the boiler by Easter. She put the accounts aside and started working out the necessary ingredients for tonight's session when Brian came in from outside.

'Another flat taken,' he said, pulling off his jacket. 'I really am looking, Theresa, but every time I see a suitable place by the time I get to the agent the place is gone. I was this close today.' He held up his finger and thumb with a fraction of air between them.

'Oh, Brian, don't be silly,' said Theresa. 'You can stay as long as you like. You're always so helpful around the house and you make very good tea.'

'Is that a hint?' asked Brian, moving towards the kettle.

'Good idea,' said Theresa, shuffling her papers into some order. 'Look at the time. I've got to dash out for tonight's stuff.'

'The Huit-à-8? I wouldn't. I passed it on my way down. That tramp's been prowling round outside, shouting obscenities at everyone going in and out. The police are there, taking statements.'

'Really?' said Theresa. 'I thought they said he wasn't dangerous?'

'I wouldn't be so sure.' Brian filled the teapot with hot water and rinsed it out. 'Look how many places have been burgled lately.'

Theresa crossed her fingers. 'I know. It makes one feel so nervous when there are shady characters lurking round the place. But anyhow I'm heading into town for the market,' said Theresa. 'The produce is much fresher and I need a huge box of watercress. I'm making soup.'

'Yum,' said Brian.

Naturally, that night at the Cookery Club, the tramp was the main subject of conversation.

'I hope he's not burgling us all while we're in here,' said Zoe. 'It's hardly worth losing all your valuables for a bowl of home-made soup and a glass of plonk.'

'Oh, I'm sure we'll be all right.' Brian beamed. He seemed pretty certain. 'So do we leave this watercress in the iced water, Theresa, or just rinse it?'

'They're watching him, Zoe,' said Ted. 'If he tries anything, the gendarmes will be all over that *clochard*, like flies round . . .'

'Thank you,' said Theresa, putting a hand up. 'Not while we're talking food.' She peered at the work top in front of Sally. 'You're very behind . . .'

'Well, they will,' said Sally, hacking into an onion and throwing the pieces into an oiled frying pan. 'Jolly good thing too. I know, I know. I won't be a minute.'

Theresa looked around for some spare space to put down her board, and shifted the answering machine along. She noticed its little red light was blinking. In the rush of getting things ready she hadn't bothered to check it between getting in from town and the first people arriving.

Ah well, she thought, there's nothing so desperate that can't wait an hour or so. Anyhow, everyone she knew was here in the room, so it was probably only a wrong number or someone asking if she wanted double-glazing.

'Mine's all ready,' said Carol. 'I'm absolutely ravenous. Can we get on?'

'Put a sock in it, 57,' said Ted, lifting his bowl of ingredients high above his head, like a champion. 'Even a Neanderthal like me is ready.'

'Everybody, leave the ingredients in the ice bowl.' Theresa tried to bring the club back to order. 'Now, folks, as I only have one blender, we're going to have to stagger the next process. So, in the meanwhile, let whoever isn't at the blender, sit at the table and enjoy a *verre du vin*. Perhaps Ted and Jessica could pulverise first?'

'I don't think that's such a good idea,' said Sally, briskly stirring in her chopped watercress, and starting humming the chorus of 'Love and Marriage'.

Faith knocked over a glass of water and Zoe rooted about in her bag, pulling out an English newspaper, which she spread over the table to soak it up.

'How surprising,' said Faith. 'I didn't imagine you to be one of those nostalgic Brits, Zoe, who like to keep in touch with the homeland.'

'The *Daily Muckraker*?' snapped Zoe. 'I occasionally buy the vile, right-wing rag to remind me why I'm so happy here and why I never want to go back to Blighty and live among all those smug, self-righteous, finger-pointing prigs and prudes.'

Jessica's eyes flickered. She cleared her throat.

'Hey, Sal?' Ted called across the counter. 'Did you manage to sell the folks' old place back in Pom-land?'

'Yes. I told you, Ted, didn't I? A few months ago.'

'Yowser,' grinned Ted. 'So you must be worth a few quid, then. Like to take me on a holiday somewhere?'

Sally flicked a piece of onion at him. 'Always worth a try,' he laughed.

'I'm buying another place out here with it, Ted. You know that was always the plan. Anyway, the money's all gone now.'

She exchanged a look with Faith. The deal between them was still a secret. Sally gave Faith a wink. Faith blushed a little.

Sally started singing a chorus of Madness's 'Our House'.

'I thought that the police had collared that tramp,' said Faith, in a voice loud enough to drown out Sally. For the Cookery Club, Faith was now partnered with Brian, leaving Theresa free to perform the demonstrations.

'Oh, yes,' said Zoe. 'The ruddy bastard was out there swearing at the top of his voice and the girl in the shop said that so many people complained that the police had carted the little fucker away in a van.'

'Good thing too,' said Ted, placing his hand in the small of Jessica's back to steer her across to the cooking counter. 'If I'd been the boys in blue I'd have bagged that sundowner weeks ago.'

Faith turned to Ted and asked why he had earlier said 57 in the middle of a sentence.

'Is it code?' she asked.

He jerked his head towards Carol.

'My mate, 57. Before she married David there, she was maiden named Heinz. Am I right or wrong?'

'Oh!' Carol rolled her eyes. 'Who cares?'

'*The* Heinz?' asked Faith. 'Heinz of Pennsylvania?'

Carol shrugged.

'How did I not know that?' said Zoe.

Brian smiled, and bent low over his chopping board.

'You don't have children do you, Carol,' asked Faith.

Carol shuddered. 'Allergic, I'm afraid.'

David took a deep breath.

'You cannot be allergic to children, Carol,' he said. 'You're just not adult enough to take on the responsibility.'

Carol rolled her eyes and said flatly: 'Joke!'

'That's a lovely painting on the wall, Theresa,' said Faith out of nowhere.

'My mother left it to me,' she said. 'It's a Dufy.'

'It's sweet,' said Faith.

'Do you know, Theresa,' William called across the kitchen, 'we come here week after week, and I have never yet asked you where you found this fabulous glass table?'

'I thought I'd told you weeks ago,' yelled Theresa. 'I adore it. It was from that furniture cave down near the port.'

'The one near the flea market?' asked William.

'You must go there,' said Theresa, as she helped Jessica pour her mixture into the blender. 'It's a treasure house.'

'Didn't you know? It's been shut down,' said William.

'No?' said Theresa, scraping the last pieces into the jug.

'Oh yes,' replied William. 'The owner was a crook.'

Theresa couldn't help catching eyes with Benjamin, who looked immediately at the floor.

'My glass is empty,' he said, adjusting his bow tie. 'Carol, dear, be a poppet and pass me the red.'

When Benjamin looked up again Theresa caught the fleeting glance, which was more of a glare, ordering her to drop the subject of both the table and the furniture cave instantly.

Theresa pressed the button on the blender, successfully drowning out any further opportunity at conversation for anybody in the room.

Once they had all pulverised their cooked ingredients, they stood round the table pouring the finished product into jars to take home for later, while Theresa served up a large tureen of the soup, so that they could all gather round and eat it.

Just as the last bowl had been filled with steaming green soup and they all reached out for a spoonful of cream and a sprinkle of paprika and piment d'Espelette, there was a hammering on Theresa's front door.

'Oh no,' murmured Theresa, immediately imagining Sian standing at the other side of the door with a raised axe.

Ted and Carol obviously thought the same thing, for he ducked down under the table, while she rose from her seat and took a few steps towards the door, before Theresa stopped her.

'Don't worry, Carol,' she said. 'This time I can handle it.'

The hammering continued.

'Calm down,' said Theresa, rubbing her hands down her apron, before reaching for the latch.

She took a deep breath and opened up.

Standing on the step was a gendarme.

'*Je cherche* Madame Connor,' he said. '*Elle est ici?*'

Sally's face blanched as, hearing her name, she rose and moved slowly towards the open door.

'I'm Sally Connor.' She spoke to the policeman in French. 'Is there anything wrong?'

The policeman burst out laughing and stepped aside.

From behind him stepped a tramp – a tall man with long matted hair, a straggling beard and ragged clothing. From where she stood Sally could smell him. It was not pleasant.

'Eez zat 'er?' said the gendarme to the tramp, who nodded. He turned back to Sally and said: 'Madame Connor, *je vous presente un cadeau*. I 'ave a present for you.'

The tramp smiled, revealing perfect white teeth. He rushed towards the open door, as Sally staggered away from him.

'Thank God' said the tramp, in perfect English. 'I've been searching for you for ever.' He put out his arms and took another step towards Sally, who now stood still, agog, with her mouth open in surprise.

'Mum? It's me. Tom.'

When the gendarme had left and Sally had scooped up her son and taken him away home, the Cookery Club meeting continued.

No one spoke for a considerable time. They stood staring at each other, pop-eyed.

Inevitably it was Zoe who broke the ice.

'I've always said there are two mistakes no one ever admits to, and one is having had children.'

There was a long pause, till Jessica asked what the second was.

Zoe gave an insouciant shrug. 'Having a sex-change operation, of course.'

'Do you really think he's the burglar?' said Carol briskly.

'In my humble opinion thieving bastards are lower than a snake's belly,' growled Ted.

'Scum of the earth,' said David.

'Piece of shit,' said Brian.

'He certainly smelled like a sewer,' said Zoe, laughing. 'It is funny really when you think how pristine Sally always is.'

'I'm sure there's a good reason behind it all,' said Theresa, as she poured wine into every glass. '*Bon appétit, mes amis.*'

As they quietly supped they all heard footsteps again, coming up the path.

Everyone held their breath, each imagining it would be Sally back with explanations.

There was a sharp rap on the door.

'Uh oh!' Ted winced, knowing that that was not Sally's knock. 'Please not chapter two.'

'But of which problem?' Theresa wiped her mouth and stood, ready for the fray.

'Let me,' said Brian, moving briskly towards the door and opening it. 'Hello,' he said, gruffly. 'Can I help you?'

Everyone knew from his tone that, whoever stood behind the door, it was no one he knew. Theresa came up beside him and peered out into the dark, at the outline of a person in the gloom.

'For goodness' sake, Mother,' snapped the woman in the shadows of the doorstep. 'It's me. Imogen. The children are tired and hungry, would you kindly get this man out of the way so that we can come in?'

WATERCRESS SOUP

Ingredients
1 small onion – chopped
Bunch watercress – stalks removed
Handful of spinach
Butter
Salt and pepper
Ice
Cream or crème fraiche
Paprika and/or piment d'Espelette

Method
Gently fry the onion in the butter till translucent.

Bring up the heat and add the watercress and spinach and cook till it wilts.

Add 2 cups of boiling water, salt and pepper and boil for a couple of minutes.

Pour mixture into bowl containing ice cubes to stop cooking and retain green colour

Put into a liquidiser and whizz till smooth

Reheat in saucepan, season to taste and serve.

Put a daub of cream on top and sprinkle with paprika or piment d'Espelette.

15

SALLY SAT OUTSIDE THE bathroom, firing questions at Tom while he took a long shower.

'I don't understand why you didn't ring me or email me?'

'I told you, Mum, I was robbed. I kept in touch with you until I couldn't. I managed to get all the way from Jaipur to Stuttgart, on the train, without a mishap. I came safely through Pakistan, Iran, Turkey, Romania, sometimes on real rattle-buckets and cattle-trucks. Then I fell asleep on a fancy commuter train from Germany to Zurich and while I was snoring in the warmth some bastard ran off with my case.'

'But you could still have phoned me, Tom.'

'Well, yes, I could have done *then*, but I wanted it to be a surprise.'

Sally could hear him splashing about, before he turned the shower taps off.

'I was so looking forward to seeing you. How was I to know I'd get mugged in Genoa?'

'Mugged?'

'I was waiting at some horrid little station under the principal terminus, trying to get a late local train to

Ventimiglia and a vile gang of kids held a knife to me while they took my coat, my wallet, my trainers, my phone, my tickets, everything and scarpered. Your address, your phone number, your email, it was all on that phone.'

'Have you got enough towels?' Sally asked, pulling another one from the linen cupboard behind her and fluffing it up. 'I still don't understand how you ended up here, swearing at people, Tom? It's just not like you to be abusive.'

'I wasn't swearing.'

'You were. Everyone heard you. It was the talk of the town.'

'I was calling your name.'

Sally hesitated before replying. Was her son all right in the head, after his tribulations?

'Work it out,' he yelled through the door. 'The policeman explained it to me. It's very rude apparently. But I don't speak French, so I don't know.'

'Sally? Sally? Sally?' repeated Sally.

'I don't call you Sally. You're my mum.'

'You were calling out "mum"?' Sally tried out saying the word to herself a few times.

'Nooooo,' said Tom. 'I was yelling Madame Connor. Slowly, with a pause. Madame. Connor. I just wanted someone to say "Oh yes, I know her; she lives over there or up the road."'

'Madame Connor? Madame Connor?' repeated Sally. Then it dawned on her. The French shoppers had thought Tom was saying Connard, or even Con, both of which were pretty racy words, certainly not spoken in polite society or yelled at women coming out of shops. The ladies must have thought he was calling them Lady Motherfucker, Mrs C--t! It had never entered Sally's mind before, but in France her name was a liability. She couldn't help but laugh.

'Oh, Lord, Tom. Oh dear!'

'Anyway, I tried a train without a ticket and was chucked off at San Remo, and walked along the coast from there, sleeping in doorways, and I got here. People threw me pennies and some gave me bits of bread and cups of coffee. Then when I finally reached Nice, I realised that, although I knew you lived just outside the city, I had no idea in which town or village. I thought it might have a B or V, but so do lots of places, and there are so many with a Sur-Mer tacked on. The only thing I knew for certain was that from your window you could see the sea.'

Sally could hear the scissors chopping. He must be cutting his beard off.

'So I went to every little Sur-Mer town radiating out from Nice and looked for a likely place, calling out your name, and looking through windows.'

'Poor darling,' said Sally. 'So how long have you been so near me, without my knowing?'

'About four weeks.'

'Four weeks!' Sally felt her heart stab, thinking of how many times they might have been a few hundred yards away from one another, round a corner, and not known it.

The door opened and the real, recognisable Tom stood before her. Wrapped up in Sally's white towelling robe, his beard and hair roughly chopped, he looked so sweet and lost.

'I'm going to take you up to the barber's in the morning. Then we'll go into Nice and get you a set of clothes,' said Sally. 'But now let's go downstairs and I'll make you a square meal, while you tell me everything.' She laughed and slipped her arm round his waist. 'You know, Tom, now that I think about it, if you'd called out Sally they'd have thought you were up to no good too. It means salted, or, depending on the word that comes next, exactly what you were when you arrived at Theresa's – dirty!'

The Cookery Club meeting had dispersed pretty quickly after the arrival of Imogen.

Never had a roomful of people slurped up a bowl of soup and tossed down a glass of wine with such speed.

When the door slammed after Zoe, always the last to go, Brian slipped quietly into his room.

'Who is *that*?' hissed Imogen. 'You didn't tell me you'd taken a lover.'

Theresa made a sshh sound. 'If you must know, he's my lodger. His rent brings in a bit of money.'

'Fine,' said Imogen, watching the children tearing at bits of bread and cheese left on the table. 'So where are our rooms?'

Theresa was at a loss.

'I had no idea you were coming, Imogen, or I'd have got something sorted.'

'I phoned ahead from Gatwick. You've had all evening. If you weren't so busy carousing with your friends.'

Theresa looked at the red flashing light on the answering machine. Well, there was that query answered. The message must have been from Imogen.

'For goodness' sake, you're always inviting me here, Mother. It's Easter. Last time we spoke you said "Come at Easter". So here we are!'

'But I . . .'

Theresa didn't know how to tell Imogen that, apart from Brian's room, there was only her bedroom and it had only one bed. If she'd had warning at least she could have got some little put-me-ups for the kids.

'Look, Imogen, I'll phone up to the hotel just above me. They might have a room.'

'A hotel? After the day we've just had?' Imogen shook her head as though Theresa was an idiot. 'If anyone's going to a hotel I'm afraid it will have to be you. Look at the children. They're exhausted.'

Theresa looked down at the three little pairs of eyes which looked anything but tired, rather, they appeared fired with exhilaration.

'Can we have an ice cream?' asked Lola.

'I want to go swimming in the sea,' said Chloe. 'I've got my certificates.'

'I've got sessisicakes as well.'

'No you haven't,' Chloe sighed. 'You have to be over nine and pass a test.'

'Well, I'm hungry.' Cressida started to cry. 'I want Verdi cakes.'

'Do you have fruit?' Imogen enquired. 'Just something to take the edge off. And where are the bedrooms?'

Theresa knew that her daughter wasn't being exactly straight with her. Theresa might do things on a whim, but Imogen had always been one for diaries and long-ranging appointments. She never would just arrive at the airport hoping for a flight. Something was going on.

'Aren't you going to explain anything to me?' asked Theresa, buttering pieces of baguette and handing them to the girls. 'What on earth has happened?'

'Nothing.' Imogen did not look her in the eye.

'You suddenly arrive on my doorstep with the children at eleven o'clock on a Wednesday night? It makes no sense.'

'We'll have all the time to talk in the morning,' said Imogen, taking off the children's coats. 'Now we really must get some sleep.'

Feeling more suspicious than ever, Theresa ushered them into the bedroom. Only a few hours ago it had seemed so charming, but now looked dingy, cramped and claustrophobic.

'This won't do after tonight,' said Imogen. 'But we can discuss that when you come back for breakfast.'

Theresa knew there was nothing else for it but to trudge up to the Hôtel Astra, and hope that, on the night before Maundy Thursday and the start of the Easter break, they had a room free, or she would be sleeping on the street.

Sally and Tom talked till late into the night. While in India he had taken up painting, studying with a local Italian who had run away from life as a banker to concentrate on art, living his life in the style of Paul Gauguin, except painting the slum-dwellers of Bombay and the fishermen of Goa, rather than Polynesian girls.

It was this teacher who had made Tom realise that he too had run away – in his case, from his father. Now, with his father dead, Tom had no reason to stay away. More to the point, he wanted to come to the place that had attracted all those painters in the nineteenth and twentieth centuries.

On top of everything Tom said he wanted to see his mother again.

Sally couldn't have been happier.

She slept lightly and woke with the sun, immediately jumping from her bed, convinced the events of the previous night had all been a dream. But Tom's filthy, ragged clothes were still there, sealed in a plastic bag in the bin.

She let herself out as quietly as possible and ran up to the bakery to get a fresh loaf, and some treats, then returned to lay up for breakfast before Tom woke.

He came down, bleary-eyed, at 7.30.

'I'd better get a job of some kind,' was the first thing he said. 'Do they need anyone changing beds or something at the hotels? Dishwashing. Anything.'

Sally winced. 'I'm sure I can find you something better than that.'

Tom sat and spread apricot jam on a croissant. 'I just need something which could earn me enough to pay my way and get me a bit of money for paint and a few canvases. Then I can sell the paintings and I'll be all right. You'll see.'

Sally feared that Tom was being rather optimistic about the idea of painting as a career.

'I can give you the money for a canvas and some paints right away,' said Sally, pouring coffee. 'You can stay here and eat here, so you don't need any money really.'

Tom held up his hands. 'I don't think you understand, Mum. I want to support myself. I have to get a room somewhere, and be independent. I won't be kept by you. It's what Dad was always accusing me of. I came back to show you I am not a leech.'

Sally moved across to the sink for no reason except to hide the tears welling up. She had never thought for a second that Tom was a leech, was very happy to have him here, and was so sorry that, simply because of his father's attitude, he had stayed away for so long.

'It'll also make seeing you more fun. I can come to yours, and you to mine. I'll cook you a curry.'

Sally's landline phone shrilled.

Tom scuttled off to get dressed in whatever he could find that wouldn't be embarrassing.

It was Marianne on the line. Sally tried to signal to Tom, but he was gone. She told her daughter all about the excitement of Tom arriving, missing out the bit about his being picked up by the police.

'Enough about him, Mama. I was thinking about coming over for Easter,' said Marianne. 'In fact I'm arriving tonight.'

16

A ND ARRIVE SHE DID, rapping at Sally's door shortly before midnight on Maundy Thursday.

She didn't want to talk. 'Exhausted!' she said, and went straight to bed.

In the morning of Good Friday, Sally happily made early breakfast for her son and daughter, and was thrilled to have her whole family united once more. She had persuaded them both to come in her boat to go into Nice to see the Passion Week processions.

While Carol filled her car, taking William and Benjamin, both squashing into the back seat, Ted packed the boat with almost everyone else.

'Where's David?' asked William.

'Boys will be boys,' said Carol. 'He wants to play with the new toy.'

Benjamin snorted a noise of disdain.

'I'd have sat in the front if I'd realised,' said William.

'Mind you,' said Carol, swinging on the road up the hill. 'I wouldn't mind a go on the boat too.'

'Then who would drive?' asked Benjamin. 'Please, could you drop me off at Garibaldi, Carol? I want to nip down through Old Town.'

David was at the harbourside, helping Ted make checks on the engine, while the rest of the gang climbed aboard. Faith and Zoe arrived wearing sunglasses and headscarves, looking like elderly auditionees for some 1950s spy film, and sat happily together on the back bench.

Sally proudly introduced both her children, while trying to tell everyone the safety warnings, as she had been instructed. She pointed to the box full of life-jackets, the emergency bag, the inflatable raft. But no one was interested.

When Ted emerged, covered in engine oil and wiping a rag round his neck and chin, Sally introduced Marianne.

'My daughter. This is Ted, my partner-in-boat.'

Marianne seemed to freeze, before politely holding out her hand.

'So you're the man who led my mother astray?' she said.

'I try to lead everyone astray,' he replied, with a wink.

'Not *everyone*, I hope,' said Marianne curtly.

When Sally went to pull up the fenders, and untie the mooring lines, Marianne sat beside her and hissed into her ear, 'Is that the same Ted you always talk about, Sian Kelly's husband?'

'That's him. He's a bit of a rogue, but ever so nice.'

After casting off, Tom, Sally, David and Marianne crowded into the little wheelhouse, to look at the gauges and switches, while Ted took the wheel. He was in the middle of manoeuvring away from the mooring when he put the boat into reverse thrust.

'What's happening?' cried Faith.

Ted stretched out an arm, pointing towards the sea wall.

'Look!' he said, steering the boat back to the harbour side. 'We almost forgot Jessica.'

As the boat bumped sides with the marina wall, without making any attempt to secure the vessel first, Tom stretched out an arm to help Jessica jump aboard.

Sally shouted, 'That's absolutely *not* the way to do it, Tom. Someone will get hurt.'

Jessica laughed and tumbled into his arms, knocking him flat to the deck.

From her prostrate position she called through to the wheelhouse. 'Ted! I can't believe you forgot me. You knew I was coming.'

Marianne whispered into Sally's ear. 'Who is that?'

'She's very sweet,' said Sally. 'Jessica comes to all Theresa's Cookery Club things. Ted's rather taken her under his wing.'

Marianne nodded and asked: 'Do we get a drink on this boat or is it merely for transport purposes?'

Sally pulled a bottle of fizz from the fridge, and popped the cork.

Zoe took a glass and held it out. 'I like your son, Sally,' she said. 'He's fit.'

Tom had heard and turned, giving Zoe a dramatic wink.

'See,' said Zoe, quaffing her drink, and nudging Faith. 'I've pulled.'

Theresa, having a late-rising daughter and three grand-children in tow, went into town by rail, which entailed much hysteria in the girls, who were crazy about the double-decker train, and spent the fifteen-minute journey hysterically running up and down the steps playing 'He'. They also enjoyed the subsequent trip down through the town on a tram.

'Is it a bus or a train, Granny?' asked Lola.

'Both at the same time. Bit like the trams in Wimbledon.'

'No, these are much swishyer,' grinned Lola.

Imogen had not spoken much since her arrival, but Theresa had gleaned enough to realise that her son-in-law, Michael, had gone off for a 'bit of space', and 'room to breathe'. She also knew that, by searching through his emails and text messages, Imogen had discovered that the room in which he intended to breathe was, in fact, in a five-star hotel in Sorrento, where he had booked a 'romantic weekend break' with the children's new pretty Italian nanny, Verdiana.

Theresa had wanted to remind Imogen that, if the episode with Annunziata and Imogen's father was anything to go by, hiring a young pretty Italian to loll about the house in her nightgown in the presence of her husband was not the best idea. When it came to nannies, what you really needed was a clod-hopping overweight hunchback with a heavy moustache and eyebrows to rival Frida Kahlo's.

On the day after Theresa's family's arrival in Bellevue-Sur-Mer, Brian had done the gentlemanly thing and moved out. He had, he said, quite by chance, bumped into Stewart, an old friend from Glasgow, who had a little place in the city and he was going to base himself there till he found a suitable place to buy in Bellevue-Sur-Mer. Imogen took over his room, while the three children took Theresa's. Theresa hastily bought a blow-up bed, a thing she had no idea even existed before, and she slept in the living room, tucked into the corner beneath the glass-topped table.

Today, as they strolled through the maze of crowded streets in the Old Town, Imogen marched grimly, tight-lipped, glancing into windows displaying brightly coloured bonbons, clothing and pottery, without the shadow of a smile. Meanwhile, Theresa zigzagged ahead of her, attempting to control the three kids, who were like wild dogs on a rampage and clearly having a whale of a time.

When the family arrived in the packed Cathedral Square, Theresa knew there was little hope of meeting up with her neighbours. People were jammed together.

She, Imogen and the three girls were squashed in against the glass windows of an ice-cream parlour. The girls faced away from where the procession was due. They looked at the ice creams and bawled.

Luckily, after a few moments, Imogen decided to leave the children with Theresa while she went down to the market 'to get a coffee somewhere'. Theresa tipped her off which place to choose so that they could rendezvous there later. Carol and David were heading there too.

As soon as Imogen disappeared, Theresa quelled the children by buying them each an ice-cream cone of their choice. Then they stood, happily quiet, watching the procession. The whole proceedings seemed rather *gai* for a Good Friday, Theresa thought, especially as the whole shebang was led by a group of young men and girls in the traditional Niçoise folk costumes. The boys wore loose-fitting white shirts, pink breeches and red Phrygian bonnets, while the girls sashayed past in embroidered boleros and enormous pink-and-white gathered skirts, looking like sexier versions of Sandra Dee in her heyday. Then came the bowed priests and altar boys with their shrouded cross.

When the procession went into the cathedral, the majority of the crowd dispersed either into the cathedral after them or into the nearby cafes. Theresa decided to take the kids for a quick walk up the steep alleyways leading up to the hill, at the top of which was a cemetery and a park with ravishing views. The hope was that the walk up would tire them, thus enabling the family to have a lovely lunch in the restaurant on the Cours Saleya.

Theresa clapped her hands. 'Come along, girls, we're going for lunch!' The three girls scuttled along narrow dark streets where shards of light spilled in, creating black shadows. As the twisty streets became steep lanes where the tall houses seemed to meet at the top, squeezing out the sunlight, people became scarce. Theresa paused for breath at an intersection. There was a concrete bollard on the corner, so she sat while the girls happily played 'He', criss-crossing the lane, hopping up steps and down again. She looked ahead, along an intersecting lane. In the dark shade of a tall building about fifty yards away there was a man standing in a doorway. He wasn't doing anything, just standing there. He pulled out a mobile phone and started stabbing at it, texting perhaps. Theresa knew she had seen him before somewhere, but couldn't be sure where. He wore pale, ripped denim, with a worn brown leather jacket. He had a heavy moustache.

The man put the phone away, took a cigarette from a pack in his pocket, lifted it to his lips and lit it. As he breathed in, his head turned and he looked down the alleyway in Theresa's direction.

For a millisecond, they caught eyes. And in that instant she recognised him. It was the man who had robbed her on the steps in Bellevue-Sur-Mer.

She realised that he didn't know her, though. His head turned lazily in the other direction as he fumbled to replace his flick lighter in his jacket pocket.

Theresa looked about her, wishing a gendarme would appear. No one else was in sight but the children, who were energetically clambering up the steep steps.

She wanted to go along and confront this man. She decided that was what she must do.

Looking up the hill, the children naturally chose that exact moment to vanish round a corner.

Taking another glance at the man Theresa stood up, just as a second man appeared, running along to join him.

The robber had been expecting this man. He tapped his watch and gave an indignant shrug.

The other man shrugged and threw his hands out in a 'sorry there was nothing I could do' gesture.

He lifted his head, and Theresa could see his face. She recognised him instantly.

It was William's partner, Benjamin.

Theresa shot a look up the hill, where one of the children, still playing 'He', dashed out of a doorway and scurried to join the others.

There was a swift exchange between the two men. Benjamin handed the thief something. Money?

Wishing she could stay where she was and observe, Theresa knew she had no choice but to follow the girls up the hill before they got hopelessly lost in the maze of dark alleys that made up the Old Town.

She gathered her skirts and dashed to catch the girls before they disappeared altogether.

When Theresa and the girls finished their cat-and-mouse game through the steps and alleyways of the castle hill, she made them join hands and they descended together arriving in the Cours Saleya to find Imogen sitting on a sunny terrace enjoying a salad at a table with Carol, William and some other woman who Theresa didn't recognise.

Imogen gave them a bright wave, but as there was no adjacent table for four, Theresa went with the girls to an empty table at the far end of the terrace.

The children eagerly inspected the food on the neighbouring tables.

'I want a pizza,' said Lola.

'I want a pizza too,' echoed Cressida.

'They're all made of frogs' legs and snails,' said Chloe haughtily. 'That's what French people eat. I know these things.'

'French people eat slugs and poo,' said Lola.

'Now look what you've started.' Theresa gave Chloe a stern look. Her mind was still churning over the implications of Benjamin being friends or having some unexplained business with the man who had deliberately pushed her over, stolen her handbag and caused her such distress. She glanced over towards William, wondering should she tell him about Benjamin and the thief. He was laughing at something Carol was saying.

Theresa also knew that Benjamin had been up to something clandestine with Pierre in the furniture cave. Benjamin certainly had secrets to keep from William.

Was it her business to expose them?

But then he *had* been talking, exchanging money, with the man who robbed her, so . . . ?

William saw her looking at him and gave a little wave, and a look of sympathy, presumably because she had been relegated to the kiddies' table. She decided she would tell him later, whenever they got a moment alone. If she was William, she'd want to know.

The waiter arrived and Theresa ordered a large pizza and salad with three knives and forks for the three girls. For herself she first chose a piece of fish, then changed her order. She had decided to have some fun and so, instead, picked a local speciality, *merda de can*.

The pizza arrived and Theresa helped cut it up so that Lola had a chance of getting some.

After they had devoured a few mouthfuls Theresa's dish arrived. *Merda de can*, a kind of special Niçoise version of gnocchi, is made with chard so that it comes out an off-green brownish colour, a tad darker than khaki. The literal translation of the name from Nissart, the ancient Niçoise language, is dog shit, which it resembles in every way but taste.

Theresa tucked in.

'Granny?' Cressida glanced, then stared at her plate, cocking her head. 'What's that?'

'It's a special dish you can only get here,' she replied.

'Looks like poo,' said Chloe.

'It's called dog poo in the local language, but it tastes delicious,' said Theresa, taking another mouthful. 'It's like spaghetti, but it's a French joke.'

Lola leaned in and sniffed Theresa's plate. 'I want some.'

'No problem.' Theresa took a spoon and dropped a little on the plate beside the pizza. Lola ate.

'Mmmmmm!' She gave a naughty grin. 'That's a good joke.'

Theresa nodded towards the pizza.

'If I can have some of yours, you can have some of mine.'

Theresa and the three children happily tucked in, attacking each other's plates with gusto.

'Granny,' said Chloe. 'You have to promise not to tell Mummy about this. Then when we come back we can pretend it's real dog poo.'

Theresa took the last bite, just as Imogen arrived at the table.

'What on earth are they eating?' she moaned

'It's delicious, Mummy,' said Cressida. 'Look, we finished everything.'

'We like it in France,' said Chloe.

'*Merci beaucoup*, Madame!' said Lola. 'See, Mummy! I can speak French, too.'

'They'll be getting tired,' said Imogen. 'Give me the key and I'll take them back for an afternoon nap.'

The strangest thing then happened. The three girls pulled the faces they usually reserved for Theresa, but instead directed them at their mother.

As Imogen got them up from the table, they clung to Theresa.

'We want to stay with Granny,' said Lola. 'We like her best.'

Imogen yanked Lola's arm and dragged all three children (now yowling and yearning back in Theresa's direction) into the throngs of the market and away.

Theresa moved over to sit with Carol, William and the other woman.

'Theresa,' said Carol as she arrived, indicating the stranger. 'This is Sally's daughter, Marianne.'

'Did you come over by car?' asked Theresa.

'That depends what you meant by "come over",' said Marianne. 'I flew in from London last night; however, this morning, I came here to Nice with my dear mother in her new boat. My mother is ditzy enough, but Ted was at the wheel and had a strange fit of manliness.'

Carol gave a quizzical look.

'As we came into port he declared he was going straight out again to, in his own words, "put the old girl through her paces". I asked to be put ashore.'

'Who on earth was he talking about?' asked Theresa. 'Jessica?'

William gave an explosive laugh as Carol spurted her drink out, and started frantically dabbing at her chin with a pale turquoise handkerchief, which matched her silk blouse.

'Theresa, dear, now we know what you've been thinking during all your Cookery Club meetings!' William shot her an old-fashioned look. 'I imagine Ted was actually talking about the boat.'

Theresa felt herself blush a deep red.

'Look, the others are on their way over, with their hair in the air,' laughed Carol, pouring some rosé from a carafe into an empty glass for Theresa.

Sally approached, looking windswept, with Jessica in tow. Carol gave them a vigorous wave, but Jessica glanced at the table, shook her head, exchanged a few words with Sally and strutted off alone, stabbing a number into her mobile phone.

'I think Jessica looks a little green around the gills,' said William. 'She's clearly no sailor.'

'Missing Ted already, perhaps?' suggested Carol. 'Who else is on the boat, Marianne?'

'My hippy brother and some idiot called David, who's acting like Ted's personal puppy dog. That girl was clinging all over Ted. It was sickening. I told her, in no uncertain terms, to leave the poor man alone.'

Carol opened her mouth to speak but Theresa noticed William press down hard on her leg.

'A butch boys' jaunt,' said William. 'What fun . . . not!'

'It's not all boys,' said Marianne. 'Those two ancient raddled viragos are still on board.'

If this was how she described Zoe and Faith, Theresa didn't like to think what descriptions Marianne would be coming up with about her as soon as she was out of sight.

Sally squeezed through the rows of tables, and indicated that she was going inside to use the ladies' room before joining them.

'Poor Ted.' Theresa sipped her drink. 'It must be terrible to live your life on the edge like he does.'

'Do you mean his womanising?' asked Marianne.

'No, I meant being stalked by a girl who's working for his own wife.'

'So Sally's told you about Sian's spy, too.' William leaned in to Theresa. 'What do you think? This is Sian Kelly we're talking about, by the way, Marianne, the famous entrepreneur.'

'I do know,' said Marianne starting edging her chair back. 'I'm in business myself.'

'How rude you must think us.' Theresa turned back to Sally's daughter. 'What a lovely surprise for your mum. My daughter arrived for Easter too. Are you here for a holiday?'

'Not exactly,' said Marianne. 'I'm working on a business franchise and renewing some contacts pertaining to my project.'

'Really?' Theresa sipped her wine. 'How exciting. What's the project about?'

'Errrm . . . business.' Marianne glanced at her watch.

'What kind of business?'

'I'm checking out . . . wedding venues.'

'How lovely,' said Theresa. 'Who's getting married?'

'If you must know . . .' Marianne downed her drink and smoothed down her tight skirt, ready to stand up. 'I am.'

Carol, William and Theresa all grinned and said 'congratulations' and at this moment Sally emerged to join them on the terrace.

'Sally must be so excited.' Theresa twisted in her chair to smile at Sally.

'Not at all. In fact, she doesn't know. I haven't had a chance to tell her. She's been too busy fussing over my delinquent brother and playing with her toy boat.'

Marianne was already standing. She tossed a twenty-euro note on to the table and gathered up her things. 'Now I'm going to see whether I can tear her away from all this gay camaraderie long enough for us to have a serious chat.'

In silence, Carol, William and Theresa watched Marianne walk over to Sally, and whisper something in her ear. Flustered, Sally glanced in their direction, gave a farewell wave and left with her daughter.

Carol, William and Theresa all remained mute for a few seconds but, once Marianne and Sally had vanished into the crowd, they turned to one another and pulled faces.

'Good Lord,' said Theresa, realising that Imogen was probably making just such a bad impression on her neighbours.

'Puppy dog!' said Carol. 'Bloody cheek.'

'She might be up for Businesswoman of the Year, but she certainly won't be winning the Miss Congeniality prize any time soon.' William pulled his fingers across his closed lips. 'As to the wedding, my lips are sealed.'

'Makes you wonder who'd marry her!' Carol laughed.

'Change the subject.' Theresa downed the rest of her glass. 'We'll all just have to pretend to be very surprised.'

MERDA DE CAN

Ingredients
1.5kg floury potatoes
500g swiss chard (or spinach and lettuce mix)
350g flour
1 egg
1 tablespoon olive oil
Salt and pepper
Parmesan, grated

Method
Peel and boil potatoes till soft.

Blanch the chard in boiling salted water for 4 minutes.

Squeeze in towel, finely chop and leave chard in a sieve to drain.

Purée or mash the cooked potatoes, and add flour, lightly beaten egg, drained chard and olive oil. Season to taste.

Make sure it has a firm consistency. Then leave to rest for half an hour.

Roll out into long tubes, and shape to dog-turd form.

Drop into boiling water and cook till they bob to the top.

Drain.

Sprinkle with parmesan.

Serve – with sauce of choice or plain with butter.

17

S ALLY COULDN'T MAKE UP her mind whether she was quite over the moon now that her daughter had come to Bellevue-Sur-Mer to tell her she was getting married. For a start, Sally had never before heard a word about her proposed son-in-law-to-be and Marianne still wasn't letting on any details. Plus it all seemed very rushed. Though, who knew, perhaps Marianne had been seeing this mystery man for years and had only now decided to marry him.

Marianne had given Sally her news in the taxi back from town.

As they walked through the marketplace in Nice, Sally had been told, in no uncertain terms, that nothing on earth would persuade Marianne to climb back on the boat 'with that bunch of imbeciles', so Sally left Ted to take everyone else back on his own. Sally hoped they'd be all right, as Ted was rather cavalier about checking the charts and screens for depth and hidden obstacles, although he did know a fair amount about the finer technical points of engine maintenance.

'You could always have the reception at my house in

Bellevue-Sur-Mer,' Sally had suggested to an icy reception from her daughter.

'I want somewhere with a five-star reputation,' replied Marianne. 'This is going to be a special day. Let's face it, I could come to your place any time I wanted.'

'Where will everyone stay?' asked Sally. 'Hôtel Astra?'

Marianne looked Sally in the eye. After the smallest hesitation she said: 'That dump? Are you joking?'

Crushed, Sally took out her local guidebooks and placed them in a pile.

'It's not that bad,' she said.

'It's creepy,' said Marianne.

'If you've never stayed there how would you know?'

'Everyone knows.'

Sally gritted her teeth. 'If you say so.'

She decided to stop coming up with ideas and just be happy that her daughter had decided to have the wedding nearby, rather than in London. So she sat at the kitchen table with a notepad and a map, preparing to note down all the nearby posh restaurants and potential wedding venues from the fancy guidebook Marianne had bought, while Marianne herself sat in the corner reading a brochure she had picked up from a five-star hotel in St-Jean-Cap-Ferrat.

'Will my hippy brother be here for ever?' Marianne asked. 'Or could you encourage him to go on his travels again . . .'

Sally was stabbed to the heart by this. She had only just got Tom back. How could she send him packing just because Marianne wanted him out of the way?

'If you don't want him here, Marianne, I'm sure Tom will be happy to go out for the day.'

'Aren't you friends with Sian Kelly?' asked Marianne out of the blue.

'Yes,' said Sally. 'And Ted.'

'Good.'

'OK,' said Sally, smelling fear. 'Is there any particular reason you ask?'

'What's the time?' Marianne glanced at her watch. 'I forgot to change regions. Are you an hour forward or back?'

Sally saw the avoidance technique, which made her all the more worried about everything to do with this potential wedding and especially the groom. Why wouldn't she talk about him? Why had Marianne not even proffered a photograph? Was he very old, very ugly, a jailbird ... what was wrong with him, that Marianne chose to avoid the subject?

'Is he handsome?' asked Sally. 'Tall? Clever? Don't you have a photo?'

Marianne shook her watch at Sally, who timidly said 'Forward an hour.'

'What's *she* like?'

Sally was taken aback for a moment, then realised that Marianne was harking back to her neighbour, Sian.

'Sian is very nice,' she said, despite the niggles in her head. Her conscience prickled too, because Sally disapproved of the way Sian had set up that girl as a spy on poor Ted.

'That's not the impression I got from the others in town. Among other things, they called her a dragon.'

'She's very protective of Ted. Overprotective really. It's her big weakness. Apparently she's set up some girl to report back on her husband's behaviour in her own absence.'

Marianne smiled. 'I'd heard.' Marianne laid down her brochure. 'You know what's really odd, Mum? Sian Kelly runs one of the most prestigious businesses in Britain. And yet she is married to her own Achilles heel. Now there's irony for you.'

Sally knew that often marriages didn't work. Husbands and wives lied to one another. Husbands and wives strayed. I mean . . . she had the evidence of her own failed marriage to go by, and yet, somehow it seemed to Sally quite immoral, and at the same time pointless, that Sian had gone to these lengths. But she was puzzled about why any of this would matter to Marianne.

'So why, all of a sudden, are you so interested in Sian and her husband?'

'Because, Mama, Sian Kelly is one of the UK's top businesswomen.' Marianne picked up a pencil and started doodling. 'And then, one day soon, you watch me – I'm going to have a business empire even more successful than hers.'

Sally gulped.

After Carol had driven Theresa back to Bellevue-Sur-Mer, with William in the back seat, they stood on the quay and watched Faith and Zoe getting off the boat.

Zoe gave an expansive wave. 'What a marvellous day. Hey, you three!' she called to them. 'Come on. Let's get drunk and disorderly.'

As they reached the harbourside terrace bar–brasserie, Zoe plonked herself at a sunny table.

Faith stayed standing and said: 'It's been a gorgeous day, Zoe, but a bit too exhilarating. I really should take a little nap.'

'Sleep?' Zoe screeched. 'We've got eternity to sleep, woman. Come on.'

Faith sat, taking a seat next to Carol, while Zoe ordered a bottle and six glasses.

'How did David do?' asked Carol. 'Did Ted let him have a go?'

'The men had a great time. They're going out again. Look!' Zoe shaded her eyes and pointed in the direction of the boat, which was already pulling out into the choppy waters of the bay with David and Tom standing near Ted in the wheelhouse. 'Those men and their machines.'

'They're all still boys at heart,' said Faith.

'Except my husband,' added Carol. 'Apparently he's a puppy dog.'

'He *is* rather cuddly,' said Faith, not picking up Carol's irony. 'I suppose they want to enjoy a bit of speed without us old ladies on board.'

'They had speed enough on the way out, didn't they?' asked William.

'Not as much as we'd all have liked,' said Zoe. 'Too many dramas.'

'Dramas?' William leaned in.

'Jessica wasn't too bright on the way out. I suppose you either have sea legs or you don't.' Faith grimaced. 'She seemed upset. I think the real problem was something that Sally said to her.'

'Sally?' William was perplexed. 'What did she do wrong?'

'It was odd,' said Faith. 'The boat hit some wash and lurched, and Jessica sort of clung on to Ted, and when she recovered her equilibrium, Sally said something that had a huge impact on her.'

'Don't leave us on tenterhooks, Faith,' said Carol. 'Spill!'

'It was something like: "I know what you're up to and who you really are." Then Jessica hesitated, as though she was going to make an announcement, but instead smiled, and took a few steps away, then turned back and shot her *such* a look.'

William leaned in. 'What kind of look?'

'It was a mix of being scared and being full of spite. She kind of shrank and grew at the same time. Very strange. Then she moved to the back of the boat, sat looking out at the sea with tightly pursed lips and refused to communicate with anyone till we got off. But she had an air of malevolence about her. No one dared go near.'

'Does anyone know where she is now?' asked William.

'Are we talking about that ghastly blonde bint who's always making dewy eyes at Ted?' Zoe, who been gazing out to sea, suddenly decided to rejoin the conversation. 'I last saw her down near the port, when we pulled in so that the blokes could pick up a few bottles. Face like fury, waiting at the bus stop, gabbling into her mobile phone. I pity the poor person on the other end of the line.'

Theresa, William and Carol all caught eyes. They

each knew it had to be Sian on the receiving end. Her own silly plan to set up Jessica as a bait-cum-spy on Ted had obviously backfired.

The worm had turned.

Before they could continue a shadow loomed over Theresa's shoulder.

She turned to see Brian, blocking out the sunlight.

'Sorry if I startled you, Theresa, but I appear to have left my passport at your place. Silly me! It must have slid under the bed in my room or somewhere.'

Theresa took him along the road to her flat and she was surprised to find that Imogen and the kids weren't there. Theresa took the moment to use the lavatory while Brian disappeared into his old bedroom looking for the passport.

When she came back into the living room Brian emerged from Imogen's room, waving his passport in the air.

'Thank goodness for that,' said Theresa. 'Now, Brian, promise me you won't vanish away out of my life, just because my family turned up.' Theresa opened the front door and they both stood on the step looking out at the seafront. 'We must keep in contact. Do you have a number or address, so I can invite you over sometime?'

'Don't worry.' Brian smiled. 'I'll still be coming over for the weekly Cookery Club. Look!' He pointed towards the beach. 'Your daughter and the children appear to be enjoying themselves.'

Theresa had to blink to believe her eyes.

Imogen was happily sitting on the sands under a little parasol, which she must have bought at the local shop. At her side the kids were engrossed, earnestly making sandcastles.

Theresa gave a wave, hoping that someone would notice.

Chloe looked up and gave her a huge grin and a wave back.

'Come and have a drink with the gang, Brian,' suggested Theresa.

'I only have enough time for a quick one. I need to dash up to the station,' said Brian. 'Got an appointment with the lawyers – hence the need for my passport.'

Theresa and Brian went back to the brasserie and sat at the end beside William.

Brian waved gaily at everyone and ordered a couple of bottles of wine for the table. He drank half a glass then excused himself.

'I'll just use the gents, then I'll slip off,' he whispered into Theresa's ear.

Theresa watched him go inside. He certainly was a fine figure of a man, with a broad back. As he vanished into the shadows she turned and whispered into William's ear. 'I saw something today and I'm torn as to whether or not to tell you about it.'

'Now that you've said that, of course, Theresa, you know you *have* to tell me.'

'In the Old Town at Nice ... I saw the man who robbed me.'

William drew back to look more closely at Theresa's face. 'What's that got to do with me?'

'I ... er ... well, I have some information about Benjamin.'

'Yes?' William's eyes were slits. He barely moved a feature. 'Like what?'

'It may mean more or less to you, and I don't want to stir up trouble, but I saw Benjamin too. In the same place.'

'In the same place as what?'

'As the man who robbed me.'

The two turned their seats slightly out of the circle as Theresa explained how she had seen the man who had robbed her, and then seen Benjamin coming along for an apparent liaison with him. What she really wanted, she explained, was to track that thief down and put the police on to him. Maybe Benjamin could help her?

William's lips tightened. He didn't say a word. His breathing became shallow and tight. Then suddenly he banged his fist on the table, causing everyone's glasses to rattle.

'Fuck it!' he said under his breath, as he flung a euro bill on to the table and stood up.

'What's happening today? Why is everyone behaving like a prima donna?' Carol reached out to William, who roughly pushed her hand away and stalked off. She turned and spun back to Theresa. 'What on earth did you say, Theresa? My God, he's gone off like a volcano.'

'I told him I'd seen Benjamin in the alleys of Old Town, talking to the man who robbed me.'

A loaded silence reigned at the table until Zoe broke it.

'Well done, Theresa, darling,' she said, with a kitten-ish smile.

'I don't understand,' said Theresa. 'I only thought I was giving William a warning, and rather hoped that Benjamin could lead me to help get that thief taken off the streets.'

'Oh, you stirred up a little more than that, my dear. Now all I can say is: "You lit the blue touch paper, now let's all stand well back."'

As a shadow had fallen over the proceedings, which appeared to be her fault, Theresa felt awful. She waved to the waiter to get the bill. It would cost a packet, but the least she could do was pay for everyone's drinks and hope everything would lighten up a bit.

The waiter arrived and told Theresa that there was nothing to pay. The tall gentleman with grey hair had already paid.

Brian!

How sweet, thought Theresa. He didn't even really have a drink, yet bought for the whole table.

18

I T SEEMED THAT EVERYTHING always arrived in packs, just like they said of London buses. After years here on her own, Sally now had both Marianne and Tom staying, and soon possibly she would have another visitor: Marianne's mystery beau.

Marianne had supper with her mother and then, despite much protesting from Sally, ordered a taxi to take her to her hotel a few miles away somewhere just outside Beaulieu. She wanted to see whether it was as pleasant as it seemed in the brochure. 'These things lie,' she said.

Sally was left pondering the whole mysterious business of children. As their mother you felt that they somehow belonged to you, were part of you, and yet, as they grew up, you were forced to realise that they weren't. They were just other people, with their own thoughts, desires and secrets. Sally felt she could just about understand Tom, but Marianne was like an alien. The ruthless determination was quite frightening to behold. Sally dreaded Sian's reaction if Marianne was to make good on her threats. But then, at the start of her own acting career, wouldn't she herself have gone to some extreme lengths to further her chances? She remembered hugging information to herself so that she might get to an audition, while her friends didn't. Perhaps Sally had had that naked ambition too, just had forgotten it over the years of being out of the business. Well, if Marianne could be as successful as Sian, that would be one thing. Sally only hoped she would be happier in her personal life.

She wished she knew more about the mystery man, but knew also that asking too many questions would only drive Marianne further away.

Sally sat up waiting up for Tom to come home, but when an hour or so later she woke to find herself sitting in the armchair dribbling, with the television blaring a football commentary, she gave up and retired to bed, leaving a note for him, telling him that they'd have breakfast together in the morning, before going into town looking for canvas and paints.

Sally was woken just after midnight by a violent banging on the front door. As she wrapped her dressing gown round her and shuffled towards the door she feared that this must be Tom back, maybe drunk, perhaps having mislaid his keys.

She opened up.

Carol stood there, looking agitated, but, as ever, beautifully turned out.

'Is Tom back?'

Sally shook her head.

'Nor's David. And I can't get any response out of his phone.' Carol bit her lower lip and pressed her gloved hands tight together. 'You don't think they're still out there, at sea, do you?'

'Oh God!' Sally immediately understood the connotations of this. 'What's the sea like? Rough?'

Carol nodded. 'Pretty choppy.'

Sally cursed herself for trusting Ted. Who knew what might happen out there at sea in the darkness? And Ted had had no formal training, only the Australian male ego.

'Tom doesn't have a mobile. I'll try Ted.' Sally grabbed her own phone and dialled Ted's number. It rang out for a long time, then went to answer-phone.

'What else can we do?' asked Sally. 'Phone the coastguard? Do they even have a coastguard in France?'

'I thought of trying something like that, but what if they've come ashore and are stuck in some disco, where they can't hear their phones, or . . . I don't know . . . just drunk somewhere, or simply asleep?'

Sally put her coat on over her pyjamas and dressing gown, and grabbed her keys. 'Let's go and see if the boat's there.'

Carol pulled a face. 'Why didn't I think of that?'

The two women ran along the sea wall to the port de plaisance, where Sally and Ted had a mooring.

Their space was empty.

'What now?' said Carol. 'Perhaps they came in up the coast, in Monte Carlo or somewhere.'

'Perhaps. I'm worried that Ted got pulled in and asked for his certificate.'

'And?'

'He doesn't have one. I do.' Sally took out her mobile phone. 'You keep ringing David. I'll keep ringing Ted.'

They sat at the harbour side, repeatedly dialling.

After about five minutes Ted picked up.

'Ted?' Sally screeched into the phone. 'Where the hell are you?'

Ted groaned.

'Um. Not sure.'

'Ted? Where's David and Tom?'

'Oh, those two Boy Scouts? They're asleep on the boat.'

'But where's the boat?'

'I don't know,' said Ted.

Carol, who had been squeezing her face close up to Sally's to listen in, took this moment to grab the phone from her and bellow into it.

'Where have you left my husband, Ted? And Tom? Are they safe or are they lost at sea? We have to know where they are, before I dial the police.'

'Oh jeez, don't do that . . .' Ted's voice changed from the voice of a person lying down to someone sitting up. 'No the boat is all safe and tied up, and they're on board.'

'And where the fuck are you?'

'Easy on, easy on now, Carol. Don't throw a wobbly at me. The boat is in the harbour.'

Sally took the phone back. 'No, Ted, the boat is most definitely not in the harbour, because we're standing right beside the empty mooring.'

'Did I say Bellevue-Sur-Mer harbour? No. It's in another one.'

'Another what?'

'Another harbour.'

'Which harbour?'

'I don't know. We just ran out of petrol and pulled

in at ... Cap Martin, Cap Ferrat ... Cap-something, Cap-wherever it was.'

Carol took over yelling into the handset. 'Why aren't you with them, Ted? You're the fucking sailor.'

'I got a bit interrupted on my way back to the boat. But, hey, they're both fine, so what's your problem?'

'If you would only let me know where they are, Ted, I could get into the car and go and get them.'

Ted groaned. 'Oh no, Carol, please don't do that. Blokes like sleeping on a boat, you know? It gives them a sense of adventure. Come on, gals. Stop giving me such an earbashing and give them a bit of space. I'll make sure they're back with you for breakfast. OK?'

Sally and Carol accepted Ted's promise, but both really wanted to know the exact details of what had happened and why the men hadn't simply come back home.

'You realise what's probably happened, don't you?' said Sally.

'No.'

'Ted's hooked up with some floozy.'

Carol held up a hand. 'Don't get me started.'

Realising they were going to get no nearer to finding out what had actually happened till the morning, they both retired to their homes.

Sally was sorry that she was alone in the house, knowing that both children were so near. But she also knew she had somehow to stop thinking of them as children. They were grown adults, with their own plans and hopes and dreams, just as she had had at their age.

With a heavy heart, which was somehow at the same time light and full of joy, she pulled off her coat and made her way back to bed, where she lay awake for hours.

Meanwhile, Theresa, who was also awake, sitting at her table looking out at the bay, while the snores of Imogen and the children resounded round the flat, saw the two women pass on their way back from the mooring. She noted that, for some reason, Sally was in her pyjamas.

She herself was still worried about her earlier exchange with William. She had gone back over all the little signals Benjamin had given her in the past in front of William. And those signals told her to shut up. She thought of the first time she had set eyes on Benjamin, when he had been so unpleasant to her in that second-hand furniture shop and how when the subject of the table had come up later he had stopped her mentioning it to William.

Was Benjamin sleeping around? Could that be it? Was he having an illicit relationship with Pierre of the furniture cave? She supposed that that would be reason enough to send William off in a temper. First doing it with Pierre in the shop and then maybe the robber fellow up the alley. But, though she couldn't speak for the man who had knocked her over and robbed her, Pierre didn't seem at all the type to go for men, in a sexual way. But when it came to sex, who knew anything?

She wondered about Brian too. How lovely of him to buy everyone's drinks today. Had he ever been married? He seemed very eligible. It was strange for him to be left on his own at his age. She wondered where he was now. Where was he staying? Would he come back when Imogen and the children went back to Wimbledon?

How complicated the lives of people were: William and Benjamin, Michael off in Rome with the Italian nanny, Verdiana; Imogen, middle-aged but still running to Mummy in time of trouble. Sally and Carol obviously also in the middle of some crisis up the road. Ted and Sian, his rightly suspicious termagant wife, and Jessica who was perhaps sent here to lead him on, acting as Sian's agent provocateur while spying on him and all his other women.

It all made the drunken antics of Zoe seem like a rather pleasant and sane way to grow old.

In comparison to everyone else, things didn't seem as complicated for her. She had Imogen here, and the grandchildren were finally coming round to liking her too.

That thrilled her.

Yes.

Things weren't so bad after all.

19

THE NEXT COOKERY CLUB was held at Sally's as, with Imogen and children in Theresa's flat, it didn't seem quite right to hold it there and, more importantly, Theresa was worried that Imogen might start interfering and sending everyone home if she believed that the noise was keeping the children awake or on some other pretence. Mind you, while Theresa was making the phone call to Sally to ask her, she pondered on Imogen since she had arrived in Bellevue-Sur-Mer and how much she seemed to have softened. Her only complaints so far were about the loud voices she could hear from the Hôtel Astra, above. Everything else appeared to please her.

Perhaps it was the pain of an injured psyche, after her husband had vanished with the nanny, or maybe it was simply that Riviera touch, the same magic which had soothed Theresa when she first arrived here, that had softened her.

Theresa had done a quick phone around, and the usual gang assembled, with a few extra live-in strays: Tom, who decided to act as a kitchen help, and Marianne, who sat in the corner ignoring everyone, reading a book.

Theresa phoned Brian's mobile and persuaded him that he must come, things wouldn't be the same without him, and he duly arrived, a little early, and appeared to be even more assiduous in his gentlemanly ways, pulling out a chair for Jessica when she came in, handing round the plate of nibbles, and making sure all the glasses were kept topped up.

They were making another Niçoise speciality, a pissaladière, and having finished rolling out the pastry, had moved on to chopping onions.

Zoe sniffed first, while beside her, Faith rubbed her eyes. A general sniffing started.

Tom started to laugh.

'Listen to you all!' he exclaimed. 'It sounds like some drug den full of coke heads.'

'I'm sorry?' said William, looking up through bleary eyes. 'What do you mean?'

'It's just funny, that's all. Sniff, sniff.' Tom held one end of a knife to his nose and mimed out sucking up cocaine.

'Leave it,' said Benjamin. 'We're preparing onions, for God's sake, William. We're going to sniff a bit, aren't we?'

'I just think . . .'

'Leave it!' snapped Benjamin.

Changing the subject, Benjamin asked whether the sailing party had enjoyed their night camping on board.

'I feel as though I'm still on the ruddy boat,' said Tom, wiping a tear from his cheek. 'I'm rolling about the streets like a drunken sailor. How are you getting on, Dave?'

Carol raised an eyebrow and turned to her husband. 'Oh, yes, "Dave", do tell.'

'We had great fun,' David replied, ignoring Carol's sarcasm. 'It was good to have a bit of man time.'

Carol gave a little snort and exclaimed 'Lordy Lord! I never realised that being a Boy Scout was equated with manliness. When are you getting a tent and a woggle and joining the jamboree?'

'Shut up!' said David, his face now flushed, and his eyes red with onion tears.

'Don't you tell me to shut up, "Dave". I also think,' continued Carol without pause, 'that manliness, or even being in the Boy Scouts, might just include the basics of being able to operate a mobile phone to alert people about your safety – or otherwise.'

'We were fine,' said David with an extended sigh. 'Why would we phone?'

'You knew that,' snapped Carol, sweeping the paper-like peel into the rubbish sack. 'Sally and I did not. In fact we were so worried that we were parading along the seafront in our pyjamas.'

'That's a sight I'd like to have seen,' said Ted.

A silence followed, while everyone concentrated on peeling, chopping, wiping their eyes and blowing their noses.

Ted broke the embarrassing pause filled only with sniffs. 'All my fault, folks. Look, to tell the truth, we ran out of petrol and I went off to get some, and, well, I got a little bit waylaid, but I knew the blokes were happy and tucked up with a bottle of the old vino, so . . .' His voice faded out.

'You didn't need to go off wandering, Ted. You

should have been able to get fuel at the marina,' sniffed Sally, onion tears streaming down her cheeks and dripping on to her chest.

'Well, I . . . It was cramped in there.'

'For goodness' sake!' Marianne rose from her seat in the corner and grabbed a knife. 'I thought this was a Cookery Club, not the Marriage Guidance Council? Come on, let's cook!' She rolled up her sleeves and started stabbing at an onion.

Theresa finished rubbing the last tin tray with butter, while the others lined theirs with pastry and, in the corner, next to Ted, Jessica sniggered into the counter.

Ted hushed her.

Theresa had an idea to change the subject again, and said brightly 'Guess what, Brian? Do you remember when you so kindly came to my rescue after some nasty bloke knocked me down and stole my bag? Well, I saw the man in Old Town on Friday. Got quite a good look at him, actually. And I think, well, I'm pretty sure he's a drug dealer.'

Brian looked blankly in her direction. It was almost as though she was speaking a foreign language.

'Really?' he said, after a long pause. 'The man from way back? On the steps? Surely you can't be certain it was him. It was a very long time ago.'

'Oh, it was him, all right,' said Theresa pressing pastry into the tin. 'I'd never forget him. The face, the body shape, the gait, even the smell of him.'

'I see.' Brian looked quite concerned. 'Did you tell the police?'

'I didn't actually. Do you think I should have done?'

'I can't imagine there's very much they could do

about it now,' he laughed. 'Anyone need a top-up?' He grabbed the wine bottle and did the rounds with it.

Benjamin glared at Zoe, who was staring in his direction.

'And what are you looking at?'

Zoe pursed her lips. 'A cat may look at a queen,' she said.

'That's enough,' said Benjamin, ripping his apron off. 'Enough, enough, enough.'

'Sorry everyone,' said William. 'We're off.'

They both marched to the front door and out.

'Exeunt the Flowerpot men,' said Zoe.

'Is that because of their floral shirts, Zoe?'

'William and Benjamin,' said Zoe. 'Bill and Ben. Don't know why I didn't think it up months ago.' Zoe left a little pause then said beguilingly 'Weeeeeed! Which I must say, in Benjamin's case, is rather apt.'

'Now, everyone,' said Theresa in a louder than usual voice. 'Let's get those onions into the frying pans.'

'This is the best fun we've ever had at Cookery Club,' said Zoe, dumping a mound of onions into the pan. 'Who's going to kick off next?'

During the silence which followed they all stirred, one frying pan on each of the four burners.

'Where's it all going to lead?' asked Faith, under her breath.

'I hope it leads to a drink,' replied Zoe.

'You crack me up,' said Tom to Zoe.

'Go on, Ted,' said Sally, dragging the conversation back to the night on the boat. 'Where *did* you sleep then?'

'A five-star boutique hotel, of course,' said Ted.

'Mother! For goodness' sake!' Marianne rushed to Sally's side and hissed in her ear. 'Why must you go on about it? Leave him alone.' She turned to the frying pan and, pushing her mother out of the way, started stirring the hissing onions.

'There wasn't room on the boat for all of us,' said Tom, joining the fray. 'Not to sleep, anyway, unless we were going to play spoons, which no one fancied. Why the fuss? We were all incapable of driving the boat home. Did you want us all to drown?'

'No!' shrieked Sally, through the hanky she was using to blow her nose. 'I just want to be kept in the loop about my boat.'

'It isn't *your* boat, though, Sally, is it?' Ted brought his chopping knife down hard into the block causing the chopped onions to jump and spread over the counter. 'It's *my* fucking boat, and I'll do what I bloody well like with it, even if it's just saving mollycoddled or henpecked men from their female jailers.'

Sally and Carol gasped in unison.

'Sorry, mates, look at yourselves' said Ted, taking off his apron and strutting towards the door. 'There's 57 dressing David up in fancy dress, as though he's some fucking Barbie doll she just bought, while Sally behaves as though Tom is still a twelve-year-old kid. He's thirty years old, for fuck's sake. But if you don't like the truth, nick off.'

He went to the front door and left, slamming it behind him.

'Farewell to the Lizard,' said Zoe.

'Sort of Lounge Lizard, do you mean, Zoe?' asked Faith.

'No. The Lizard of Oz, or course.'

Tom guffawed.

'Good grief!' said Brian, downing his wine.

Carol turned on her husband. 'Did you tell that uncouth Australian that you were henpecked?'

'If the cap fits.' David shrugged. '"57".'

'What fucking cap?' said Carol. 'If anyone's henpecked, it's Ted. Look at him! His wife is so barking mad she thinks he's bonking Theresa!'

It was Theresa's turn to gasp.

'There you go, Carol. Or should I say, Adolf? I'm not your puppet you know, but you treat me like one.' David spoke staccato-fashion, while shaking pepper on to his onions. 'America is a classless society, you know. Yet you always assume superiority, and we always do what *you* want to do. Living with you is like living with Stalin.'

Carol turned and slapped David so hard across the cheek that he staggered into Sally, knocking her into Jessica.

'And if we're talking about manliness, Carol,' David nursed his ruddy cheek with the palm of his hand as he made for the exit. 'For all your feminine airs and your just-so clothes, you've a punch on you that would put Mike Tyson to shame,' he called out his parting gift before slamming the door behind him. 'Very feminine!'

'And then there were six!' With reptilian eyes, Zoe scanned the room. 'Anyone else fancy a bout in the ring?'

To get out of the fray, Tom started ladling out and spreading the cooked onions on to the pastry tins.

Theresa knew she was supposed to be in control of things. In a desperate attempt to re-establish an equilibrium, she asked loudly 'Everyone got their olives and anchovies ready?'

Sally turned to apologise to Jessica, who hastily scrambled about with her handbag, which had shot along the counter in the scuffle and came to rest on the stray onions. Something fell to the floor. Sally stooped to pick it up, bumping heads with Jessica who also reached for it.

'Your phone,' said Sally, picking it up. 'Wait a minute!' She gripped the thing and turned away from Jessica. 'What's this?'

'Nothing,' said Jessica, stretching to grab it from Sally's hand.

'I know what this is. It's a Dictaphone!' Sally staggered backwards as Jessica snatched the little machine from Sally and slipped it into her handbag. 'You're taping us!'

'You're paranoid, Sally,' said Jessica calmly, snapping the bag shut. 'It's a phone. A newer, more modern model than you're used to, I imagine.' Jessica moved forward, pressing past the others, also heading for the front door. She turned, and waved. 'The Bellevue-Sur-Mer asylum is too much for me, tonight, too, I'm afraid. Bye, bye.'

And she also left.

'There she goes – the Jezebel!' Zoe knocked back the rest of her wine.

'I thought her name was Jessica,' said Faith, laying her olives in a row.

'A Dictaphone, eh?' Zoe popped open the jar of anchovies. 'Hmmm. Something fishy.'

Tom laughed again.

'If it really was some sort of recording device, why would she want to tape *us*?' said Faith. 'We're all so dull.'

'Speak entirely for yourself,' said Zoe with a floppy pout.

Sally answered. 'It won't affect us, Faith. It's for Sian, I presume, about Ted. In Jessica's position as spy-in-chief.'

Carol, who was mopping at the corners of her eyes with a pretty lace-edged handkerchief that matched her blouse, let out a sudden sob.

Brian rushed forward. 'Carol? Perhaps you'd like a brandy.'

'It's the onions,' said Carol. 'Onions make me cry.'

'Even when you're crying,' he said, 'you are very beautiful.'

'I thought you said *you'd* bought the boat,' said Marianne, returning to her book. 'But just now Ted said he had bought it. What's that about, Mother?'

'Oh . . .' Sally fussed with things on the countertop. 'Ted and I share it.'

Marianne laid her book on her knee. 'But that doesn't explain why you have no money left. Does it? How much is half of a thirty-nine-foot motor cruiser these days? Where did the rest of the money go?'

'What do we do with the flans once we've laid out the fish and olives on top?' asked Faith, in an uncharacteristically loud voice.

'They go in the oven, Faith,' said Theresa. 'Could everyone please calm down.'

Marianne stood up and loomed over Sally.

'Faith, Zoe, Carol?' said Tom hastily. 'While the pissaladières bake, perhaps I might buy you all a drink down the road. Brian, Theresa, shall we?'

Sally knew she was cornered, and, as the other members of the Cookery Club left the house, she realised that she was going to have to come clean with her daughter about where all her money had really gone.

In the bar by the seafront Tom sat chatting with Zoe, while Carol and Faith gazed out on the still waters of the harbour.

Brian sat close to Theresa.

'Since I moved out I've missed all the hurly-burly,' he said.

'Isn't that kind of thing reserved for witches' covens?'

'If the pointy caps fit!'

'And what are you in all this, Brian? Chief warlock?'

Brian laughed. 'What did he look like?' he asked, while brushing a piece of dust from his shoulder.

'Who?' Theresa stared blankly. She had no idea what he was talking about.

'The man who knocked you over and took your bag? You said you saw him again.'

Theresa shrugged. 'Scruffy. Torn blue jeans, leather jacket. About five foot ten. In his forties maybe. Reddish hair. Hopeless description really. Could be anyone of millions. It would have been a waste of time reporting him. Just lots of form-filling for nothing.'

Brian stretched out a finger and stroked Theresa's cheek.

'I do hate to think of harm coming to you,' he said. 'I'm very fond of you, you know.'

Theresa blushed.

What a turn up – at this age to be flirted with by a handsome eligible bachelor!

'Look at them.' Brian nodded towards Zoe who was cackling loudly at one of Tom's remarks. 'And tell me you're not part of a coven?'

Theresa cradled her wine glass and stared out to sea.

'I tell you what we should do,' whispered Brian in her ear. 'Get Carol and David to join us and go out for a ride in that lovely sports car with a huge picnic one afternoon. Up to the woods on Mont Boron or somewhere,' he said. 'What do you think?'

Theresa smiled.

'I think it's a splendid idea.'

When Theresa got home she found a dark, quiet house. Imogen had left her a kind note, beside an uncorked bottle of wine, an empty glass and today's local newspaper. The kids were all in bed asleep and they were all very happy to be here, said the note. Imogen wished she and the kids could stay here in Bellvue-sur-Mer for ever. It suggested Theresa finish the wine, as there was one glass left.

Theresa felt so happy she could cry, and there wasn't an onion in sight. In one night she was being courted by a gentleman, and wanted by her daughter and grandchildren. Who could ask for more?

She looked down at her pissaladière. It looked pretty good, if she did say so herself. She'd managed to get two, as so many people had walked out of the club tonight. She put both tins into the fridge for the family to have tomorrow.

Then she put her bed out on the floor, and lay down. She tried to sleep but it was impossible. After the roller-coaster evening she knew she wouldn't, so, by the light of the street lamps, she got up again and cut herself a slice of the onion tart and laid it out on the glass table with a small glass of red wine. While she ate she decided to read the paper Imogen had left out, even if she only glanced at the headlines.

She switched on the small table lamp and took out her reading glasses. She found reading the paper rather a useful method of polishing up her French. The pictures frequently gave a clue to the story.

Today it was all the usual stuff about politics, finance, sport and national plans for road-building. A page was devoted to the worries of local restaurateurs about the disappointing outlook for the forthcoming year's tourism, another to some celebrity film gala and a folklore festival up in the mountains somewhere.

Theresa turned over to the page which concentrated on local issues: births, marriages, deaths and court cases.

There, in the middle of the page, was a picture of a man who resembled the owner of the furniture cave. Without thinking, she stroked the glass top of the table which she had bought in his shop and leaned in to take a closer look at the newspaper. It was him, surely. She glanced over the article but there were too many French words which were beyond her vocabulary. But then she saw his name was Pierre. So she went to the bookshelf, took out her dictionary and translated the adjacent text, as best she could.

Well!

What a shock!

The furniture shop had been shut because the owner, Pierre Delaville, had been arrested. It appeared that Pierre was using the back room of that very shop as a kind of drug exchange. He was part of a group with links to a criminal gang who operated out of the port and trafficked with dealers in Corsica and Africa. Pierre was the middleman. He sold drugs to locals. In the police search of both his apartment and the store rooms of his shop, they had picked up massive bags of cocaine, hashish and heroin. Pierre had been sent down for ten years.

Theresa took off her glasses and rubbed her eyes.

My word! There we had it. It wasn't a love affair going on behind William's back. Benjamin must be on drugs.

Everything Theresa had witnessed on the day she bought the table would fit together with Benjamin's being a drug addict. When he had emerged from the back room he was certainly behaving in a manic fashion. She'd never seen him cavorting about like that since.

And now, Benjamin's usual supplier had been banged up, so he was buying from some other man lurking in the alleyways of Nice's Old Town. A man who Theresa knew was on the wrong side of the law, as he had pushed her over and stolen her handbag. Yes. That all made perfect sense. And if maybe William had struggled before this to get Benjamin off drugs, then that would really explain his fury yesterday. His anger wasn't so much directed at her as towards Benjamin.

And tonight! All those references people were making to cocaine and sniffing.

Oh Lord! Poor William.

Theresa folded the paper.

What could she do to help?

She put her head in her hands.

What a mess!

No point helping. She'd interfered enough already.

She lay down on her air-mattress and gazed through the windows at the moon, shining in the black sky like a silver coin.

A song was running through her head. She couldn't get it out of her mind.

'Somebody loves me; I wonder who?'

PISSALADIÈRE

Ingredients
Roll of puff pastry*
Onions
Garlic
Small black Niçoise olives
Jar of anchovy fillets
Olive oil
Thyme
Salt and pepper
Dash of good thick balsamic vinegar, velours or glaze

Method
Roll out pastry to cover a pizza pan, and blind bake.
Chop onions and fry in olive oil.
When they are soft, add a squeeze of garlic, salt and a good grind of black pepper, and a dash of balsamic vinegar.
Sprinkle with thyme.
Spread mixture on to the pastry.
Arrange the olives and anchovies on the top.
Bake at approximately 180°C for 20 minutes or until golden.
Cut into slices and serve.

---

* The traditional recipe uses a kind of pizza dough. I prefer puff pastry.

20

Next morning Sally bumped into William in the boulangerie. He was standing in the queue to be served. They both wore dark glasses.

'Benjamin's finally come clean, and told me he's back on cocaine,' said William. 'If I can borrow Carol's car today he's going back into rehab.' He nodded towards Sally's eyewear. 'And you?'

'I had a huge row with Marianne,' she said. 'I didn't tell anyone what I'd done, because Faith and I made a pact. But the truth is Faith's son wanted her to buy a house here while she only really wanted to rent. As you know, I've been looking to buy for so long, so we went to the lawyer together. I bought the house, and she rents it from me so we're both happy. Marianne didn't like it at all.'

'Why's it any of her business?' asked William.

'Yes, why? That's a point,' said Sally. 'Her life may be all sums and interest rates, stocks and bonds and all that financial jargon, but I can't live like that.'

'And why should you? Look at all you mothers being bossed about by your children. Faith's son, for instance. What business is it of his if she rents or buys? It's not right. Parents should leave their children alone, and children should have the decency to do the same in return.'

Sally made a quiet sound of approval.

'Why was her son so keen on her buying anyhow? To get her stuck over here?'

'From what I gathered, it was more that he didn't want her frittering away "his inheritance". But poor old girl, she wants to make the most of her last years, and why not?'

'I think you did the right thing, Sally. You were worried about leaving all your money in some bank. Well now it's safe, you get a decent income from the house, the capital's still there, and Faith can live the high life. Everyone's happy.'

'Except Alfie and Marianne.'

'Alfie doesn't know, nor did Marianne till Ted opened his enormous Ozzy gob.' Sally sighed and said, 'Marianne went on and on about property values and sitting tenants.'

'Oh poo! You now possess a valuable house instead of a dodgy bank account. I wonder in the light of all the recent bank collapses how these financial gurus have the nerve to keep going on about banking and stocks being the answer to everything.'

'I agree,' said Sally. 'But I suppose it's Marianne's job and I don't want to upset her. I always feel you can have fun with a house or a painting or *things*, but having money in the bank makes you feel like Fagin.'

'If she's so worried about sitting tenants, remind her that Faith's knocking on a bit.'

'She's of an age with Zoe,' said Sally.

'A hundred and four, you mean?' William laughed. I don't think Zoe's face is any indication of anything, with the Botox and the lip plumpers, and those nasty injections she has in Switzerland.'

'Oh, by the way, take care when you see Carol,' said Sally, paying for her baguette and cramming it into her shopping bag. 'I think that spat with David last night really hurt her.'

'Oh, I know,' said William, ordering a couple of croissants and a seeded loaf. 'As I came up here I saw David heading off towards the boat just now with Ted.'

'Why did I ever take those power-boat classes?' Sally grimaced. 'This is all my fault.'

'Come on, Pandora,' said William, linking arms with her and swinging out into the alleyways of the Old Town. 'I don't think we can quite lay all the troubles of the world on your shoulders ... yet.'

Sally got home and laid out breakfast for three: herself and her two grown-up children, then sat down to read the paper.

After a little while Marianne emerged from her room, looking sombre and wheeling the same suitcase with which she had arrived a few days before.

'Oh, Mum, you shouldn't,' she said. 'I should have left you a note. Have to fly out this morning, so I won't have time for breakfast.'

'You're not leaving because of our row about me buying that house, are you?'

Marianne looked surprised. 'No, actually. After sleeping on it, I think it's a better idea than when you first told me. It gives you an income, and you still have the capital. Plus you make that old woman happy. Well thought out, Ma.'

Sally felt a gush of relief, not only that the quarrel with her daughter seemed to be resolved, but that Marianne was not the total monster that so many people in the financial sector appeared to be.

'You're not worried about Faith being a sitting tenant?'

'She's respectable and she's old. She might die soon, and if she doesn't, it wouldn't be too hard to get her out, if we needed to.'

Sally shuddered and said, 'Shall I come with you to the taxi rank, or the station?'

'Really no. David's giving me a lift.'

Marianne brushed her lips across Sally's cheek.

'I thought he was in the boat with Ted?'

Marianne shrugged. 'I know nothing,' she said.

'They're not thinking of taking you there by boat, are they? You can't land a pleasure craft near the airport, you know!' said Sally. 'Security—'

'He's taking me in the car.' Marianne talked to Sally using a face reserved for addressing idiots.

'Marianne? About the wedding ... When will I meet your young man?'

Marianne glanced at her watch. 'Look, I'll be late. It might not happen. Don't waste any time on it.'

She wheeled her case to the front door, turned back and mimed a phone, using a finger and thumb, her usual goodbye gesture.

'I'll call you, Mum. Thanks for the mini-break.'

Sally stood dumbstruck for a few seconds then Tom shuffled in from his bedroom, wearing jeans and a T-shirt, running his fingers through his shaggy hair.

He looked down at Sally's breakfast spread. 'I couldn't face any of that.' He glanced at the oven clock. 'Got to rush. I'm going out on a jaunt—'

'Don't tell me,' said Sally. 'In the boat with Ted and David.'

'No.' Tom gave her a second version of that 'reserved for idiots' face, then poured himself a glass or orange juice and drank it in one quaff. 'Actually I'm going on a date.'

'Oooh!' cooed Sally. 'How exciting. May I ask who's the lucky girl?'

'The lucky girl who what?'

Sally wondered if there was something wrong with her accent. Maybe too long living here and speaking fluent French had messed with her English accent. How else to explain why this morning no one seemed to understand her?

'The lucky young girl you're taking on a date?'

Tom rubbed his eyes, snatched up a croissant and took out a huge bite.

'Who said anything about a young girl?'

He chewed the mouthful and swallowed before striding across to the front door.

'I'm going on a date with Zoe.'

Before Sally got her breath back, Tom was gone.

As Imogen was going home on a late flight out that evening, she asked Theresa if she'd mind taking care of the kids while she spent a final day on the local private beach, being pampered.

Theresa gladly agreed and after Imogen left, the kids all got together and helped Theresa to create a picnic.

Just as Theresa had packed up and was leaving, the phone rang. It was Brian. She explained that, inspired by his suggestion, she was going for a picnic up at the arenas in Cimiez.

'I don't suppose you fancy joining us?' she asked him.

'Which way will the car come?' asked Brian. 'I could wait along the road, in Nice.'

'Oh, no,' said Theresa. 'We're going by bus.'

'Carol's going by bus? *Pourquoi*?'

'Oh, no. It'll be just me. Me and the kids.'

There was the briefest of pauses on the line.

'OK. Fine. So where do I hop on?'

'At the 22 bus stop. Massena.' Theresa hesitated for only the slightest moment before posing her question for him. 'My lot go back to England late tonight. Would you like to have your old room back?'

'Not sure,' said Brian. 'I'd have to give notice where I'm now staying . . .'

'I understand. Just in case . . .'

Another pause, which Brian broke. 'So, then, I'll see you later?'

As she replaced the receiver, Theresa looked down at the three eager faces waiting by the front door.

'I don't want to go home,' said Chloe.

'Nor me,' said Lola.

'Nice is nice,' said Cressida.

They rode on the bus into Nice and Theresa tried to work out whether she was misreading Brian or had something just gone wrong during their phone call? Of course, wherever he had moved to, he must be happily settled. And why would he want to be a lodger when he could be an independent man? She wondered where he stayed now. He'd said in Nice, near the port, so perhaps he lived in one of the side streets, the bus was passing at this moment.

Theresa didn't want to be nosy, but equally Brian had been keeping rather private about himself and his whereabouts in the few days since he had moved out.

Theresa's musings were brought to an abrupt halt when, just as they were coming past the port, heading up towards Place Garibaldi, the bus driver stopped the bus and grumpily told the passengers to descend as it was *'terminée'*.

Theresa and the three girls marched along. Up one of the side streets a little band was playing, so the children naturally ran towards the music.

They caught the tail end of some marching display by some boys in the junior department of the Foreign Legion, which, till this moment, Theresa had always thought was a jokey thing from history, not a military reality still going in the present day.

'Granny?' asked Lola, squinting upwards. 'Who is that woman up on the wall?'

Theresa dreaded to think but her eyes followed Lola's gaze to a giant bas-relief statue of a woman holding something like a cricket bat and a gigantic flag.

'I have no idea,' said Theresa. 'But I can see from the sign that she was apparently a laundress called Catherine Ségurane and she had repelled an invading Turkish army with nothing but a flag and a washing beater. Come along. Brian will be waiting.'

Theresa picked up the picnic basket and marched onwards. 'We have another bus to catch – then it's lunch.'

Brian was duly waiting, waving at the bus stop. Once they arrived in the olive grove of the old monastery gardens and spread out their plates and sandwiches, Brian looked around. 'Pity there isn't a bar, and I could buy us a bottle.'

'I shouldn't,' said Theresa. 'Not when I'm in charge of the kids. Maybe this evening, after they've gone?'

Brian thought for a little while.

'I have a little business this evening. I doubt I'll be through before about ten.'

Theresa felt that she had been pushy, and regretted it. She'd forgotten all the rules of dating. It was like being a teenager again.

'Another time,' she said, and felt better for being more cool about it.

While they ate, Theresa and Brian talked about Bellevue-Sur-Mer and its inhabitants.

After a few words with Chloe, Brian lent her his phone so that she could look up the story of Catherine Ségurane.

'Wow,' she said after a few minutes. 'Listen to this. To frighten away those invading armies, that woman we saw on the wall pulled up her clothes and bared her bottom at an army of men – and they all ran away.'

The three girls giggled wildly, and munched on.

'We love France,' said Lola.

The other two nodded firmly, their mouths too full to speak.

Once Imogen and the children had climbed into the taxi bound for the airport, Theresa felt empty and disillusioned. She pottered about, cleaning the kitchen tops, putting away her blow-up bed and changing the sheets in her own room.

Once it was made up, she flopped down on her bed, and lay gazing out of the window at the sheer wall of the Hôtel Astra. She could hear a couple up in the hotel room there chatting away. The well gave a strange echo today. It was like hearing voices from a television set next door. They were English, debating what to pack, and what to ditch.

She bent her head to look up to the light flooding out of their open window.

That really was some leap that Ted had made, to land on his feet, though naked as a jaybird, in her little yard. She hoped the girl had been worth it.

Imogen and the children must be touching down soon in London. She was glad to have at last found the grandchildren good company. They were, in fact, rather a delight. And now that Imogen had been hurt so badly she also seemed much kinder. Theresa wondered whether they would all come back, for the summer, perhaps, or Christmas.

It was too depressing lying there, fully dressed, alone. She got up and went out to walk along the seafront in the dark. She took a book, though really she hoped that maybe one of the gang might be already in the bar and she could sit up and chat with them for a while.

She pushed open the door. Sally was there, sitting in the corner, deep in conversation with Carol and Faith. Theresa was glad she wouldn't have to sit alone with a drink like some desperate character in a Jean Rhys novel.

'My son is arriving on a late plane tonight,' said

Faith, as Theresa pulled out a chair. 'It was too nerve-racking just sitting waiting on my own. Then the girls walked past my house, heading down here, so I came out and joined them.'

'My lot have just gone back to London,' said Theresa, 'so I was restless for the other reason.'

'We all have our little burdens,' said Faith. 'But it's nice to have some camaraderie, isn't it?'

'I'm an empty-nester too,' said Sally. 'Marianne left this morning.'

'But you still have lovely Tom,' said Theresa. 'He's a charming boy.'

'Lovely Tom has gone off for a dirty weekend with Zoe,' exclaimed Sally. 'He phoned to tell me the gory details.'

'Not the actual gory details I hope,' said Carol, crossing herself.

'Almost. I couldn't listen.'

'And those were his exact words,' asked Carol. 'A dirty weekend?'

'A dirty weekend.'

Carol gave her familiar low laugh. 'Oh, dear, Sally. I wouldn't worry. As long as he doesn't come back with a glassy smooth brow and a new pair of lips.'

'Men are certainly strange creatures,' said Faith.

'Well, Zoe is also a pretty strange creature and my son is very impressionable.' Sally knocked back the rest of her glass. 'She must be about ninety-nine, for God's sake.'

'Not so much,' said Faith. 'I believe we are of an age.'

'They've gone to St-Paul-de-Vence.'

'Maybe they're going to see the art?' suggested Theresa.

Sally snorted. 'That's a new word for it.'

'I'd say it gives us all hope, Sally.' Carol picked up a cocktail stick and used it to stab an olive. 'With that acid tongue, and a face that looks as though she got stuck in a wind tunnel, if Zoe can pull a handsome young blade, we might all still be in with a chance in the romance stakes. Look at us. We're all stuck. Dinosaurs, rotting away in a lonely paradise.'

'Oh, what are you on about, Carol? You're all right.' Sally put up her hand to call the waiter. 'You have David. We're the old maids.'

'Hmmm,' replied Carol. 'Frankly, I feel done in, and in need of a change.' Her phone, sitting on the table in front of her, buzzed – a text. She picked it up and looked at the small screen, then tapped in a few letters.

When Theresa tried to top up Faith's glass she put her hand on top.

'I'd better be getting back,' she said. 'Alfie will be arriving any minute, and I should be both present and sober when he turns up.'

Sally also rose from the table. 'I'll pay for everything so far, girls,' she said. 'But I'm turning in too. I'll walk you back home, Faith.'

The two women left, leaving Theresa alone with Carol.

'I'm ravenous,' said Theresa. 'Would you share a bowl of frites?'

Carol glanced at her watch.

'I shouldn't – the figure, you know.' Carol took a deep breath. 'But what the hell? I need a little comfort food.'

Soon after the waiter arrived bearing chips, the

bar door opened and Brian stood on the threshold, beaming.

'Ladies!' he said. 'What a lovely surprise. Had a little business in the area and thought I'd pop in on the off-chance, little thinking I would actually find my favour-ite two women in Bellevue-Sur-Mer, locked in a nocturnal tête-à-tête. What will you both be having?'

Theresa's heart skipped a beat. Brian had come look-ing for her, after all!

She decided to throw caution to the winds and asked for another glass of rosé.

'Did Theresa tell you about our glorious pique-nique today, Carol? We had a lovely time, didn't we? Your grandchildren are enchanting. Rather like you. Did they all get off all right?'

Brian arranged the three glasses on the table and sat next to Theresa, facing Carol.

'Husband still off, sulking?' he asked. 'It's a madman who'd let *you* down,' he said. 'Cheers!'

Theresa loved the way Brian was always so gallant.

'Sometimes things are meant,' said Carol, her face resigned. 'He misses America, I think. It was me who wanted to live in Europe. He'd prefer to be wandering round Greenwich Village eating bagels, not tucking into bowls of olives in our little French town. This row has stirred it all up again. Last night he threw down the gauntlet. He wants us to move back to the States.'

Theresa noticed that Carol was wearing the same red dress she had bought on the wet afternoon when she persuaded Theresa to buy the turquoise mac. Theresa did that, too, wore bright clothes to cheer herself up.

'Why is life so complicated?' said Carol quietly into her drink. 'I was so happy here.'

No one could answer. There was a long silence.

'Sounds like my business plans,' said Brian, in a voice that was aimed at lightening the tone.

'If only we could simply map out our future, like a train timetable,' said Theresa. 'It would be so much easier.'

'I agree,' said Carol with a doleful smile.

'You're both wrong,' said Brian. 'It's allowing change in which makes life so wonderful. Look, you both took the plunge once before and came here.'

Carol shrugged.

'Yeah. I suppose we did.'

'It was very sudden and spur of the moment for me,' said Theresa. 'No one wanted me to. But the risk seemed worth it, in exchange for a clean slate.'

'It's kismet, you see.' Brian looked Theresa in the eyes and said: 'Sometimes something comes along, and you have to seize it, or you'll regret it for the rest of your life.'

Theresa tingled inside.

This was a proposition.

She was certain.

'I see what you're saying, Brian.' Carol looked up from her drink and gave a weary smile. 'There comes a day when you realise you've been so busy clinging to the life raft that you missed the passing ship. So where are the flares? I'm looking to get picked up by that ship.' She gulped down the last of the wine in her glass and stood up. 'Anyhow, I'm bushed. I'm going to turn in.'

'Yes,' agreed Brian. 'It is late.' He looked at his watch. 'I might just make the train back to Nice.'

He helped Theresa into her jacket, then stuck out his elbow. 'Allow me to walk you to your door, madam.'

Carol gave them a little wink and a wave as they went their different directions.

Brian took Theresa to her front door and waited for her to open it.

Her heart beat as she stepped across the threshold and he followed.

Before she had a chance to flick the light switch, his lips were on hers. It was the briefest of kisses, but it was a kiss! Theresa felt like a teenager again.

'Goodnight then, Theresa. Don't want to miss that train,' he said, pulling the door shut after him as he left.

She heard his footsteps running away.

What a turn up!

She lay on the bed fully clothed, staring up the blank wall of the Hôtel Astra, wondering what would happen next.

Within minutes she was asleep.

After leaving the bar, Sally and Faith meanwhile had had a much more eventful half an hour than they would have wished.

When they arrived at Faith's house, Sally could see that the house was dark but the front door was ajar.

Faith stepped forward to go inside.

'Wait!' Sally commanded, pulling Faith back from entering. 'They may still be in there. Does Alfie have a key?'

Faith shook her head. 'Maybe I didn't shut it properly,' Faith suggested.

'It's not worth the risk, Faith.' Sally dialled the gendarmerie to report a burglary.

Meanwhile they both sat on the wall opposite Faith's home, looking at the windows for signs of movement.

The police arrived remarkably quickly.

'Second one tonight, third one just reported,' said the sergeant. 'Whoever they are, they've been busy.'

Holding torches, the gendarmes swept into the house and a few minutes later were back at the front door.

'No one inside,' said the sergeant. 'But they've left quite a mess. Change the lock in the morning.' He tore a piece of paper from his notebook and scribbled on it. 'Here's the form for your insurance.'

Minutes later they were gone, bar one officer who was taking fingerprints, leaving Sally and Faith in his wake picking through the emptied drawers and rearranging the upturned furniture.

'What a scene for Alfie to arrive to,' said Faith. 'I wanted it to be so nice for him.'

'We should be making a list of what's gone, Faith. Alfie will understand.'

The two women started downstairs, Sally writing while Faith called out the missing items.

It was a shambles. The obvious things – the radio, the television – were gone. Drawers emptied and pulled out, the contents spewed across the floor.

Upstairs things were not so bad.

'They were interrupted,' said the officer pointing towards a laptop computer on the dressing table in

Faith's bedroom. 'Otherwise that wouldn't still be here. Or that.'

He pointed to a boxed smartphone, the latest model, unopened.

'It's a present for my son,' said Faith. 'It was something he said he needed the money for.'

A loud rap on the front door silenced them.

'That will be him,' said Faith, slipping the phone into a drawer.

The police officer led the way downstairs.

He stood behind Faith while she opened the door.

It was Alfie.

'I came here about an hour ago,' he said to his mother, with a smile. 'But you were out. I got an earlier flight.' He then saw the gendarme. 'What's going on?'

'Your mother was burgled this evening,' said Sally.

'When you were here before,' asked the policeman, 'did you see anything?'

Alfie shook his head. 'The house was dark and silent. Nothing unusual at all. Except that my mother wasn't inside.'

'If I'd known you were going to be early,' said Faith. 'I would have been here.'

'If this was happening when I was outside I'm very glad you weren't here,' said Alfie. 'It could have been serious.'

After the gendarme left, Sally made tea for Faith and Alfie, then left, turning down the hill towards her own place.

Sally was thinking about Tom and Zoe, and cocky little Alfie, and how there was no predicting how your children turned out or what they would want in life, when she saw the detectives again. They were all gathered outside the house next door to hers. This place must have been the thieves' third outing of the night.

Now Sally felt very lucky.

The burglars had not picked her house to turn over.

21

WHEN SHE WENT OUT early to get her morning loaf, Theresa saw Jessica strolling along the seafront in deep conversation with Ted.

She gave them a little wave but they were so engrossed that they didn't even notice her.

She watched them turn into a street heading up towards the Old Town, and then she sat alone on the sea wall for a little while, watching a pair of fishermen coming in and offloading their early morning catch. She looked at the swimmers out in the bay, and the sunbathers putting up their umbrellas and rolling out their towels on the patch where only the other day Imogen had been playing so happily with her children.

She wondered where Brian was now. Was he thinking of her? Would they meet again soon? Would it go further, maybe turn into a romance or even a marriage?

She was interrupted from her reveries by her mobile phone ringing in her handbag.

It was Imogen.

'It's your fault!' she cried. 'Why did we ever come out to horrible France? It must have been that dump of a vile brasserie on the seafront. I thought that waiter had a shifty look about him. The whole place is crammed with crooks and criminals.'

'I'm sorry, Imogen,' said Theresa, interrupting the deluge of vitriol emanating from the phone. 'I have no idea what you're talking about.'

'My bank,' snapped Imogen. 'I've been cleaned out. Someone cloned my debit card. They've taken thousands.'

Theresa's heart skipped a beat. 'It happened here?' she asked.

'Yes. According to the bank,' said Imogen. 'I've been on the phone to them for the last two hours, trying to go through everything. The first use of it, the card, was at that nasty brasserie next door to you.'

'Are you sure?'

'Of course I'm bloody sure,' Imogen yelled down the phone. Theresa had to hold the receiver away from her ear. 'All of the other withdrawals happened in Nice, Antibes and Monte Carlo.'

'But we didn't go to Antibes or Monte Carlo.'

'Exactly,' said Imogen. 'Anyway I can't talk now. I have to get on to the insurance company and the police, and everyone else. I've got a day from Hell ahead and I am so angry with you.'

Theresa spoke, apologising, but realised that Imogen had cut her off.

With a dry mouth, she sat holding the phone in both hands and taking deep breaths. Should she go into the brasserie, where only last night she had been so happy drinking with Brian, and tell them there might be a thief among their staff, or should she leave it to Imogen and the police to deal with?

Theresa decided against making waves. After all, no one knew for sure that it was definitely the waiters in the bar who cloned the card. Theresa decided to warn her friends to be careful, but before doing anything else to wait till the police or bank report might pin down the culprit more surely.

As soon as she was dressed, Sally phoned Faith asking whether she needed any help, but Faith told her that Alfie was being wonderful and that she was fine. 'It was only things,' she said. 'No one was hurt.'

But Sally felt on edge, nonetheless, and when her front doorbell rang, she jumped.

Sian stood on the threshold. 'Came in on the red-eye,' she said. 'Ted is out, probably fiddling about with the boat and I'm still on Los Angeles time, so I'm ready for a late-night cocktail.'

'You'll only get tea, I'm afraid,' said Sally inviting her inside. 'It's already on the table.'

Sian slumped into a chair. 'I hear that in my absence Ted's been a very good boy.'

Sally thought of all his flirting with Jessica at Theresa's Cookery Club, and said nothing, but made a fuss with the teapot, pouring out the tea, going into the cupboards for biscuits.

'It's been rather cheering to hear how good he's been.' Sian opened her bag and laid her mobile phone on the table. 'My secret assistant is a hundred times better than anyone I've ever employed,' she said. 'I adore her.'

Sally wondered whether she should tell Sian that the very girl she appeared to be paying to keep an eye on Ted was the one with whom he seemed to be philandering. She decided against it, and instead told her about the burglaries at Faith's house and next door.

'Albanians,' snapped Sian. 'They come in through Italy. It's the downside of being part of the European Union.'

Again Sally knew she had to change the subject.

'How was Los Angeles?'

'Same old same old,' said Sian with a yawn. 'How's your son? Glad to have him back?'

Sally decided not to elaborate on the details of Tom's dirty weekend with Zoe, so just said yes, and suggested that after Sian caught up with a little sleep they met up for lunch later on the terrace of the brasserie.

Theresa paced around her flat, fretting about Imogen's loss. She prayed the bank would be able to sort it all out and that anything they couldn't do would be covered by Imogen and Michael's insurance policy.

She also decided that she *would* go down to the brasserie and have a sharp talk with the manager.

Just as she was heading for the front door her phone rang again. It was Brian.

'I'd like to take you to lunch. How about it?'

'I can't really. Imogen had her bank card cloned. I have to have words with the manager at the brasserie.'

Brian told Theresa that he would help. The man must be spoken to firmly, he said. These people paid more attention to other men. It was even more reason why they should take lunch together.

Theresa spent half an hour changing, putting on

make-up and choosing suitable afternoon jewellery and still arrived early for her luncheon date.

The brasserie was already quite full. David and Carol were sitting happily chatting at a table in the sun. Carol looked radiant, and as she and Theresa caught eyes, she threw her head back in a deep laugh at something David said. Clearly the contretemps of the last few days had blown over, which was a relief to see.

Theresa wondered whether she should say something immediately to the maître d' about the cloned bank card, or wait till Brian was there to help.

She decided to go inside and have a quick word on her own. The manager told her that every restaurant along the coast and throughout the world had this kind of thing happen. He could check through the receipts but all it would show would be what she already knew. Waiters here brought the card machine to the table, they never took the card away, so they didn't have time to clone it. Someone may have used the proper card or the cloned card here but it was nothing to do with the restaurant – and he was very sorry for her loss.

She realised he was right. She made her way out into the sunshine. Just as Theresa got herself comfortable at the table for two, she noticed that, since she'd gone inside, Sally had taken one of the corner tables on the terrace and she sat chatting with William, Ted and the dreaded Sian. Sian was facing her way. Theresa didn't want a scene with the woman coming over here and giving her another slap, so she got up and changed places, now sitting with her back to the others, facing the sea.

She watched a large motor cruiser set down anchor, and some kids near the shore messing about on surfboards. A row of people in T-shirts sat on the sea wall, as though waiting for a coach to arrive. A gaggle of tourists passed close by on her side of the street, following a guide holding up a blue and white stick, cameras at the ready. One man was actually holding up his video camera, filming everything as he walked along.

As she picked up the menu, Theresa wondered how many times that man would actually watch his film of a normal street scene full of strangers.

She glanced at her watch, noticing that Brian was now a few minutes late. She wondered where he had to come from. Central Nice perhaps, or further afield? Would he move back in to her house if their friendship progressed, or was it more sensible to keep a romantic distance?

It was nice to daydream.

As she lay the menu down again she recognised Jessica sitting on the sea wall in the middle of the group of tourists. She too was holding up a camera, taking pictures of the brasserie, it seemed. Theresa gave a smile for the camera, at the same moment Brian loomed over her.

Blushing, she scrambled to her feet as he stooped to kiss her hand.

'Good day to you, my dear.' He sat down opposite her, facing back towards the other tables and flicked open his napkin. 'If I may say so, you're looking ravishing today, Theresa.' He picked up the menu. 'I thought I'd speak to the manager about your daughter's problem after we eat,' he said. We don't want them spitting on to our plates, do we? Now, what'll we have?'

He raised his hand for the waiter, and, while Theresa studied her menu, Brian whispered into the waiter's ear.

A few moments later an ice bucket arrived, with a bottle of champagne.

'There we are,' said Brian, grinning as the waiter uncorked the bottle. 'A bubbly drink for an effervescent lady.' He held up his glass for a toast. 'May all of our wishes come true.'

Theresa turned to see whether anyone else had noticed the champagne arrive. She caught Carol giving Brian a surreptitious wink. They had obviously concocted the idea together last night.

How wonderful.

She too raised her glass and, looking into Brian's eyes, repeated: 'May all of our wishes come true.'

As the dessert plates were placed on the table, Brian said 'There's a little something I need to do this afternoon, and I'm going to be rather cheeky and ask Carol if she wouldn't mind driving me up to La Turbie.'

'I've always wanted to go there,' said Theresa. 'To see the Roman Trophy.'

Brian gave her an old-fashioned look. 'Not today, I'm afraid. Let's just say there's a little something I saw in a jewellery shop up there. A gift for a special lady. So I hope to see you later when I've got . . . what I'm off to get, as it were.'

Theresa blushed.

Was he going to buy a ring, perhaps? When he came back might he propose to her?

'I was thinking, Brian.' Theresa was flustered. 'Can you give me your mobile number again?'

'Sure. Lovely new smartphone. Look!' He held up the latest model – in green. 'Do you have a pen?'

Theresa rooted about in her handbag. She pulled out a notebook, but only came up with a pencil with a broken lead. 'Oh dear . . .'

Moments later Carol and David rose to go, leaving William alone at the table. Theresa saw the pair stop for a few brief words with Sally, Sian and Ted, then they passed through the space by their table.

Fumbling in his pockets for a pen, Brian stood. 'Carol, a few weeks ago you said if we ever needed your car . . .'

Carol laughed. 'And I suppose you're asking me to drive you somewhere this afternoon?'

Brian winced. 'If it wouldn't inconvenience you too much.'

'But I was going to . . .' Carol turned to her husband. 'Oh Lord. You don't mind do you, David, darling? Look, why don't you go back to William and the pair of you polish off the rest of that bottle while I whisk Brian off to wherever it is he wants me to go?' She glanced at her watch. 'It would have to be right away, Brian.'

Brian glanced down at Theresa.

'Oops! Sorry about lunch. But you understand, Theresa, I know.'

Brian handed her a pen and as he recited the number, Theresa wrote it down.

As she looked up to hand him back the pen Theresa noticed that Jessica was still there over the road, taking pictures. She waved again.

'Who are you waving at?' asked Carol.

'It's Jessica, look. She's taking pictures of us.'

Brian put a hand up to cover his face. 'Let's be off,' he said.

Theresa held out the pen, but Brian was already walking briskly away.

'Hey, what's the hurry?' Carol put out her arm in a jokey way and said 'Be a gent, Brian, and lead me to my carriage.'

Theresa slipped the pen into her bag. She could return it to Brian this evening when he returned with the jewellery.

Then, taking the long way round to avoid direct sightline with Sian, she took the champagne bucket and edged round the tables to join David and William, who whooped.

Sian saw her arrive at the next table, and made a point of getting up and leaving. Ted shrugged and leaned back in his chair.

'I'm not going anywhere, my love,' he said to his wife.

'Sally!' barked Sian.

Sheepishly, Sally rose. She was torn, but chose to go with Sian. As she stepped out into the street she too noticed Jessica and her camera.

'Why do you need photos of us all?' she asked Sian.

'What on earth are you talking about?' snapped Sian as she strutted away.

Ted shrugged, then slipped from his table to join Theresa and the men.

'I wonder why she's staying over there, taking pictures of us all,' said Theresa, looking in Jessica's direction.

'Oh, that one?' said Ted. 'If you ask me, she's got nits

in the network. Always asking bloody questions. She's driven me up the wall.'

'I thought you two were close.' Theresa tried to say this as politely as possible.

'Yeah. Not sure what all that was about. All you girls got it into your heads that I was giving her one. But frankly she's not my type. Too nosy. These two know how I feel about her, don't you, fellas?'

'She's sort of come on to all of us,' said David.

'Even me,' added William.

'Hush!' Theresa put on a smile, seeing that Jessica had crossed the road and was heading straight in their direction.

'Hi there, you guys,' Jessica called. 'I just thought I'd come over and say goodbye.'

Ted rose and held out a formal hand. 'Been nice to know yah,' he said.

'Well, anyway,' said Jessica, shuffling from foot to foot. 'I'm off, so . . .' She gave a little wave. '*Ciao*. See you.'

Without turning round, she walked away.

William shrugged. 'What was that all about?'

'Like the lady said – she's off.'

'I'll have to find you a new partner at the Cookery Club,' said Theresa. 'Maybe Brian?'

The three men made a hmmm noise and took a swig of their drinks.

'He's sweet, isn't he?' said Theresa, not really expecting a reply. 'Like a great big faithful Labrador.'

'Brian?' said Ted. 'That scumbag? He's no Labrador. Believe me, Theresa, he's a dingo.'

Theresa was shocked. 'I think he's sweet,' she said.

'He's been very kind to me. Perhaps he's one of those women's men.' Theresa decided to be daring and let them know how she felt. 'As a matter of fact, I have to confess I've got a little crush on him.'

'You'd do better to have a crush on a rattlesnake,' said Ted.

'Women's man?' William snorted into his drink. 'I'd have more chance with him than you. He's as camp as a jamboree, isn't he?'

Theresa didn't know how to reply. All gay men seemed to think that every attractive man was gay.

'I saw him in town at that gay bar in the market the other day with some bloke,' said William. 'Scruffy leather queen. Scottish I think he was. They looked pretty damn close, to me. In fact, I saw that same bloke that he was with in the Huit-à-8 this morning buying fags. Nasty-looking type.'

Theresa knew William must be wrong.

Brian had made it very plain that he was after her.

She could not possibly have misread the signals.

Sally left Sian who was walking along the street ignoring her while she took some important business call, to go up the hill and make sure Faith was all right.

She passed Carol and David's home and noticed that the door was ajar. That couldn't be right. David was still in the brasserie and Carol had gone off in the car with Brian. Aware of the spate of burglaries in the town last night, she walked gingerly up the path, gripping her phone, ready to call the police.

Just as she pushed the door open Carol came bustling out carrying two suitcases.

'Oh my God!' cried Sally, startled, her knees buckling beneath her. 'What's going on?'

'I could ask you the same, darling,' said Carol. 'Are you checking up on me?'

'I thought you were being burgled.'

'I'm leaving home.'

'What?'

'I'm eloping.' Carol turned and locked the door behind her. 'It's really romantic and the most exciting thing I've done in years, so I beg you not to waste your time trying to stop me.'

'But David—'

'He'll get over it,' snapped Carol. 'These moments only come along once in your life. It's kismet, you see. Fate. He adores me, worships me, he said. I've never felt so alive.'

Sally caught Carol's arm. 'I'm sorry if I've missed something, Carol, but I have no idea who you're talking about.'

'Brian, of course. We spent the night in the Astra last night. It's true love. Capital L. Really it is. This man is the Mr Right I've been waiting for since I was a teenager.' Carol shook off Sally's hand. 'Must dash. He's waiting in the car.' She gave Sally a brisk smile. 'I'll pop back and see you all someday. I promise. You see, Sally, what I've learned is that these moments come along sometimes and you miss them, trying to be safe and familiar. Well, I'm throwing caution to the winds. It's exciting.'

'But you can't just leave without telling anyone. At least give David a chance. We barely know anything about this other man. You can't desert David for a one night stand. How can you be so cruel . . . or stupid?'

Carol seemed to grow even taller and her lips tightened.

'And who are you? Jiminy Cricket? I've a conscience of my own, thank you very much.' Seeing that she had hurt her, Carol leaned forward and kissed Sally on the cheek. 'Thanks for being such a great friend, darling. But I really am going.'

She picked up the cases and skipped down the alley-way of steep steps.

Strangely disturbed, Sally turned and went home, where she spent the rest of the afternoon and evening tidying out her drawers.

Later that afternoon, Theresa stopped at the bank hole in the wall on the way home. She needed cash and also wanted to transfer some money to Imogen to help her out, till the bank or the insurance could make things better.

She normally understood all the French instructions, which were simple enough: 'votre code', 'code bon' and suchlike, but this time Theresa got some strange untranslatable message on the screen, which she thought might be telling her to phone her own bank.

As soon as she got home she dialled them, but got an out-of-hours message. She'd have to deal with it after eight in the morning, though of course, being an hour ahead, that meant nine.

She tidied up the flat a little, sprayed some polish to make it smell good, and then put on a bit of make-up. When Brian arrived, she wanted to look her best.

* * *

That night Sally lay in her bed, wondering how far Carol had got. Were the odd couple heading for Paris, Vienna or maybe taking the coast road into Italy? Did they have somewhere to go, or were they going to stop at hotels along the way? She wished now that she had asked for a few more details of Carol's crazy elopement.

She wondered too how David was feeling. Several times she had considered phoning, but then, if Carol hadn't left him a note, Sally thought it was not her business to tell him and, if she had, if she now phoned, wouldn't it make her look like some harpy? Perhaps he'd think she had known about it all along, and how could she prove she had not?

With a jolt Sally realised that she had been so shaken by Carol's announcement she had not gone up the hill to check on Faith.

Still, Alfie was there, so he would surely be helping her clear up and, if anything was wrong, surely by now she would have heard.

She wondered again whether Carol had left David a farewell note or just taken off without a word.

A few hundred yards away, in her own bedroom Theresa also lay awake.

Brian had not phoned to make the dinner appointment she was expecting. Nor had he turned up at her front door bearing a small box containing a ring, and fallen to his knees and proposed.

She worried that perhaps Carol's car might have broken down or been involved in an accident.

Why hadn't he called?

Several times she had rung the mobile phone number Brian had given her, and kept getting a French female voice which told her that the number was 'not attributed'.

When Brian had recited it to her, the moment was so quick and muddled, Theresa thought she must have written it down wrongly.

Anyway, Brian had left her guarding his pen, which was a good one, a turquoise Parker. No doubt he'd call back for it soon. It was a lovely pen. Just like the one Mr Jacob had given her as a leaving present.

A turquoise Parker – exactly like the one she had lost.

Theresa sat up and pulled open her handbag.

She took out the pen Brian had lent her.

She looked closely.

It was the one she had lost, she was certain. Yes! It *was* her own pen, Mr Jacobs' present to her. There, on the little silver band, were her own initials.

How on earth did Brian come by it?

Silly! He must have picked it up and taken it accidentally while he was a lodger here in her flat.

Theresa put the pen down on the bedside table, threw her bag to the floor, turned off the light and lay back.

She could hear earnest voices coming from the hotel room above.

The man had an Australian accent. It sounded a lot like Ted. She hoped that if it was him he wouldn't be dive-bombing naked into her yard again in the middle of the night.

Whoever it was, he was with some woman, and they were talking very seriously.

Sian was in town, so surely it couldn't be Ted. He wouldn't be that callous. It must surely be some other Australian male.

She heard a door slam and then there was no more talk, although one person was still there in the hotel room above her. She could hear a woman's voice humming to herself.

Theresa craned her neck and could see the silhouette of a woman moving about.

Not Sian, then.

But it seemed that the woman was now on her own.

Theresa turned over and, in the gloaming, gazed at her pen. How lovely to get it back. Dear Mr Jacobs. She must invite him over here for a weekend during the summer. Perhaps he could help her through all the legal business if she married Brian.

Poor Brian. He was probably tired out after shopping, or maybe there had been some problem with the car. No doubt he would phone in the morning, or even arrive on the doorstep with hot croissants and an engagement ring.

She smiled, shut her eyes and swiftly fell asleep.

22

S ALLY WAS WOKEN AT around seven by the shrill ring of the doorbell and the flap of her letterbox.

A letter lay on the doormat. She stooped to pick it up and opened the door, but no one was there.

The envelope was handwritten. Sally tore it open as she slopped into the kitchen to make herself a coffee.

The letter was from Ted, telling her that he had caught an early flight for Australia and he was giving her the deeds for the boat, which were at the notary's office at the top of the town. He said he was planning on starting a new life, in Oz.

What was happening in Bellvue-Sur-Mer?

First Carol, now Ted!

Sally swigged back the coffee and hastily dressed.

She wandered down to the seafront, hoping to bump into William or someone to talk to.

In the distance, up the hill she heard the undulating wail of an ambulance or police vehicle.

Theresa was sitting alone in the brasserie, nursing a *café crème*. She too looked pretty agitated.

'Mind if I join you?' asked Sally, pulling out a chair.

Theresa gave a nervous smile.

'I think someone must have put something in the water,' said Sally. 'It's been a real night of goings-on.'

'Really?' Theresa bit her lip. Sally was always in close contact with Carol, perhaps she'd know if something had happened to the car and Brian had been hurt . . .

'I was wondering about . . .'

'Ted's left for Australia,' interrupted Sally. 'He left me a note.'

'Ted? He's gone? For good?'

'That's what the letter implied.'

'With Sian?'

Sally shook her head. 'I believe he told Sian in person.'

'Did he go off with Jessica, then?' asked Theresa. 'Jessica's gone too. She announced her departure to the men yesterday afternoon, at the end of lunch. Ted had a strange reaction, now I think back. He tried to tell us he'd never liked her.'

'Really? Jessica's also gone?' Sally was shocked. She hadn't bargained for that scenario at all. 'That sounds as mad as Carol, then.'

'What about Carol?' asked Theresa.

'She's eloped with Brian.'

Theresa felt the blood drain from her face. 'Carol? Eloped? With Brian? My lodger Brian?'

'Exactly! Can you imagine anything so absurd? They both drove off into the sunset yesterday afternoon. God alone knows where they are by now.'

Before Theresa could find words to reply, William appeared, running round the corner, frantic, his face white as a sheet. He was yelling for Sally.

'Sally! I've been searching for you. It's terrible. Come quick.'

'Oh God, what's happened now?'

'It's Faith.' William stopped at the edge of the terrace and stooped, holding his knees and taking deep breaths. 'I just bumped into Alfie. He arrived home early this morning to find his mother lying on the bedroom floor, covered in blood, unconscious.'

Theresa and Sally both rose hurriedly.

'Is she all right?' they asked, in unison.

'The ambulance has taken her off to the hospital in Nice. It appears she was attacked early yesterday afternoon, and has been lying there ever since. The police are all over the house. It is pretty serious.'

Part Three – Mayday

23

F AITH REMAINED IN A coma, unable to provide any information about what had happened when she had been surprised by whoever had come into her house and attacked her.

The one certain thing was that either Faith had left her front door open, or the perpetrator had had keys, so naturally Alfie was brought in for questioning. Later in the afternoon he was arrested, taken into the police station and subjected to hours of questioning about the assault upon his mother.

Once the police had finished making their forensic investigations in the Bellevue-Sur-Mer house, Sally and Theresa went in to clean up the mess.

Sally found herself again rearranging Faith's things which had been swept on to the floor, and folding clothes to put back into the open and sometimes upturned drawers. Up in the bedroom there was a lot of blood. The mat had to be destroyed, as it was sodden. They changed the sheets and blankets on the bed, which were also bloodstained. Whoever had attacked Faith had obviously surprised her while she was having a nap, or lying on top of the bed reading.

Theresa and Sally spoke to one another in short sharp phrases – horrible, oh dear, look at this, shall we? Neither woman could really take in what appeared to have happened here: a frail old woman battered by her own son.

Both women were spinning the facts through their heads, sorry that they had been so hard on their own children, who were surely incapable of anything as bad as this atrocity.

'I hope it's not my fault,' said Sally.

'How could it be?' asked Theresa.

'I shouldn't have interfered.'

'You helped Faith out by buying the house so she could afford a little fun. Where's the harm in that?'

'It's not what Alfie wanted.'

'But it's what Faith wanted. We cannot live our lives to please our children. And think about it, Sally, if we all went around doing everything to please them they'd hate us for that too.'

'And, when you think about it, what difference could it make to *his* life whether she bought or rented? It's mad.'

When they had finished making the place look smart and clean again, together they phoned the hospital only to find there was no change in Faith's condition.

Then they locked up – having made sure to get a locksmith in, the same one who had fitted Theresa's lock on the day she had been attacked on the steps, and secured the door with brand-new keys.

When Sally got home, Marianne was waiting.

'I'd better tell you the truth,' she announced. 'There

isn't going to be a wedding. There never was. I made it all up on the spur of the moment. I was trying to divert your attention from what was *really* going on. But now you'll have to find out, as, it'll all become pretty obvious now that Ted's run off.'

Sally was bewildered and said as much.

'I am Sian's mystery assistant.'

'You're what?' Sally was very put out to think that she had been kept out of a secret shared between her daughter and her friend.

'Naturally when I applied for the job I used Dad's surname, not yours. But once I got the job I admitted to Sian you were my mother. I knew she was sure to find out sooner or later. Afterwards she told me she came to see you and laid down some pretty strong hints, but you never picked them up. And so she suggested we both continue to keep it quiet.'

Sally felt hurt and insulted, both by her friend and her daughter.

'You were the spy she sent to keep a watch out for Ted?'

Marianne shrugged.

'I have to say you didn't do a very good job,' said Sally.

'I did everything I could. But he's a blokey bloke. His own man. No one could have foreseen his running off to Australia like that, and once he'd decided to do it, who could have stopped him?'

'So what was the point of your spying mission then?'

'Oddly enough,' Marianne continued as though Sally had not spoken, 'I think it was your persuading him to buy the boat which started off Ted's yearning for independence. Buying the boat was the first big secret he kept from her.'

'Apart from a hundred and forty-three female tourists,' said Sally, feeling her indignation rising.

So now everything that had happened to Ted was all her fault!

'How is Sian?' asked Sally. 'Have you seen her since you came back?'

'She's pretty edgy, naturally enough. She keeps saying Ted's gone off "for some space to breathe". She keeps repeating things like "he needs to get back to his roots" and all the usual excuses middle-aged wives give for errant husbands. I imagine I'll have a lot of work to do over the next few weeks, both in providing comfort and doing the work which Sian will be unable to do.'

Sally felt appalled by her daughter's coolness, but said nothing.

'You must have arrived here in Bellevue-Sur-Mer bright and early.'

'I came back last night, actually. I was always meant to be coming here and working with Sian today. Things changed so suddenly though. Now it is vital I am here.'

'Where did you spend the night?'

'If it's any of your business, I was in a hotel.'

'You should have stayed here. You don't need to waste money on hotels.'

'It was late. I didn't want to disturb you.'

'And it was you who let Sian think that nothing was going on between Ted and Jessica?'

'Nothing *was* going on between Ted and Jessica.'

'Come on, Marianne! You saw them! Always flirting, partnering one another in the Cookery Club.'

'Oh, you and your silly Cookery Club. I have no idea who Jessica is. That she chose the same day as Ted to leave town is nothing to do with him.'

'Oh! You know that for certain, do you?'

'As a matter of fact, Mother, I do.' Marianne calmly picked up her handbag and made for the door. 'And now I'd better get back to work. I fear that today poor Mrs Kelly is going to be in no state to make sensible business decisions.'

She left, and Sally angrily threw her cup down on to the table.

Luckily it failed to break.

Theresa went up to see David. She knew it wasn't the same kind of pain, but having been duped by Brian, she felt somehow connected with David's loss of Carol, and – having been there during the whole flirtation, but blind to it all – felt almost as though it had been her own fault.

She expected to find a desolate man, alone and crying, but he was pacing the room, raging, flinging things at the wall and reacting with fury to everything other than the actual loss of his wife.

'I bought her the clothes she ran off in. And the suitcases. It's common theft. Why should that unctuous pimp swagger round carrying my Louis Vuitton suitcase?'

Theresa suggested making a cup of tea.

'I paid thousands of dollars for that car,' he snarled at her as she filled the kettle. 'It's a Jaguar, for Christ's sake. An icon. And I need it. How dare she take my only form of transport to cavort around with that libidinous Lothario?'

Theresa again tried to appease David, but his temper grew and grew, till suddenly it appeared to reach a crescendo.

Then, quietly, he sat down. 'Give me the yellow pages,' he said.

Theresa handed over the big book. David rifled through the pages.

'I'm going to put a detective on to them,' he said calmly. 'I want that automobile back. Why should that smooth-talking Limey loafer have my Jaguar convertible?'

David ran his fingers down the columns, then picked up the phone. He looked up at Theresa as though she was his secretary and said 'Thanks anyway. I'll be fine on my own from now on.'

He fluttered his fingers at her, as though to say 'You are dismissed.'

Without even taking a sip of the tea she had made, Theresa went back to her lonely flat.

She sat at the glass-topped table, winding back every conversation she had had with Brian, realising that all his lovely comments, made while drinking in the brasserie the night before last, which she had thought were for her, were actually directed towards Carol. None of it, not one word had been for her at all.

'*Sometimes something comes along, and you have to seize it, or you'll regret it for the rest of your life.*'

Brian had been talking Carol into running off with him.

Why had Theresa thought it was a coded message for her?

How stupid could you get?

Carol was sending or receiving a text too, wasn't she, a few minutes before Brian walked in. An assignation, perhaps? Or warning him that she wasn't alone?

Theresa let out a little sob. Why on earth *would* Brian have been flirting with her? Let's face it, she was fat, old and washed-up.

Theresa felt even more idiotic now, knowing that she had been overcome by wishful thinking and had let her imagination run away with her.

Given half a chance, anyone would elope with Carol. She was gorgeous. Tall, witty, slim, stylish, blonde, glamorous, with a perfect figure . . . she was everything desirable in a woman.

After about an hour mulling it all over and making herself more and more unhappy, Theresa decided she must have something else to focus on or she would go mad.

She phoned Sally to ask whether there was any news about Faith's condition. 'Should we go in and try to see her, do you think?'

Sally told her no, the hospital had been very firm that, as Faith was in intensive care, only family members could visit her.

'Oh dear,' said Theresa. 'While Alfie's helping the police, that means no one.'

'She's unconscious, I suppose,' said Sally, 'but I do think it might be nicer if someone could be there, to hold her hand or something.'

'I wish there was something we could do about it all,' said Theresa. 'Anything.'

'I know,' replied Sally. 'It's all awful. There isn't a happy face to be found in the whole town.'

When Theresa put down the phone she thought about it. What had been written in the stars above, to make today so awful for everyone?

Faith was in hospital and still in a serious condition; Sally was unhappy because of Faith being attacked, and in her house; Sally's son had disappeared with Zoe, a woman old enough to be his grandmother, not to mention as mad as a box of frogs; Theresa herself was upset about being such a fool about Brian, and feeling guilty for having had Imogen over here to stay, where her card had been cloned; William was alone while Benjamin fought his demons in rehab; David had lost his very glamorous and witty wife to Brian. And although Theresa had never got on with Sian, still she felt terrible for her. The poor woman must be in shock after her husband had upped and left for Australia without so much as a by your leave.

Theresa put the kettle on and made herself some tea. She looked down at her wonderful wrought-iron and glass table and mulled over the thought that it was odd how something so beautiful could have come from a shop run by a drug dealer.

She took her cup and sat.

She wished she had a crossword or something to pass the time. Or even better wished there was something she could physically do to make things better.

She grabbed a notepad and decided to write a

shopping list, then she could take a bus to Cap 3000 perhaps and wander round the shopping mall, anything . . . as long as she could get out of the flat and out of Bellevue-Sur-Mer for an hour or two.

She rooted in her bag and pulled out her turquoise pen – she was happy to have it back, the one little thing which brought her a tiny ounce of satisfaction on this miserable day.

As she rolled the pen around in her hand she realised that she hadn't seen it since that day months ago when she was knocked down and robbed.

It was one of the things snatched, inside her stolen handbag.

Her heart skipped a beat.

She thought back to the theft, and the man pushing her down the steps.

Brian had been the first person on the scene that day, apparently her knight in shining armour. That had been their first meeting. He had been at the top of the steps when she was pushed by the surly swarthy man in the leather jacket – the other drug dealer.

Brian didn't move in till *after* that incident.

She *had* thought Brian must have picked up the pen in the flat, when he was staying here as her lodger.

But she was robbed *before* Brian moved in.

Brian had never been in the flat at the same time as the pen.

So how had he come by it?

Certainly not by picking it up while staying in the flat.

She inspected the pen again, this time taking out a magnifying glass and double-checking the inscription on the silver band to see that those really were her initials.

T.S.

Yes. It was her pen.

It had been taken from her by the man who robbed her.

But somehow, after that, it had come into Brian's possession.

Theresa tried to calm her thoughts.

By some mad serendipitous coincidence he could *perhaps* have bought it in the junk market, on a stall made up of stolen goods.

But in her heart she knew he hadn't.

And if Brian hadn't come upon it by chance, there were further sinister connotations.

He must have had something to do with the man who grabbed her bag.

Maybe he was even the one pushed her while the other one ran down to snatch the bag?

For some moments she sat still, her heart pounding.

Theresa stood up. She would phone the police and tell them.

She picked up the phone.

She sighed and put it down again.

What would the police make of her story? 'Officer – I know the man who was in possession of my stolen pen!'

They'd laugh her off the line.

Perhaps she was simply looking out to make a villain of Brian because he had made a fool of her.

For the moment she would do nothing. But

tomorrow, when she'd had a night to mull it over, she would share the information with Sally or William or David. She had to tell one of her neighbours.

Perhaps they had similar tales which put together would add up to something really incriminating.

24

S IAN CALLED ON SALLY in the morning, for coffee. She was wearing dark glasses, which she did not take off, even though they sat together in Sally's kitchen.

'Your daughter is an angel,' she said. 'I don't know what I'd do without her. She's handling all the books, the business, everything.' Sian gave a little whimper. 'I can't seem to focus properly.'

'Have you heard from him at all?' Sally asked.

'No. Just the farewell note which he left late at night before he sneaked out for his early flight. He must have been planning it for a while. You don't just pick up tickets to fly to Sydney at the last minute.'

'Maybe he's really homesick,' suggested Sally. 'Does he have family out there?'

'Some cousins and a sister, I believe.' Sian emitted a dry sob. 'I knew he carried on with women, of course I did. But I never thought he'd just go off like that.'

Sally shrugged.

That Jessica had been a slippery little thing.

'Men can get led on, you know, Sian. It happened to me too. My husband . . .'

'No, no,' said Sian. 'There isn't another woman, I'm pretty certain. He really needed to find himself again. I realise that I overpowered him, with all my business propositions and international plans. He only ever wanted the simple life. So he's gone off to find it. He just needs space.'

And we all know where that space is, thought Sally.

'He's never been the same since he did it with that Theresa woman.' Sian sipped from her cup. 'I hope she's feeling rough about it.'

'Sian. I am certain nothing happened between Ted and Theresa. Really. Nothing.'

'Hmmmm!' Sian shook her head. 'I'm not so sure.'

'No,' said Sally firmly. What else was there she could say? 'Jessica, on the other hand . . .'

'Who's Jessica?' asked Sian.

'The slight blonde girl. She announced her departure the day before Ted left.'

'Oh,' said Sian. 'The journalist.'

'Journalist?' It was Sally's turn to be surprised.

'Oh yes. We had quite a chat about the business. She writes for one of those British tabloids, you know. Pages and pages full of nothing but rumours about celebrities you've never heard of, fashions you wouldn't be seen dead in and letters from very cross people from the Cotswolds.'

Sally remembered the fight over the Dictaphone at the Cookery Club and said quietly, 'Jessica was a journalist?'

Sian sobbed.

* * *

267

Theresa had grabbed a newspaper from the tabac before jumping on to the bus into town.

As she was feeling so shaky today, she decided on a little comfort, to read about things at home in England, and so bought one of the overpriced one-day-old English tabloids.

She stuffed it into her bag and spent the journey gazing out of the window at the unsurpassable view over the Bay of Angels.

She was heading for the Nice flower market. She planned to take a stroll through all the stalls, buy a little something, some olives or a tub of honey, then take herself to lunch on one of the sunny terraces.

She walked down through the dark alleyways of Old Town, looking at some lovely Jacquard linen tablecloths. Having chosen a nice one, and even taken her credit card out, she decided she must resist the temptation to buy. As she put the card back into her purse, she remembered she had still not phoned the bank since the message came up on that machine. As she hadn't used the card since, she had forgotten all about it. She'd have to do it once she got home.

In the bustling market she bought some olive and chilli tapenade and found a table at the bar near the end of the Cours Saleya, near the Ponchettes and the glowing yellow façade of Matisse's old Nice home.

She browsed through the menu and ordered a salad Niçoise and a glass of Côtes de Provence rosé wine. Why not?

While she waited she pulled out the newspaper and started to read the front page.

A shadow fell over her.

'Theresa!'

It was William.

'Come and join me.' He pointed towards a table near the back of the terrace. 'Corny line, but do you come here often?'

'I've passed by a few times. It always looks so lively.'

As he helped her gather her things, William whispered in her ear. 'It's a sort of local gay bar, really. Though tourists generally have no idea. You get families and honeymoon couples sitting among all the local lesbian and gay couples, totally oblivious.'

As she shoved the paper into her bag, Theresa looked around and realised William was right.

'What fun,' said Theresa. She whispered back to William. 'How is Benjamin?'

'He's OK,' replied William. 'For the moment. I'm picking him up from rehab tomorrow.'

It was during dessert that Theresa plucked up courage to ask the question she longed to ask William.

'The man you saw with Brian last week. I presume it was in here?'

William nodded.

'Perhaps they were the unsuspecting tourists you just told me about?'

'Brian had his hands all over the man,' said William. 'It was pretty revolting. It might be a kind of gay scene here, but it's not *that* kind of place.'

'Describe the man he was with again?' Theresa asked.

'Worn brown leather jacket, denim jeans, chain smoker ...'

Theresa thought it was an accurate description, but

realised it could still be anyone, not necessarily the man who robbed her.

'Anything else?'

'Swarthy. One of those passé Tom Selleck moustaches.'

It was surely the same man who had robbed her.

Brian knew him. Brian's hands were all over him.

They were a couple.

Brian had assisted the man who robbed her.

Brian was a fake.

Brian was in collusion with a crook, and might well be a crook himself.

Yet she had been fooled into taking him into her own house, believing his hard-luck story. He was a conman. She hated to think what might have happened if she'd let things go any further.

There was only one conundrum . . .

'If Brian is so into men,' Theresa asked, 'why do you think he ran off with Carol?'

'Perhaps he's bi?' said William.

'Or after her money?' suggested Theresa.

William looked puzzled and said 'What money?'

'Carol's money. Isn't she an heiress?'

William shook his head, wincing, implying Theresa was mad for thinking so.

'I rather gathered she was part of the Heinz family. American . . . Heinz baked beans, soup, ketchup and all that stuff.'

'No,' said William in a long querulous swoop.

'So why all the "57" references?'

'Her maiden name was Heinz. But so many Americans are of German descent, and Heinz is a very common name to them. It means Henry. I think she was from Pittsburgh, too, where there is a Heinz factory, but you can bet your bottom dollar a multibil-lionaire family like that would live somewhere fancy, like upstate New York, not downtown Pittsburgh.'

'So Carol isn't rich?'

'No. David is the rich one. Back in the States he was a property developer. Bought up huge properties in Soho and Noho and Tribeca, when prices were rock bottom. Did them up, and sold them on for a fortune.'

'Really?' said Theresa. 'I had no idea.'

'David is rolling and Carol was the attractive woman on his arm, whom he was always so eager to please. She certainly got lucky with him. David kept her in great style, which she liked. Naturally enough.'

When the waiter came with the bill, Theresa offered to pay for both of them. The machine was brought to the table and she put in her PIN.

The waiter shook his head.

He spoke rapidly in French and Theresa couldn't catch the gist of what he was saying.

William lowered his voice. 'He says the machine is saying "no funds".'

'No funds? But . . .' Theresa's heart skipped a beat. Her saliva dried up. Her thoughts came quickly: her turquoise pen; Brian staying in her house; Imogen's cloned card; his leaving with Carol; her own bank details kept 'safe' in the paperwork drawers in the living room and on her laptop, where Brian could easily find them.

She realised, with a sudden awful certainly, that she knew *exactly* what Brian had wanted from her.

'We're all famous!' cried Zoe, lurching along the seafront, waving a newspaper in the air.

'You're back!' said Sally, coming along the quay from the other direction. 'You Jezebel.'

'No,' grinned Zoe. 'Jezebel wrote the wicked words. Welcome to the Freakshow! Sodom-and-Gomorrah-sur-Mer.'

'You're drunk!' said Sally.

'And you're fat,' said Zoe. 'But in the morning I shall be sober.'

'So now you're stealing your jokes, Zoe, as well as people's sons. That was Winston Churchill's quip. And I'm not that fat.' Sally stood with her hands on her hips, blocking Zoe's way. 'Zoe? Where is Tom?'

'Oh, Tommasso le Grand. Yes. The little adorable thing.' She looked round as though expecting to see him. She shook her head and shrugged. 'I gave him my body, and he was satisfied. No, he's not here now. He needs time alone to touch himself up . . . I mean touch me up . . .' She cackled and lurched a few steps onwards.

Sally took hold of Zoe and shook her by the shoulders. 'Where is my son?'

Zoe wriggled out of Sally's grasp.

'He's in Villeneuve Love-it . . . Villeneuve-Louvet . . . Loubet, looby dooby doo.' Zoe staggered across the road, narrowly missing a collision with a passing cyclist. 'He's in a tent. I need to sit down.'

She threw the newspaper down on a seat at the back of the terrace outside the bar, flopped down on to the

272

seat next to it and lay her head on the table. Within seconds she was asleep and snoring.

One of the waiters shrugged. It wasn't the first time he'd had Zoe collapse, drunk, on one of his tables. But she was a good customer of long standing, and she always gave very good tips. So he put a glass of water on the table in front of her, and tidied up a little.

The scrappy, tattered old newspaper, which fell to the floor from the seat beside her, he took away and tossed into the bin.

Theresa spent the rest of the afternoon in the bank and later at the police station.

It turned out that, on the day he left with Carol, Brian had taken a substantial amount of Theresa's money. After all the work on the Cookery Club she was back to square one. It was soul-destroying.

She now had a long wait while the bank decided whether or not to reimburse her. The fact that the man had been, in their eyes, cohabiting with her would not help her cause.

Going through the accounts minutely with the manager Theresa saw that although Brian had always paid the rent on the dot, and paid in the Cookery Club money, he carefully removed small amounts of money at the same time.

What an easy ride he had had with her.

When Theresa got back to the seafront in Bellevue-Sur-Mer she saw Zoe, passed out on a table in the bar, and remembered the first morning here, when she had seen her in a similar position, passed out in the café–tabac.

Sally was at another table nearby, keeping her eagle eye on Zoe.

Theresa gave her a wave and went across to join her.

'I want her to wake up and tell me where she's left Tom,' said Sally. 'Before she hit the deck she tried to imply that he had joined a circus.'

'I've been such a fool,' said Theresa, slumping into the chair opposite. 'Brian's cleaned out my bank account. But now I have to say I feel really sorry for Carol.'

She told Sally about the withdrawals from her bank and how the same thing must have happened to Imogen. While in the bank she had consulted her diary and realised that Brian must have copied Imogen's card the day he pretended to come back looking for his passport, and then had had the cheek to use it to pay for all those drinks and the bottle of champagne.

Theresa also shared her suspicions with Sally that Brian was working in tandem with the man who robbed her, the same man who sold drugs to Benjamin.

'I wish we could contact Carol, and tell her,' added Theresa. 'She needs to be warned.'

Sally told Theresa that she had already tried many times, but Carol's mobile phone constantly went straight to answer-phone.

'They can track people down these days by your mobile phone,' said Sally. 'Maybe she thought David would find her and drag her home.'

'Pity he doesn't,' said Theresa. Then it dawned on her. 'Perhaps Brian realised that the phone could be used to trace *him*, and so he dumped it.'

Both women gasped.

Two large middle-aged men sitting at an adjacent table turned and raised their glasses.

'We're also from England,' said the shorter one, starting to stand up. 'Can we join you?'

'No,' snapped Sally and Theresa in unison.

The men each pulled a face at one another and turned away.

Within moments of having repelled the advances of the two Englishmen, Sally looked up and saw Alfie standing on the edge of the terrace, staring at her.

'Oh God,' she murmured to Theresa. 'Don't leave, please.'

Theresa spun round, saw Alfie and said quietly but firmly: 'I won't.'

Alfie swaggered over and pulled out a seat.

'How is your mother?' asked Sally.

Alfie let out a long tired sigh.

'She seems a lot better this evening.' He ran his fingers through his tousled hair as he spoke. 'The doctors seem more hopeful, anyhow.'

'But she's still unconscious?' asked Theresa.

Alfie nodded.

'The doctors told me to leave her for tonight, come home, have a good rest and prepare to be there tomorrow. They seem hopeful that she might wake up soon.'

Sally's foot was pressing hard down on Theresa's.

'The police let you go then?'

'They had to. I had nothing to do with it. I was miles away. And it was easy to prove. Passport control.'

Sally's foot pressed harder.

'But I am going to find whoever did this and I am going to . . .' He licked his lips. His mouth seemed dry. 'Well . . . I don't know,' he said. 'I just hope the police catch them and put them away for a very long time.'

He gazed down at the table for a long time then said, 'Sally, Theresa, might I ask if you could lend me a little money. To tide me over, you know, while I look after Mum?'

Theresa went to bed but couldn't sleep.

So many things went round in her head.

The nerve of Alfie asking her and Sally for a loan. Wasn't he supposed to be some financial whizz-kid? Or was that just Faith's parental pride boosting his reputation up a notch to impress them?

The thought of Carol, away, out of contact, entirely at the mercy of Brian, who might do anything to her. Theresa kept picturing Carol's mobile phone, sitting in a bin somewhere, ringing out to nobody.

The realisation that her own finances were now in a worse state than when she first arrived here in Bellevue-Sur-Mer.

The powerlessness of knowing that Brian was to blame for it all, but having no path of action against him. Theresa wondered whether his drug-dealing, handbag-snatching friend would be shadowing Brian and Carol wherever they had gone, or now that Brian had left, had he gone home to England, or Scotland, or wherever he was from?

The police still seemed very cool about the whole matter, as though this was the kind of thing that always happened here, and there was nothing they could do about it.

It wasn't at all like those TV shows where the police all spring into action.

But then, Theresa realised, the TV shows only showed the police jumping to after a murder, not something like this, which would only be classed as petty crime: theft and embezzlement.

She wanted to grab that tobacco-stinking bloke and fling *him* down some stone steps and see how he'd like it.

Her thoughts strayed next to Ted, wondering where he was now, and if he was happier being single, or maybe now he was away he might miss Sian . . .

Then the phone rang.

Theresa looked at the clock. It was after midnight.

She leapt from her bed and answered.

'It's Imogen.'

Theresa's heart beat frantically. What could have happened that she was calling so late?

'Is everything all right?'

Imogen cleared her throat. 'No. Of course it isn't.'

'What's wrong?'

'I just don't enjoy having a famous clown for a mother, that's all.'

'Imogen?' Theresa asked, sitting back on to the edge of the bed. 'Are you drunk?'

'I had a glass or two, yes, but only to help me cope.'

'Cope with what? Is it Michael again?'

'No, Mother, it is *you*. You and your inane friends. I have had the world and his wife on the blower now for two solid days, and I've had enough.'

'I'm sorry, Imogen,' said Theresa in as calm a voice as she could muster. 'I don't understand.'

'The *Daily Post*,' said Imogen.

Theresa remained silent.

'"Freakshow-on-Sea: the bizarre Riviera lives of British ex-pats"?'

'Imogen. If you have something to say, could you just spit it out.'

'It was that coy little blonde, of course. I never trusted her. I was surprised that you allowed her into your flat.'

'Imogen, please . . . Fill in a few dots for me here. I have no idea what you're talking about.'

But as Imogen started to speak, Theresa suddenly had an inkling . . .

She scrabbled about in her bag and pulled out the English newspaper, which she had carried about all day but never read. She spread it out on the bed and flicked through the first few pages.

About halfway through, there was her picture. And Sally's. In fact they were pretty much *all* there, sitting on the terrace of the brasserie, with Brian rising, ready to move away with Carol.

'I'll call you back,' said Theresa, placing the phone back in its cradle.

Her heart thumping, she read the double-page spread.

It was all there in black and white, and though it was technically true, on the page it looked so false and awful.

Theresa was the 'fat queen of costume jewellery' who ran a pathetic cookery school for bored alcoholics like antediluvian dipso wasp Zoe and faded, long-forgotten Z-list TV celebrity Sally 'of the coloured gunk and polka-dotted jumpsuits'. According to Jessica's article, Sian was a successful businesswoman by day and a screeching, malicious termagant by night, while William and Benjamin she called the camp answer to Tweedledee and Tweedledum. She even referred to 'Dee' being a father figure to the much younger 'Dum', who had an expensive coke habit. Carol was depicted as the swanky Yank with a droll but sarcastic tongue, who lugged around her cowed husband David, a man who was there only to write the cheques that maintained her expensive Riviera lifestyle.

The only person who came out of the piece with an ounce of dignity was Ted, the sadly neglected poet with no publishing deal, who 'ought to be up there with the greats', not living in a tired tourist town in the middle of nowhere, smothered by a load of failed ex-pat hicks. Jessica even told of Ted's plans to get back to his Australian roots, and talked about how she hoped one day to catch up with him again.

Theresa read the whole article again, while taking deep breaths.

The byline, she noted, was Jessica Truegold.

Truegold! Theresa was glad now that no one had ever trusted Jessica, even if it was for all the wrong reasons. The sneaky little bitch, sucking up to them all for support, while compiling this hateful piece behind their backs! The hidden recording device had certainly come into its own, Theresa saw, as, in the article, much of the dialogue from the disastrous night of the pissaladière cookery evening was reproduced verbatim.

Theresa poured herself a whisky. There were times when a glass of wine wouldn't hit the spot. She picked up the phone to dial Imogen, but instead found herself ringing Sally.

She read the whole piece aloud to her.

'I'm coming over,' said Sally when she had done. 'You don't mind me arriving in my pyjamas, do you?'

25

FAITH REGAINED CONSCIOUSNESS NEXT morning. But it was a week before she was discharged
from hospital. She was adamant that Alfie had had
nothing to do with the attack, although she could not
truthfully remember anything about that afternoon.
The first time she realised she had been attacked was
when she woke up in hospital several days later.

There was no word at all from Carol. Theresa and
Sally wondered whether she had yet discovered that
Brian was not in fact the servile, well-mannered British
gent he impersonated, but a vile, swindling conman.

Tom was still absent, though he phoned to tell Sally
to put a date in her diary, and to tell everyone else to
do so too. He had booked a minibus for her and all
their friends, to bring them up to a special birthday
treat for her. He couldn't see her till that day. When
pressed further about Zoe, Tom clammed up and told
her it was not Sally's business, but, yes, he was still
seeing her. She was his muse.

'That's a new word for it,' said Sally.

Tom hung up.

Theresa spent hours on the phone, making lengthy

calls to her insurance company and the bank. She also consulted Mr Jacobs about her legal rights, and it did seem that, by letting Brian stay in her flat, she had somehow colluded with him, and that unless he was picked up by the police and found guilty of embezzlement and burglary or anything else criminal, she would not have much chance of ever getting her money refunded.

After much thought, Theresa knew the only thing left for her to do was to try and sell the Raoul Dufy painting which her mother had left her. She would not get the money right away, but she could certainly show the bank that the money would certainly come. With a heavy heart she took the painting from the wall, and carefully wrapped it up in newspaper and bubble wrap, then she took an old towel she usually used for dyeing her hair, wrapped it round the parcel, put it in a plastic carrier bag and slid it under her bed, ready for the day she could get an appointment with a professional valuer.

Sally spent a lot of time up with Faith, making sure she was well cared for, and even she had to admit that Alfie did appear to be doing an excellent job.

Once when Faith was taking a snooze Sally sat him down in the kitchen with a pot of coffee and interrogated him. She wanted to know what he was up to.

'Nothing,' he said. But, as they say, he would, wouldn't he?

'Why were you so keen for your mother to buy this house?' she asked casually. He still did not know that Sally had actually made the purchase.

'Because it's lovely, and she is old,' was his reply.

'Yet you are always asking her for money...'

'Not any more. You haven't heard me asking for money, have you?'

'You asked *me* for money.'

'That was while Mum was ill.'

Sally noted that that in itself was tantamount to his admitting that he did ask his mother for money.

'What is the great drain on your funds, Alfie, that you always seem to need money?' she asked. 'Are you on drugs?'

Alfie replied with a loud and outraged 'No!'

'Have you lost your job? Is that it?'

Alfie shrugged. 'I move about a lot. There are gaps. Everyone at this time is having a bit of a setback in the world of finance.'

Now that his mind was on another tack, Sally came right out and asked him: 'Did you attack your mother?'

'I did not.' Alfie looked down at the table for a few moments. 'Why would I? It would be too easy to be caught doing something awful like that, and then I would be automatically cut out of my inheritance.'

What a defence!

Sally had to repress a gasp.

Theresa was set on catching Brian and his moustachioed companion. But first she needed to discover whether the despicable drug-dealing thief was still in town.

She spent much of her time sitting on the terrace of the bar in Cours Saleya, watching every new arrival. She had no luck.

The rest of the time she patrolled the upper

alleyways of the Old Town, hoping to get a glimpse of the man there.

Nothing.

On the third day she went to see William.

'I have a proposal to put to you . . .'

William asked what.

'Could you get Benjamin to go out and search for his old drug dealer, so I can see if the man is still in town?'

William's face did not move. He took a couple of deep breaths and then told Theresa to fuck off.

As she walked away from his front door, Theresa realised that William had been right to be so rude.

But her own worries had eclipsed the thought of his own.

Having put Benjamin into rehab, why would William want to tempt him back to the world of drugs in any way?

She went back into Nice alone, and spent the afternoon sitting at the terrace of the gay bar, taking coffee and lunch there.

When the evening bowls of crisps and olives came out, she was still sitting there.

Another woman who had been sitting in the bar rather a long time too, sat and stared at Theresa, then got up and asked if she could join her.

Theresa looked around at all the other empty tables and realised she was being picked up. She smiled and blurted something, which, instead of repelling the woman, made her smile and take a seat.

Oh God.

Theresa's French obviously wasn't up to discouraging lesbian advances!

She scraped about in her head for any French words she knew which might politely express her meaning: she was not there in the bar to make friends, she was actually married (mind you, what did that mean nowadays?).

However, every word she said in her faltering French seemed to come out wrong and give the woman further encouragement, for the woman smiled more and more, and shifted her seat closer.

Theresa saw that there was no point to do anything but continue to sit there sipping her drink, with some strange Frenchwoman sitting beside her, grinning like an idiot.

'*Anglais?*' said the woman.

Theresa nodded.

'*J'aime* Marks and Spencers,' said the woman.

Theresa gave a weak smile.

'Fish and chips, cuppa tea, Benny Hill,' said the woman. 'Norman Wisdom.'

Good God, thought Theresa, was she going to run through the gamut of British clichés as a pickup line?

Theresa looked up, hoping to find something else to talk about. She gazed towards the crowded street, where a set of acrobats had started a frantic tumbling act for the people sitting in the restaurant next door.

And there he was.

Brian's drug-dealing companion was sitting alone at a table near the front of the terrace, looking down while he keyed something into a green smartphone.

Theresa made a burbled attempt at '*Excusez-moi*', as she rose from her chair and squeezed through the tables and chairs, trying to get to the front. When she arrived next to him, he looked up, perhaps distracted by her shadow which fell across his shoulder.

They caught eyes.

'You thief!' she said calmly. 'Where's Brian?'

'Fuck off you stupid old cow,' said the moustachioed man. He had a thick Glaswegian accent. He swiftly slipped his phone into his pocket, and grabbed his cigarette packet, before stumbling to his feet and making off.

'Where is he?' screamed Theresa, running after him. 'Where is Brian?'

As he ran away from her, the man was gaining speed, while Theresa felt as though every person in the marketplace was standing in her way. She saw that the man didn't care who he knocked, or flung out of the way. Whatever it took to escape he would do it, regardless of who got hurt.

'Thief!' Theresa cried at the top of her voice. '*Voleur! Voleur! Au secours!*'

But she ran out of breath long before he did, and she watched him disappear into the dark alleyways of the Old Town.

She had not caught him, but at least now she knew that he was still in the area, although she also felt that it was totally depressing to have got so near to him and yet to be no nearer to catching him.

She went back to the bar and paid her tab, then caught the bus home to Bellevue-Sur-Mer, where she sat outside the brasserie terrace, hoping that William might come in and she could have another, more tactful attempt at getting Benjamin to help her set a trap to catch the thief.

The two Englishmen she'd seen before were there, sitting at the same table.

This time they had no eyes for her. They had a plan of the town and they were deep in conversation. One of them was scribbling notes into a small pocket notepad, while the other pointed out places on the map and marked them with a red X. From what Theresa could see, her own address had an X across it.

She ordered a coffee.

The man with the notebook looked up, then looked back at his notes, then looked her in the eye and said: 'Theresa Simmons?'

'Why do you ask?' she replied.

The man with the map held up an enlarged photocopy of the old newspaper article, and pointed at her picture.

'Don't believe everything you read,' she said. 'It's a pack of lies.'

'We know that,' said notepad man.

'Do you know the whereabouts of this person?' The man with the map pointed at the photo of Brian.

'I wish I did,' said Theresa. 'The bastard.'

The man with the notepad grinned and nodded to his colleague.

'He's called Brian Powell, and he ran off with all my money and my best friend,' she said.

'Well, there we have it,' said the man with the map.

'You see, one of the lies in the newspaper article is that fella's name,' said the man with notepad. 'He's not called Brian at all. His is actual name is Ronald Arthur Tate.'

The two men rummaged around in their jacket pockets. They both presented police warrant cards.

'I'm DCI Thomas and this is my colleague, DI Wilton. We're from Scotland Yard, and we've been on quite the wild-goose chase looking for this scoundrel and his partner-in-crime, Stewart McMahon. I suppose you haven't had any contact with him at all – rough-looking Scottish bloke, swarthy, about five foot ten?'

He pulled a photo from the file. It was the man who had robbed her. The very man who had just this afternoon called her a 'stupid old cow'.

'At the moment he's got a Zapata moustache,' said Theresa. 'I saw him about an hour ago. In Nice.'

DI Wilton pulled out his mobile phone and talked rapidly into it.

'He was heading into Old Town from the Cours Saleya,' said Theresa. 'Brown leather jacket, green tartan shirt, torn blue jeans. Stinks of stale tobacco.'

'You still at the same address here?' said DCI Thomas.

Theresa nodded.

'We'll see you later,' said the detective, gathering his things and loping away towards a car parked on the front.

When she arrived at her home Theresa felt excited. Maybe now she would have a chance. She realised she hadn't told them about Carol, or asked what level danger the poor woman might be in.

But she could do that later when they called to see her.

Who knew? Perhaps by then they would have picked up the Scottish scumbag and he'd have blabbed on Brian, or rather, Ronald Arthur.

There was a flashing message on her machine, and during the day a letter had been hand-delivered.

While opening the envelope she listened to the message.

It was Sally, telling her that tomorrow was Faith's birthday and that they were all going to have a blow-out girls' lunch in Monaco. Faith knew Theresa's predicament, said Sally, and really wanted to treat her and all the girls, as it was an expensive restaurant and Faith could not think of going on her own. It would be no fun.

Alfie couldn't be there, he had already left for a business meeting in Zurich, and Faith had suddenly come up with the idea of having a really extravagant lunch with Sally, Theresa and Zoe. A luxury girls' day out for the ladies who lunch.

Theresa pulled the typewritten letter from the envelope as she dialled Sally's number to respond.

Sally answered on the first ring.

'You're coming, right?' said Sally. 'The restaurant's got three Michelin stars!'

'Oh, Sally, I don't think I could. Not if I can't pay my own way.'

'Theresa, you don't understand. Faith *really* wants to do this. It's been one of her life's dreams to go with a gaggle of friends to this place and have the meal of a lifetime. It's one of the reasons she didn't want to buy the house, and why she let me buy it. So she had enough money to do things *exactly* like this. To live her life to the full. Come on.'

'All right,' Theresa shrugged. 'I feel awful about it, but you've convinced me. We'll treat her to something else in return, another day.'

While Sally gave her the details, what she should wear, where they would meet, Theresa was absent-mindedly reading the letter. It was from David, but seemed to make little sense. A second page was just a weak photocopy of an old American school yearbook. Theresa went back to the first page.

'My God, Sally,' Theresa interrupted Sally's stream of instructions. 'Have you had a hand-delivered letter from David?'

Sally said yes she had, but she had been so busy making the reservations and arranging Faith's party that she hadn't read it yet.

Theresa only said two words. 'Open it.'

She read a few sentences back again and then said 'Oh God, Sally! Read it, then call me right back.'

'Dear friends,' the letter read. 'I have left town. The house is on the market and, by the time you read this, I will already be flying over you all in a jet bound for New York. Over the years of my French exile, you have been great friends and I thank you all for your kindness, your humour and your generosity.

'You all know that, by running off with that shallow, smarmy, greasy Englishman, Carol upset me very deeply and you know also that, in my efforts to get her back, I hired a private eye.

'This man made enquiries about Carol's current whereabouts and, drawing a blank, as all detectives do also started making enquiries about Carol's past, her marriage to me, her own friends and family, and all that stuff.

'I met Carol Heinz in LA, we married in Las Vegas and, before we moved here to Bellevue-Sur-Mer, we lived happily together in New York City.

'But the person we all know as Carol Rogers, née Heinz, was in fact born in Muncie, Indiana and was christened Mark Morgan.

'Mark's father left home when the boy was five, and, soon afterwards, his mother moved to Pittsburgh, where she took a factory job at the Heinz cannery to support her son.

'I enclose a page from Mark Morgan's high-school yearbook. He's the third row down, second on the left.

'When he was eighteen, Mark came to Europe, to a clinic not so far from here, where I believe Zoe is a frequent client. There, he underwent the necessary surgery to transform himself into Carol, and that, I suppose, is when he fell in love with the place.

'The reason behind all the spurious excuses I was given by Carol, explaining why we could never have children, now become all too clear.

'I hope you understand why I have to leave Europe. I have friends in NYC who will give me the necessary support and I am confident that a good lawyer will get me a swift annulment.

'Meanwhile, I will probably spend the rest of my life undergoing therapy.

'David.'

Theresa tossed and turned all night.

A couple in the Astra were at it for hours, groaning and moaning, then, when that all stopped, chose to have a loud fight.

But it wasn't the noise which kept Theresa awake so much as a head full of thought.

Her money all stolen, catching eyes with the man who had robbed her, and then being told his name by a pair of police officers. And Brian was his partner-in-crime and was really Ronald Arthur.

Carol was really Mark.

Carol!

She worried for her, alone with Brian, wherever they had gone.

Then, of course, there was the thought of David's letter. What a surprise!

After reading it, Theresa had gone over to Sally's and they had sat together for the whole evening talking about Carol. Could it be true? Had David had a breakdown? But, bit by bit, they thought of tiny clues, which gave away Carol's dark secret: the deep voice, the broad shoulders, the long legs, the perfect make-up; Carol often wore polo-neck tops or a scarf round her neck, and always, always gloves.

'Who are we to judge?' said Sally.

'I know,' said Theresa.

'I take my hat off to her,' said Sally.

'She's a more gorgeous specimen of womanhood than any of us,' said Theresa.

Theresa lay in the dark and prayed that no harm would come to Carol, wherever she was. She had always been so tender and caring towards Theresa, always funny, and always full of grace.

Brian – Ronald Arthur – was so duplicitous, such a charming and cloying evil liar.

Theresa opened her eyes.

Why were British detectives here in France chasing two men across the continent? Surely it wouldn't be so urgent for them to fly out to the South of France if Brian (or rather Ronald Arthur) was just an embezzler, or Stewart just a petty thief or even a drug dealer? There must be some more sinister crime for which they were chasing Brian – or Ronald Arthur – and his friend Stewart McMahon.

The only one she could imagine serious enough to warrant their presence was murder.

Oh, God! Poor Carol!

26

N EXT MORNING THEY ALL met, bright and early, at the railway station, wearing their Sunday best, ready to go to Monte Carlo for Faith's birthday lunch.

Faith had specifically asked for Zoe to come to the lunch, so Sally tried to keep a quiet distance and hoped, for today at least, to be able to put all their differences aside.

Theresa had decided that although the newspaper article had made fun of her jewellery she would not be bullied into becoming someone else, and therefore arrived in her brightest kaftan, with chunky necklaces and earrings of pink, mauve and turquoise.

'Before we go any further,' said Faith, taking her seat in an upper-deck section for four, 'I just want to say that I will not accept any payment or offers of money towards this lunch. You must please realise that it had always been my dream to go to this restaurant, and, although I could have gone alone, what fun would that have been?'

'Lots of fun,' said Zoe, 'if you'd gone on your own you might have got off with one of the waiters.'

Everybody laughed.

'And we have another fun outing tomorrow,' added Faith. 'I think Tom has invited us all, and the boys, to some mystery thing he's whipped up for your birthday, Sally.'

While Zoe gave a Cheshire cat grin, Sally blushed, and said: 'I wouldn't get that excited. Tom has a weird sense of humour.'

While they were on the train Theresa's phone rang.

It was Imogen.

'The girls have been suspended from school for a week.'

'Oh dear,' said Theresa. 'What did they do?'

'They bared their bottoms at a visiting netball team.'

Theresa had to bite her lip to stop herself laughing.

The party of ladies arrived in Monte Carlo and they strolled from the station to the restaurant, the Louis XV in the historic Hôtel de Paris, where the maître d', a handsome dark-haired man in a tail suit, ushered them into the dining room, a perfect baroque salon with dove-grey panels, tall mirrors swagged with ivory curtains and framed with gilt boiserie, and crystal chandeliers.

'Would you prefer the dining room, or the terrace, Mesdames?'

'Oh, the terrace,' said Faith. 'Then we can people-watch.'

'They would do better to watch us, I think,' said Zoe. 'What will we see but a lot of blister-red, fat back-packers, and pretentious poseurs showing off their garish lime-green Porsches and their sunshine, yellow Lamborghinis, oh-so-carefully parked outside the casino? But look at us! We're gorgeous.'

Her trout-pout wobbled ever so slightly, as she tried,

and failed, to raise her eyebrows up into her glassy smooth forehead.

They walked through the French windows on to the terrace.

'Wow!' said Theresa, looking out towards the magnificent Garnier opera house and casino. 'There's a view! I blame that building for my moving to Bellevue-Sur-Mer.'

'I don't think your tiny flat quite compares, Theresa,' said Zoe.

'I had a little flutter. It put me in such a good mood I went mad and bought the flat.'

Zoe had another attempt at getting her eyebrows up. 'You won *that* much?'

'No!' Theresa laughed. 'A couple of hundred. That's all. But it gave me a kind of wild optimism.'

A waiter with a trolley topped with a mound of ice advanced towards their table. From holes in the ice, necks of champagne bottles protruded.

'Could I interest you all in an aperitif?' he asked. '*Une petite coupe de champagne?*'

'Certainly,' said Faith. 'One each, please, Monsieur. And let's all have pink.'

Sally and Theresa made to protest, but Faith raised her hand.

'Please, ladies, remember that if things had turned out a little differently I might be in my coffin now. This is important to me. I'd like us all to raise a glass . . . to life.'

The regal and impeccable luncheon proceeded: course after course of culinary perfection were laid before them.

Everyone agreed that the whole experience was faultless, this even in spite of a buck-toothed child at the next table who kept banging her doll on the table and whining loudly every few minutes that she was 'bored, bored, bored'.

'They should let her go play with the traffic,' said Zoe. 'She wouldn't be nearly so bored if a bloody big pink Alfa Romeo was coming down the hill towards her at sixty miles an hour.'

Despite themselves, they laughed.

'Are we really all going to pretend we don't know the contents of David's letter?' asked Zoe.

'Yes,' they all replied in unison.

'I have to say, he was the best-looking woman I ever saw,' said Zoe. 'Despite the size twelve feet.'

'Change the subject, please,' said Faith.

'And don't use the past tense,' added Sally. 'We really have to hope that Carol's all right.'

'I'd love to see inside the Opera House,' said Theresa as they ate dessert. 'It's where Diaghilev and the Ballet Russes were based.'

'Not to mention Mr Lermontov, Moira Shearer and *The Red Shoes*,' said Sally.

'Nellie Melba sang there too,' said Theresa.

'Really,' said Sally. 'When did you become such an expert on her?'

Theresa blushed, and was silenced. She had a little secret with Tom, which he had arranged with her weeks ago. It was especially for Sally's birthday tomorrow.

'I think we should all go to the casino, and be done with it,' said Zoe. 'We could come out millionaires.'

'Or lose the shirt off our backs,' said Faith.

'I'd be in trouble – my clothing today is a one-piece!' said Theresa.

'I think you have to have your passport, before they let you inside,' Sally added hesitantly.

'Really?' exclaimed Faith. 'Why's that?'

'The casino is the engine of the principality. Instead of taking tax from the inhabitants, I think the place gets the bulk of its income from the losses at the gaming tables. And in order for that money not to get frittered away, I believe no Monégasque may enter.'

'What's a Monégasque?' asked Faith.

'A person who lives here in Monaco.'

'A tight-wad tax-dodger, you mean,' said Zoe.

The lavish cheese trolley was wheeled to the table.

'Isn't it sad?' said Faith. 'I couldn't eat another thing.'

Theresa was still admiring the casino, with its triumphant verdigris statues, its shiny glass doors and blue-suited bellboys. Then she saw someone she recognised coming out of the shining doors.

'I say, Faith,' she said, pointing towards the casino steps. 'Isn't that your son?'

'Alfie's in Switzerland,' said Faith.

'It *is* him,' said Sally rising and waving in his direction. 'Alfie!' she called loudly, making the bored child at the next table sit up and stare at her.

But Alfie seemed preoccupied and dejected. He slumped down the steps and into the street, squeezing past the closely parked Bentleys and Ferraris.

'I'm going to get him,' said Sally, throwing down her napkin, and running back through the restaurant.

'But he's away on business, in Switzerland, Zurich,' Faith called after her.

'Well, Faith,' Zoe peered out into the crowded square, scrunching up her face to focus. 'It certainly *looks* like him.'

Sally ran through the lobby of the hotel and down the marble steps into the square.

She could see Alfie, heading round the side of the Opera House, on the wide curving pavement which sweeps down to the Condamine.

She followed.

About halfway down Alfie flopped on to a bench and sat gazing out to sea.

Sally came and sat next to him.

He looked up with a weary shrug.

'It's your mother's birthday, today, you know.'

Alfie made a face as though to say 'OK, you win, I surrender.'

'She saw you. We all saw you, coming out of the casino. And let's put it this way: you didn't look as though you'd broken the bank.'

'That's putting it mildly,' said Alfie.

'Ah, I am understanding now, Alfie? I realise that you could easily prove where you were at the time your mother was attacked, because you were here, and they had registered your passport. Am I right?'

'What do you want?' said Alfie savagely. 'Why won't you ever let up?'

Sally took a deep breath. 'Because I am very fond of your mother, and I have a interest in her well-being.'

Alfie was puzzled. He turned and looked at Sally but said nothing.

'You need money from her to pay for your addiction to gambling. The big question is, how far are you prepared to go, to get more money?'

'I have borrowed from some pretty mean people,' he replied. 'I keep thinking that if I win more I could get myself out of the hole.'

'But you never will, though, Alfie, will you? Not this way.'

Alfie slumped forward and put his head in his hands. 'All I need is just a little luck.'

For a moment Sally left him to his thoughts.

'You still haven't explained why you wanted her to buy that house, which, as you know, is way too big for one person. Why couldn't she simply rent somewhere? Somewhere smaller? It would have left more money . . .'

Alfie sat up and turned to face Sally.

'Do you really want to know? You read the papers. We all know that old people are fleecing us, the young. They're all frittering away our inheritance.'

Sally winced. 'What you like to think of, Alfie, as "your inheritance" is in fact your mother's life savings. Why can't she have a bit of life now that she's old? You are fit and healthy and have a whole life ahead of you, and if you stopped wasting your time and money at the gaming tables, you could have a bit of a nest egg too. If your mother's lucky, she's got twenty years . . . maximum.'

'She tried to write me out of her will,' Alfie interrupted. 'But, over here, she can't do that. Parents *have* to leave the house to their children, it's the law.'

Sally smiled, and wondered whether she should tell him, or keep Faith's secret to herself. She decided she would tell him how his mother had kept all her money in an English bank and that she herself had actually bought the house in Bellevue-Sur-Mer. But not today. In a few days' time, calmly and privately, once Alfie had taken steps to control his urge to gamble, Sally would tell him the whole truth.

'We're all enjoying a birthday party for your mum,' she said. 'I think you should come and join in the toast to her life.'

She stood and held her hand out to him.

Sheepishly, he too rose from the bench.

Sally linked arms with Alfie, 'The other thing you should do is talk to William and Benjamin, they might have a few ideas to help you deal with your addiction.'

'I don't have . . .'

Sally grabbed him by both wrists and said calmly: 'You do, Alfie. You are addicted to gambling, and you act like a little baby, always running to your frail mother for money. No more faked suicide bids, please.'

'But I—'

'I know exactly what you did, and it's unforgivable, Alfie. It's nothing but a pathetic form of blackmail, the kind that only little kids can get away with. Be a man, for God's sake. Now, come back with me to the restaurant and tell her you came here to Monte Carlo on purpose, looking for her, to celebrate her birthday with her. She adores you. Now go on and deserve it.'

... That that

27

D ETECTIVES THOMAS AND WILTON were waiting on the terrace of the bar for Theresa to come home.

Despite the fact that she was tired from the excitement of the day in Monaco, also from eating and drinking so much, she went over and sat down with them.

She wanted some answers.

'We were in the dark till that newspaper article came out,' said DCI Thomas. 'One of the lads saw the photo and recognised Ronald Arthur right away.'

'And that's why we're here,' said DI Wilton.

No, they had not yet located Stewart McMahon, but had spoken to people here who had had dealings with the man. They had also put the local police on alert. Having gone through various files with them, much evidence pointed at Ronald Arthur and Stewart being responsible for the serious attack on Mrs Faith Duckworth. There was a bloody fingerprint. The MO was the same as another case they were working on back in the UK. It also appeared that the pair had used the new smartphone, stolen in the second raid, for calls to one another.

Theresa remembered Faith having talked about buying the phone for Alfie. She also remembered Brian holding a brand-new green phone that afternoon, just before he ran off with Carol, which must have been shortly after he had attacked Faith. Stewart was holding an identical phone – probably the same one – when she accosted him in the bar in Nice.

Theresa told them.

'It's in the newspaper photo,' said DI Wilton. 'Look! He's holding it.'

'We reckon that that photo of you all was taken minutes after the attack on Mrs Duckworth, while Stewart McMahon was still in the house.'

Theresa's stomach flipped.

'But Brian, er, Ronald seemed so calm and affable that day. To think that he'd just . . .' She put her face in her hands.

'Mrs Duckworth was lucky,' said DCI Thomas. 'Their last victim, a lady in Chelsea in January, wasn't so fortunate.'

Theresa gave an enquiring look.

'Murdered,' said DCI Thomas. 'In her bed. She surprised them. They didn't want to be recognised. They'd done work for her previously. Looked at the plumbing or something. They'd copied the keys and, when they thought she was away, they let themselves in. But she had had a cold, and stayed home.'

'They'd attacked Faith for a phone?' It really didn't seem possible.

'They're a pair of chancers. They were after her jewellery, but she hasn't got much but a wedding band.

303

They like living the high life, those two, but they prefer other people to pay for it.'

She told the officers about Carol.

'We've already put out an alert with Interpol,' said DI Wilton. 'Her credit card was used to empty her account in Naples night before yesterday, and the Jaguar he stole was sold for cash yesterday morning in Palermo.'

'Palermo, Sicily?'

The detectives nodded.

'Did the car dealers see Carol?'

The detective shook their heads.

'But they did give a perfect description of *him*. He was alone.'

Theresa saw from their faces that they did not think this was in any way good news.

'We have the Italian authorities searching the sea on the ferry route.'

Theresa understood what they were implying: that Brian had killed Carol and thrown her overboard.

She asked a question that had been nagging her.

'Do they usually work together, Ronald Arthur what's his name and Stewart?'

'They *always* work together.'

'So if Stewart is still here, in Nice, why isn't Brian, sorry, Ronald Arthur, here too?'

The detectives exchanged a look. 'We believe there's been a falling out among thieves, so to speak. Ronald Arthur Tate seems to have had a plan to work alone and keep all the takings for himself. From what we gather, Mr McMahon isn't a very happy bunny. All he got was the smartphone.'

Back in the flat, Theresa made some tea, and lay on her bed to think.

But after a sleepless night and the heavy lunch, she quickly fell asleep.

When she woke, it was dark and the cup of tea on her bedside table was cold.

She wanted to get up and get herself some water, but felt heavy and tired and unable to rouse herself.

She fretted about poor Carol.

Theresa prayed that Carol was OK and not floating face-down in the Tyrrhenian Sea.

She rolled over, facing the window.

All the lights in the Hôtel Astra were out.

The whole town was asleep.

Theresa sighed.

Then her sigh came to a stop.

The strange thing was that the sound of her sigh seemed to continue.

It was as though there was another person in the room with her, breathing quietly, inches away.

She turned back to face the room, and she saw, standing above her in the ghostly light, the man who had robbed her – Stewart McMahon.

They caught eyes.

There was no way she could pretend to be still asleep.

He had seen her.

In the micro-second in which he raised his fist, Theresa sprang forward, using her shoulder to knock the man off-balance. He staggered slightly, while she scampered out of bed.

Her mouth opened but she could not utter a sound. All her attention was focused on getting away from this lethal man, getting out of the house, surviving.

She took a few strides towards the living room, but, before she crossed the threshold, Stewart had grabbed her by her hair and yanked her back into the bedroom, flinging her on to the bed.

Theresa writhed around as Stewart punched and kicked her, grabbing at her arms to keep her under control.

He tried to twist her arm behind her back. She kicked backwards like a donkey, and managed to catch him where it hurt. He staggered backwards into the wall, yelping.

Then, in the total darkness she leapt from the bed and ran forward with all her strength, into the black-dark living room, making for the front door.

She was only a few feet away from the handle when she unexpectedly bumped into something.

What could be in the way? It felt like a man. But Stewart could not have outrun her.

A strong pair of arms flung around her, gripping her so tightly that she was unable to move at all.

'Where is it?'

It was Brian's voice, but that voice was cold and rough and there were no shades of the suave charm he had always used before.

She peered up in the darkness and could see the outline of his face.

He raised his fist and gave her a hard slap across the head.

She felt the bones in her neck crack.

He slapped her next on the other side with the back of his hand.

306

His breath was hot, damp and rancid on her face.

'Where the fuck is it. Tell me NOW!'

Theresa's heart thundered. Her voice came out in painful gasps.

'I don't know what you're talking about.'

He took her by the shoulders and shook her, while leering into her face.

'The painting. The Dufy. Where have you put it?'

Theresa's heart thundered. 'I sold it,' she whimpered.

'No you didn't.' Brian shook her violently. 'You wouldn't.'

His eyes flickered up and he stopped shaking her.

Theresa's heart was beating so hard she felt it might burst through her ribcage.

Calloused hands slid round her neck from behind, and she smelled the familiar scent of stale tobacco. She could feel the bristles of Stewart's moustache against the skin of the back of her neck.

Stewart whispered into her ear. 'If you can't tell us, where the fucking painting is, bitch, we can just dispose of *you*. Then we'll have all night to look for it.'

'All right, all right,' she said, her voice coming out in a wavery whisper. 'Let go of me and I'll show you.'

Brian nodded.

She took a step towards the back of the flat. The hands round her neck tightened.

'It's OK,' said Brian. 'There's no other way out.'

'The door?'

'Just a place to put the bins.'

The hands slipped away from her neck.

Theresa turned and faced the bedroom.

Brian gripped one forearm, Stewart had her wrist.

She staggered forward.

'Through here,' she said.

It felt terrible, giving away the picture her mother had left to her, giving it to these vile men, but she wanted so desperately to *live*.

As she reached the doorway of her bedroom Theresa remembered what the detective had said about killing that woman because she had seen them . . .

She realised with a jolt that if she showed them the hiding place they would take the painting, and kill her anyway.

They had no respect for her or anyone.

They killed the woman in Chelsea.

It was a miracle that Faith survived.

Why did she think she was so different?

Theresa's mind was set.

She was *damned* if they were going to kill her.

She was going to put up a fight.

'Through here,' she said, walking past the bedroom towards the back door. 'I have a safe box out here.'

'No you don't,' said Brian.

'I do, Brian. I bought it after what happened to Faith,' she said calmly. 'I hide it behind the bins – where no one would look.'

The two men shoved her roughly against the back door.

'Show us,' hissed Brian.

'You'll have to let go of my hands,' she said, 'or I cannot unlock the door.'

Brian stood behind her, blocking her way back into the house as Theresa pulled open the door and led them out into the tiny yard.

'I need the key to the safe,' she said. 'It's hanging up in the kitchen.'

She turned to go back in, and Stewart hissed, 'Oh no, you don't.'

He ran in front of her, leaving her alone with Brian.

Theresa pointed to a pitch-black corner. 'The safe is down there.'

As he stooped, to crawl behind the bin, Theresa kicked him hard in the backside and then opened her mouth and screamed for all she was worth.

'HELP! HELP! MURDER! MURDER! *AU SECOURS!* HELP! HELP ME! *M'AIDEZ!* HEEEEELLLLLPPPP!'

Above, in the Hôtel Astra, windows were flung open.

Brian and Stewart lurched towards Theresa, shoving her into the dark corner.

As she was slammed back, hitting the stucco wall, a whistling sound came from above, and, seconds later, a naked man landed in their midst.

He had jumped from the hotel window above.

The man battered the surprised Stewart and Brian, kicking and grappling with his fists. He then grabbed both men by their hair and slammed their heads together. Brian and Stewart collapsed into a heap.

'Get yourself outta here, gal,' the naked man yelled to Theresa. 'Get gone before they come round – the nasty scumbags!'

It was Ted.

'They're both out for the count. Come on.' Ted grabbed Theresa by the hand and looked up to the window from which he'd jumped. 'Bugger me, that's a long way up. Hey, Marianne,' he called. Have you called the plods?'

As Ted hauled Theresa into the house she caught a glimpse of Sally's daughter, Marianne, leaning from the window, holding a phone to her ear and nodding frantically.

28

S ALLY WAS WOKEN IN the early hours by frantic banging on the front door. She opened up. It was Marianne.

'Ted just saved Theresa's life.'

Sally rubbed her eyes.

'Marianne? Are you drunk? It's the middle of the night. And Ted is in Australia.'

'No, Mum. He's with the police in Theresa's flat.'

'Slow down.' Sally shut the front door and shuffled into the house. 'Is Theresa all right? Should we go there?'

'They have it all under control,' said Marianne. 'Thanks to Ted.' She paused and said, 'He's my lover.'

'Ted? But he's married.' Sally could see that once again she was in for revelations. She sat Marianne down. 'You'd better explain.'

'Pour us a glass of something, Mum.' Marianne looked down into her lap and started her explanation. 'It started months ago when I came down for an interview with Sian. She put me up in the Hôtel Astra.'

'You could have stayed here . . .'

Marianne held up her hand. 'After the interview I was planning to give you a surprise, but there was no reply – you were out. While your number was ringing there was a bleep on the line and it was Sian telling me the job was mine. So, while I waited for you to come home, I sat in the hotel bar and treated myself to a drink. A friendly Australian bloke came to my table. I was on cloud nine and he seemed ever so sweet. Well, one thing led to another and we ended up in my room in the Hôtel Astra. An hour or so later, Sian took it upon herself to arrive at the hotel with a portfolio of work for me to start work on. Ted recognised his wife's stentorian tones, barking into her mobile phone as she came along the corridor towards my room, and then, to use his own words he jumped down "bollock-naked" into Theresa's backyard for the first time.'

'You were the tourist . . . ?' Sally put her head in her hands, thinking of how this was all going to go down in the town gossip mill.

'Our romance, and it *was* a romance, Mum, blos-somed, by phone and email.'

'How could you?' Sally flopped down on to the sofa and passed Marianne a glass of whisky. 'Sleeping with your boss's husband?'

'No, Mum. I never put two and two together. He's such a daredevil madcap . . . And before he jumped out of the window he hardly had time to explain who he was. I had no idea that Ted was Sian's husband until that unsettling trip out on your boat. And seeing how he was with Jessica that day I began to doubt him. But, once I knew who he was, I was put in a very odd position with Sian.'

Sally took a slug of whisky. 'I cannot imagine why neither of you told me you were Sian's assistant.'

'Sian wanted total secrecy. You see, one of my duties was to keep an eye on Ted.'

Sally snorted. 'You appear to have rather overdone yourself on that score.'

Marianne chose to ignore Sally's barb. 'Anyhow, I decided to try keeping both the job and the man. Eventually Ted made the decision to leave Sian and marry me. He went to Australia. We were going to set up life out there. But once he got there he realised he didn't actually like the old country. It didn't match up at all to his rosy childhood memories of the place, so yesterday he came back to Bellevue-Sur-Mer. We had had a romantic reunion at the Astra, which was lucky, as it led to a second jump, and saved Theresa's life.'

'You realise at any moment Sian will be hammering on my front door?' said Sally.

But at that exact moment the doorbell and phone rang and Marianne's mobile bleeped.

'Oh help!' said Sally.

'I'll go.' Marianne strode to the front door.

'It's me, Ted.' Ted called from the street. 'I need some clothes.'

Back in the living room Sian's voice screeched out of Sally's answering machine. Sally was an evil bitch and her 'spawn' Marianne was 'a Gorgon'.

'Glad that's cleared up,' said Ted, talking over the message. 'I'd shake your hand, Sally, but if I let go of this police blanket I'd be in danger of exposing more than a mother-in-law is entitled to see.'

Sally stepped back and turned to Marianne who was looking down at her mobile phone. 'So you really *are* getting married?'

'Well, there's a first!' said Marianne. 'I've been fired by text message.'

'Yeah. We're hoping to have the wedding in that fancy five-star hotel where I went the night I ran off and left the blokes and the boat,' he told Sally. 'Cap Ferrat, d'Antibes or Martin or whichever Cap it was. Marianne and me had a little romantic liaison, there that night.'

'Thank you, Ted,' she said putting her hands up to cover her ears, 'I have no desire to hear the sordid details.'

Marianne glanced at the clock. 'Four a.m.! Isn't it your birthday now, Mum?'

'Oh gosh.' Sally remembered that Tom had a treat in store for her later in the morning. 'I think it's time we all went to bed. In a few hours we've got to be on that bus.'

29

A MINIBUS WAITED IN the street near the Gare Maritime.

Zoe was already seated inside, decked out in her evening gown and all her jewels.

'It's ten o'clock in the morning, Zoe,' said Sally. 'We're not going to the Prince's ball.'

'How do you know?' said Zoe. 'Actually, we're going somewhere much better than that.'

'I thought we were going for lunch,' replied Sally.

'We are heading for An Experience.' Zoe gave Sally a salamander-type eye-roll and sat back in her seat. She looked at her watch and said sharply 'Come along! Where is everyone?'

Faith and Alfie were heading along the seafront towards the bus, chatting seriously with William and Benjamin. Sally was very happy that she had helped make things work out for them. Last night, before Marianne and Ted arrived and dropped their bomb-shell, Sally had effected a terrific reunion between Alfie and Faith, and, with the help of William, created a mutual support pairing between Benjamin and Alfie, both now determined to fight their addictions together.

As to the situation between Marianne and Ted, Sally had decided there was no point putting up a fight, as they both seemed utterly set on being together.

They were sitting together now, gazing lustfully into one another's eyes.

She turned away, looked out of the window and saw Theresa coming out of her front door, carefully double-locking it behind her. She was dressed elegantly, with all her usual abundance of colourful jewellery, but her make-up couldn't disguise a huge purple bruise on her cheekbone.

'Ouch, Theresa! I didn't expect you'd be up for joining us this morning, after all that.'

'Do you know, I don't want to talk about it,' Theresa said to Sally. 'It was a long night for all of us. But, look! I'm here!'

Theresa was excited about today's trip, and, despite the night from hell, was damned if it turned into yet another thing Brian stole from her.

Since Theresa had been rescued by a naked Ted, and Brian – or Ronald Arthur – and his partner-in-crime had been arrested and taken off to prison in the early hours, there had been many questions and lots of explanations.

While she gave the police her statement Theresa had been checked over by a police doctor. The police also brought in the locksmith who fitted another new lock.

But Theresa also had a little secret. An hour ago, when she was dressing up, ready to join the bus party, her phone had rung.

It was Jessica.

'I'd like to make you an offer to sell us your story about living with the criminal Ronald Arthur Tate.'

'No thanks,' said Theresa.

'We can offer you a substantial amount of money,' she added.

When Theresa heard the figure, she accepted, thinking of the money as compensation for all that Brian had stolen.

She turned to Sally. 'I hope *you're* all right?'

'In so many ways, we're both so lucky,' said Sally. 'And I'm rather nervous but excited about the mystery tour!'

Tom had been organising this special surprise for Sally's birthday since the day he arrived. Theresa already knew about one part of it, having been asked over the phone a few days ago to contribute a little of her expertise.

She kissed Sally a happy birthday and climbed back towards the rear seats of the bus.

Then the driver, finishing off a cigarette out on the street, asked Sally to be sure and to check everyone off the list.

Sally knelt on the front seat and facing back into the bus, called out everyone's name.

'William, Benjamin,' she said.

'Flobbabdobb!' said Zoe. 'Fluddububbb!'

'What's the matter with her?' Benjamin nudged William.

'Sounds like she's still having trouble with the new lips.' William arched his brow as he spoke.

'Ted, Faith,' Sally continued calling out her list and ticking off.

'Weeeeeed!' said Zoe, falsetto, reverting to her normal alto to say: 'And I think the little house knew something about it! Don't *you*?' before singing 'Bill and Ben, Bill and Ben, Flowerpot men'.

'Zoe!' snapped Sally. 'Will you please shut up!'

When Sally finished her roll call, she instructed the driver to leave.

He stubbed out his cigarette and slid the door shut, then made his way round the front and climbed into the driver's seat.

As he turned back, leaning his arm along the front seat, preparing to reverse out of the space, he cursed.

Someone was banging very hard on the back window.

Sally turned to take a look.

Someone was making their way around the bus.

A fist hammered on the window beside her.

'You're not going to leave without me, I hope, my darling, even though I am a total fool.'

Carol, as impeccably dressed as ever, climbed in to the front seat, next to Sally.

'Shove up,' she said. 'Happy birthday, darling! May I beg all your forgiveness for my abrupt departure. But now I'm back!'

The journey to Villeneuve-Loubet was taken up with Carol's tale of her escape from Brian.

She and Brian had driven as far as Naples, heading for Sicily, which Carol had always thought would be a very romantic place.

'We were on a car ferry, waiting for it to depart. Those Italian ferries are mad, they let you on and then just sit there in port for three hours. So we'd checked out the cabin and we were heading down to the bar. I went into the ladies' powder room . . .'

'Oh, really, did you?' said Zoe. 'Wrong door?'

William kicked her in the shin and Zoe said 'Ouch'.

'Anyhow the door to the men's room and the ladies' room were miles away, on this boat, but strangely, once you got inside, they were right next door and had a small gap at the top of the wall for ventilation.

'I was at the basin washing my hands, when I heard Brian's whole phone call. He was telling some friend how he was planning to "do me in". When it was dark and we were miles out to sea, he was going to take me up on the deck, kill me and throw me overboard. Then the plan was that he'd get all of my vast supplies of money out of the bank, using my card and ID. Well, as you all may know, I don't actually have that much money, so that part didn't bother me considerably, but as to the dying part, well, I've been through quite enough in my life to realise that I have no desire to depart this world quite yet.'

'So how did you escape?' asked Theresa.

'I told him I wanted to get myself dressed for dinner and needed an hour or so on my own – a little woman time.'

Zoe opened her mouth; Benjamin raised his eyebrows to silence her.

'I said I'd see him in the dining room at nine. The ship was due to sail at eight, and it was a few minutes before that. So I went to the cabin, grabbed my things and rushed down to the place where the last cars were driving on and then, well, I simply strolled off the boat. Immediately went to an ATM and got all my money out of the bank, which wasn't much – a few hundred euros. I didn't have enough money for a flight so I sat at the railway station all night and got on the first train out. I would have phoned but my phone disappeared on the day we left Bellvue-Sur-Mer. Last time I remember having it was at a service station while we were filling up with petrol in Ventimiglia. I had to change trains all over the place. It's taken me days, but anyhow I got here in time for this celebration, so ...'

There was a long silence which no one knew how to break.

In the end it was Carol who spoke again.

'You may or may not know that, while I was away, David left me. And I don't blame him. We hadn't been getting along so famously lately. Plus, he always wanted to go back and live in New York, so I suppose me being such a fool over that crook, and taking his precious car was as good a reason as any.'

'I could think of another ...'

Zoe suddenly cut short her sentence and looked very pained.

The bus turned off the main road into the little town of Villeneuve-Loubet.

'There's Tom!' cried Sally. 'Now we might find out his big surprise.'

Tom was standing in the main road, directing the traffic down into a car park, behind which stood a large tent. He was wearing a pink-and-gold version of a ringmaster's costume.

'I am so excited I could explode,' said Zoe.

'I wish you would,' said William.

Everyone climbed out of the bus and admired the huge tent.

A large circus-style banner fluttered over the entrance. It read : 'Les Dames de Bellevue!'

Tom took his mother's hand.

'My first big exhibition,' he said. 'You're getting the private view. It opens to the public and critics this afternoon.'

Sally was led into the tent, followed by the other ladies, and William, Benjamin and Alfie.

Everyone gasped as they looked around.

The tent was decked out in bright circus-like colours, with ribbons and streamers dangling and circus marches pumped out of hidden loudspeakers.

The centrepiece was a shiny great tableau like the *Last Supper*, in which all those gathered round the table were the inhabitants of Bellevue, with Sally in the centre, sitting behind a shiny red table laden with all the dishes they had all cooked in the Cookery Club.

In a roped-off gallery on one side of the tent stood a huge colourful sculpture of Sally wearing a pirate costume at the helm of a speedboat, with Ted, complete with kangaroo legs, clinging on to the engines at the back.

Next to it another vibrant statue, this time it was a fat woman with lots of eye make-up, in turquoise earrings and a kaftan, wearing an apron and a wielding a frying pan.

'That's you!' said Tom to Theresa, who wasn't quite sure how to take the compliment.

The other side of the tent had a partition wall which was hung like a conventional art gallery with huge paintings of Zoe, naked.

'The result of our so-called "dirty weekend",' said

Tom. 'I got dirty with paint while Zoe bravely bared all, for hours on end, allowing me to paint her.'

'Anyone else ever made an exhibition of themselves?' cried Zoe, posing fully clothed in front of her naked self.

'I heard about your ordeal last night,' said Carol quietly to Theresa. 'I am so sorry. I feel somewhat responsible.'

Theresa squeezed Carol's gloved hand. 'Don't be silly. We were both stupid fools who should know better.'

There was a roll on the drums and Tom stood on the central podium.

'And now,' Tom indicated a row of waitresses who emerged through a flap in the tent, 'As this exhibition is taking place in the birthplace of the world's greatest chef, Auguste Escoffier – pardon me, Theresa, but I'm sure you won't disagree that he was the top – we are all going to have some champagne and, to celebrate my darling mother's birthday, I propose the perfect dessert: Peach Melba!'

Theresa and Sally took a glass and a dish each from the proffered trays and perched on the red velvet circular banquets in the middle of the tent.

They could see Ted, sitting on the other side of the room, his arm around Marianne. The couple gazed into one another's eyes.

Tom was laughing, waving his pink-and-gold top hat, while Zoe cavorted in front of the portraits of herself, performing for Faith, Alfie, William and Benjamin.

'It's all very sweet, isn't it?' Sally sighed and took a

mouthful of ice cream with raspberry sauce. 'We all panic, but our kids are fine, really, aren't they?'

'They are,' said Theresa.

'I have to learn to be less judgemental,' said Sally. 'We're all just human, after all.'

'I know.' Theresa took a bite of vanilla-syruped peach. She had to say, her recipe wasn't at all bad, but when you were following the rules of a master, how could a perfectly constructed dish like this fail?

Theresa's phone rang.

It was Imogen.

'Mummy?'

'Yes, darling?'

As the day had started so well, Theresa prayed it wouldn't be bad news.

'You know I said the girls had been suspended from school and, I think I told you a few weeks ago, that, since the trip out to see you, they all seemed to be doing rather well at French . . .'

'Yes?' said Theresa.

'I'm finally facing up to it: Michael isn't going to come back, is he?'

Theresa quietly said no.

'So I've made a decision,' continued Imogen. 'We, that's the girls and me, well, we've decided we're going to move to France.'

Theresa gulped, took a deep breath and said, 'That's nice.'

She scooped the spoon round the bowl and opened her mouth.

'No, not exactly Nice, but, like you, somewhere near,' said Imogen with a laugh in her voice. 'Like

Bellevue-Sur-Mer. I've already phoned the estate agent and they say there are two rather good houses that have just gone on the market.'

Theresa thrust the laden spoon into her mouth.

'And, you know what's so wonderful about it, Mummy. You'd be able to babysit again!'

Theresa's mouth was so full of Peach Melba she couldn't manage a reply.

PEACH MELBA

Ingredients
2 whole white peaches
Caster sugar
Vanilla pod
Raspberries
Lemon juice
Vanilla ice cream

Method
1. Peaches
Bring a pot of water to a simmer. Put peaches into the simmering water to blanch for 1 minute.

Drop peaches into a bowl of iced water, then peel. Cut them in half and remove stones.

Make a caramel by burning some caster sugar in a pan. When brown and starting to bubble, add a little water till it is a syrup and put vanilla pod into this.

Add peaches, simmer, stirring occasionally, till peaches are soft (and slightly firm) generally about 5–8 minutes.

Remove from heat, strain, cover and set aside till peaches cool, then chill.

2. Raspberries
While they are cooling, purée fresh raspberries in a blender, and strain through a sieve into a bowl.

Add 4 teaspoons sugar and lemon juice and stir to dissolve the sugar.

3. Serving

Put a ball of vanilla ice cream at base of each bowl.

Drain and arrange two peach halves on top of ice cream.

Pour raspberry sauce over peaches.

Decorate with spun melted sugar or chopped almonds – but *never* whipped, or any other, cream.

Acknowledgements

Angus
Christopher
All my friends at *La Civette Du Cours*
Constance
Fidelis
Gilbert
Jose Mari
Josey-Anne at the Language School
The bus drivers on the Lignes d'Azur
Lima, meilleure pour autant que je sache
Maître d' at Alain Ducasse Restaurant, Louis XV, Monte Carlo
Nerys and Patrick
Raymond
Richard
Les sauveteurs des plages de Nice
To all my friends at Le Safari Restaurant for always giving me an extra special welcome and desserts
Sebastian

A Note on the Author

Celia Imrie is an Olivier Award-winning actress best known for her parts in the films *Calendar Girls* and *Nanny McPhee*. In February 2015 she returns as Madge in *The Second Best Exotic Marigold Hotel*. Her roles on stage include Dotty in *Noises Off* and Mrs Tilehouse in *The Sea* and, on television, Diana in *After You've Gone*, Vera in *A Dark Adapted Eye* and Miss Babes in *Acorn Antiques*. Last year she brought her cabaret/revue *Laughing Matters* to Crazy Coqs and then to the St James Theatre. Her autobiography, *The Happy Hoofer*, was published in 2011.

www.celiaimrie.info   ©CeliaImrie